I0630920

Bound By Flames

Hidden Realms of Silver Lake
Book 8

Vella Day

Bound By Flames
Copyright © 2019 by Vella Day
Print Edition
www.velladay.com
velladayauthor@gmail.com

Cover Art by Jaycee DeLorenzo
Edited by Rebecca Cartee and Carol Adcock-Bezzo

Published in the United States of America
Print book ISBN: 978-0-9899759-8-8

ALL RIGHTS RESERVED. No part of this book may be used or reproduced in any manner whatsoever without written permission of the author except in the case of brief questions embodied in critical articles or reviews.

This is a work of fiction. Names, characters, places, and incidents either are the product of the author's imagination or are used fictitiously, and any resemblance to actual persons living or dead, business establishments, events or locales, is entirely coincidental.

What's a guy to do when the woman he wants refuses to listen to reason?

Dragon shifter, Logan Caspian, has his hands full with journalist Wendy Oprander. Sure, she might be a wolf shifter, but that doesn't mean she can't be killed. And it would be an understatement to say he was upset when he found out she was investigating the same dangerous case he was working on. Naturally, Logan was quick to suggest she drop the story, but that discussion did not go over very well at all. Not to worry. He could be just as stubborn as Wendy. After all, Logan was a Guardian and her mate.

Considering everyone she talks to seems to be lying, Wendy is struggling to figure out who to trust. Having the super-hot Logan hovering over her isn't helping one bit. Her focus has to be on getting the scoop on this big conspiracy and not on him.

When someone tries to kill her, she has to decide if she is willing to risk it all for her dream job or chance losing the man she wants more than air itself.

Chapter One

WENDY OPRANDER'S PHONE rang, jarring her out of her musings. Ever since she'd submitted her piece about the slave ring run by Gregory Malpan to the local newspaper, her journalistic muse had up and run off. Considering she worked on commission, she needed to get her act together. And soon.

She refused to believe her writer's block was because she was still reeling over her own capture during that slave operation. Her cousin Danita tried to tell her it was natural to be messed up from it. Anyone who'd been kept in an underground cell for a week would have some form of emotional baggage.

Only Wendy didn't—or so she wanted to believe. Could she be in denial over the whole affair? Sure. Was it possible the reality of it all would slam into her at the worse possible moment? A definite maybe.

It was why she really needed to work on something big, something important, something that would take down another crime lord. A new challenge would help her find a different purpose in life and take her mind off her troubles. The big question was who or what was big enough to do the trick? It wasn't like serial killers or human traffickers grew on trees.

For the past couple of hours, Wendy had been looking through all of the news outlets and still came up with nothing. Whenever that happened in the past, she often turned to her source at the Avonbelle Province Police. But first, she had to answer her cell. Damn. She was losing it.

Wendy lifted her phone and checked the caller ID. Crap. It was the editor at the Edendale Herald. Stanton Everhart was probably wondering when he'd receive her next article. He'd really like her last exposé.

"Hello?"

"Wendy, Stanton here. We'd really love to run another one of your stories. Do you have anything for me?"

"I'm working on something." Okay, that was kind of a lie, but in her defense, she was doing research.

"I'm glad to hear it. One of my fellow editors over in Thedia called to say he'd read your Malpan exposé. To say the least, he was impressed. Keep this up, and I'll have to hire you full-time." Despite his uncharacteristic chuckle, he sounded sincere.

Her heart almost stopped at the possibility of being a full-time journalist. It was her life-long dream. Wendy was convinced that if she had a steady paycheck coming in, the lack of pressure would help with her productivity.

"You know I'd love to work full-time."

"I know. Just get me that headline-worthy story, and we'll talk."

That wasn't going to be easy. She smiled, but it definitely had been forced. Good thing Stanton couldn't see her expression since this was a voice-only call. "I'm on it."

When Stanton disconnected, she slumped in her seat. Where was she going to find a breaking story? As much as she didn't want to be beholden to Officer Brent Shepard, she needed his help. While she'd sent him information in the past when she found something useful from one of her sources, asking him out right for help wasn't her style. If they hadn't dated in the past, she might have been more willing.

The reason for her hesitation had merit. She'd been the one to break up with him. Truth be told, there had been no deep connection between them. The part she felt the guiltiest about was that Brent believed they belonged together. He'd said they were perfect for each other, but leading a man on wasn't in her makeup, so she'd broken it off.

Wendy inhaled, pushed aside her reservations, and called him.

Brent picked up right away. "How's my favorite journalist?" he asked with way too much cheer in his voice.

Crap. She could only hope he wasn't happy to hear from her because he thought she was calling to ask him out for a date. Fingers crossed it was for another reason. She remembered him telling her that he was desperate to become a detective under Anderson Caspian and that any information he learned on his own—whether it be from a lead she'd given him or some other avenue—the better it would be for his career. However, if he was relying on her to help him reach that goal, Brent would fail.

"Hey, Brent. I need a little favor."

"Oh. What do you need?"

From the way his voice trailed off, she hadn't given him what he'd wanted. "The editor at the Edendale Herald is bugging me to write another exposé, and I'm clear out of ideas. Any juicy stories you can point me toward?" She worked hard to keep her voice upbeat.

"I might have something."

Her pulse shot up. "What is it?"

Brent said nothing for a few seconds. "How about coming in so I can show you what I have?"

Wendy didn't have time for him to be coy. He might not even have anything. Brent probably just wanted to see her. "Can't you just tell me over the phone?" she asked as nicely as possible.

"Nope."

The sad truth was that she needed to find out what he knew. From the excitement in his voice, he might actually know of something big. "Okay, I'll be right over."

"Great. I'll be here."

"I NEED YOUR help," Anderson Caspian said.

This wasn't the first time Logan Caspian's detective cousin had asked him to use his *special* talents to help out with a case. Just to be clear, *special* often meant deep dive hacking. It was something no one at the station—including Anderson—was capable of doing as well.

Logan scooted his chair closer to Anderson's desk and leaned forward. The police department was not only noisy, there were too many people around who didn't need to learn that he would be involved in one of their police cases. "What do you need?"

"Last night, two teenagers were found dead of an overdose."

"Shit. What kind of drug?" Any kind was bad, but lately there had been an increase in a certain drug that was potent, cheap, and quite deadly. Kids loved the high, but they didn't seem to understand how lethal it could be.

"Crenathum."

That was his worse fear. "How can I help?"

"I have two officers on the streets right now trying to find out who might be distributing the stuff."

"What do you know so far?" Logan asked. While the Avonbelle Province Police did great work, they were short-staffed. In addition, not all of the workers were shifters, which often hindered their investigation.

"Both of the young men were at the same party last night. When we received the distress call, we rushed right over, but they were dead when we arrived. The officers searched for drugs but found none."

"That doesn't surprise me. No one wants to be caught with something like Crenathum. My guess is that someone moved the stash."

"I agree. So far, no one is talking, and the parents weren't home during the party. They claimed they had no idea their son would be holding a get together, mostly because Mike was a model student and a top athlete. This means it's up to us to find out where this stuff is coming from. I was hoping you could do your computer magic."

He figured as much. "I can try to find out who these kids called recently. They'd have to have a dealer somewhere, and the calls would still be on their phones." He didn't want to believe the dealer was a fellow high school student. That would make things more difficult to track down.

"I asked the parents for permission to check their cell messages, but they stonewalled us."

"Why the hell would they do that? I would think they'd want answers as to who sold their kids the drugs."

"Apparently not."

"You don't think either family could be involved, do you?" Logan asked.

Anderson shook his head. "Not really. Mike Evans' dad is an attorney, and Tom Sanderson's father is a banker. Both families are quite well off. They each have big careers, which means I don't see them as the type to jeopardize that by being anywhere near drugs or drug dealers. Besides, Mike Evans has helped us out in the past. However, that doesn't exonerate either of them."

Even wealthy folks did illegal activities for power, but he'd keep that to himself for now. "Even if we find the name of the person who sold them the drugs, we'd still have to find the source."

Anderson nodded. "True, but right now I'd be happy to arrest a street pusher. Then we'll go after the big guy."

Easier said than done. "From what I've heard, the mushrooms used for this drug thrive in the cold," Logan said. "Which means the source probably didn't come from Avonbelle. I'm guessing Thedia."

"Yes, but the Trilox that's added to the mushrooms to enhance the high can be manufactured anywhere," Anderson said.

A little uncertainty never stopped the Guardians. "I can have our team do a little reconnaissance of the area. Someone in the farming community must know something."

Flying to Thedia would take time, but any one of his family members—especially Stone—would be up for the adventure. Logan always believed his cousin would have had a more fulfilling life if he'd been a private investigator. Sitting behind a desk crunching numbers wasn't really his thing, but he was good at it—really good.

Anderson leaned back in his seat. "That's what I was hoping

you'd say."

"If you want me to gather the family so you can address them, let me know."

In the past, it was more effective when Anderson met with the Guardians. Having everyone on the main page always helped.

"I will when I have more information." Anderson tapped the desk. "You might want to look into the bank records of known drug dealers to see if they received any payments recently," he said softly. "I'll send you the list of who has been on our radar."

Logan already had that on his to-do list. "I'll do my best."

"I appreciate it. Time is of the essence."

"Isn't it always?" Logan pushed back his chair.

While he loved helping run the Caspian Mines, working on a case always excited him, and he couldn't wait to get started.

Once outside, Logan was closing his car door when he spotted Wendy Oprander walking up the stairs to the police station, and his dragon instantly shot hot fire into Logan's gut.

Stop it, Logan commanded. His dragon was so damned impulsive.

Mate, mate.

From the first moment he met Wendy a few weeks ago, he thought that might be true, but he wanted to spend more time with her to confirm his belief. So far, she hadn't accepted either of his two invitations to go out. Wendy was a wolf shifter, which meant she would have felt the draw too. So why had she been so hesitant?

Logan's instinct was to jump out of the car and talk to her, but their last conversation made him think twice. He'd actually waited a couple of weeks after her release from captivity at the mines before he called her the first time. While she'd sounded in good spirits, she'd told him she was working on a piece about Malpan, the man who'd taken her, and that she didn't have time to be social.

Logan could respect that, but it didn't mean he had to like it. The problem was that after her piece came out in the paper, he called her again. She gave him another excuse about needing to write something else. He had yet to figure out his next move. He totally understood that when he was in the middle of something important, he'd pushed aside his animal urges. What could she be dealing with now that would make her deny her inner wolf?

Maybe she's scared because she knows you two are mates, his dragon said, his tone less sure than usual.

That's possible.

You need to talk to her again, and tell her you'll give her all the time she needs, his dragon urged.

I will just as soon as the timing is right, Logan answered, though he didn't believe his dragon really meant that he could wait much longer.

As soon as Wendy stepped into the station, he slumped against his seat, and tried to push her image out of his mind. Shit. He really needed to keep his head on straight if he had any chance of solving this drug trafficking crime. The family of the two teens needed closure. Once he helped Anderson figure out where the drugs were coming from, he could relax and focus on being with the woman of his dreams.

His dragon remained silent, but the intense clawing in Logan's gut implied someone wasn't happy with that decision. Stupid dragon. *Stop it, you oaf. Be patient.*

She's so hot.

Logan couldn't believe how much his animal could whine. *Yes, she is.*

Logan started the engine and pulled into the street, hoping nothing bad had happened to Wendy that would cause her to have to go to the cops. The woman had been through enough turmoil in the last month or two to last a lifetime. At some point, he might have to call Anderson and ask if he'd spoken with her.

When Logan arrived back at work, he entered the office at the Caspian Mines. He, Stone, Griffin, and the rest of the family members had offices in the main SinCas building in town, but the three of them liked the working conditions at the mines more. The foreman and other workers could find him quicker if they were there.

As soon as Logan reached his office, his cell rang. It was his mom. While he and his family were super close, Logan wasn't in the right frame of mind to talk to her, so he let it go to voicemail. He needed to ignore the rush of hormones that were racing through his system at seeing his mate and pay more attention to both the work at the mines and what he'd promised Anderson. Being productive would hopefully take his mind off his hard-on.

The first thing he did was research the drug Crenathum to make sure he understood which ingredients besides Trilox were needed to synthesize it. That might give him a clue what to look for going forward. His job was to find a trail of drugs, and that was what he planned to do.

He'd been at it for a good hour when cousin Stone, who was also his assistant, cleared his throat. "Didn't you hear me bang on your door?" he asked as he stepped inside the office.

"No."

"I knocked a few times, but when you didn't answer, I came in. I'd seen you enter an hour ago. You looked like you were in a trance just now."

He had been in a daze. Every time he reached a dead end in the search, his mind automatically shot back to Wendy. Logan hadn't seen her in a few weeks, and the image of her in those tight jeans and long-sleeve body-fitting shirt stirred something deep inside of him. When he'd first encountered her, he thought his imagination had run rampant from his success at freeing the slaves from the Malpan Mine. It was possible that was why he'd believed Wendy was his mate. To her credit, even after she'd been saved, and despite looking broken and tired, Wendy's resolve to help locate the other captives had jackknifed his interest in her. But did that mean they were fated for one another?

Yes! his dragon shouted at him.

When she'd shown up at his office a few days later to ask about the freed men, Logan began to think maybe it hadn't been his imagination. Wendy really was meant for him.

I told you she was our mate, his dragon chimed in again.

"Hey! Where did you go?" Stone asked waving a hand in front of Logan's face.

Shit. Logan looked up. "Sorry. Anderson has me working on a case."

Stone smiled and pulled out a chair in front of Logan's desk and sat down. "Oh, yeah? Can I help?"

That brightened Logan's day. Stone loved nothing more than a case. "In fact, I could use your help."

"Tell me."

Chapter Two

"LET'S TAKE THIS discussion someplace else," Brent Shepard said.

Ugh. As much as Wendy wanted to remain in the open, he was right. A police officer, probably shouldn't be seen discussing an ongoing case with a reporter, especially in his workplace. "Sure."

Brent smiled. Okay, he might be good-looking and kind of charming, but he didn't rev her engine like her former boyfriend Deke Darnell had—or Logan Caspian did for that matter. Comparing the men was not a luxury she could afford though. She had to focus on writing this article.

When Brent led her outside, she almost told him she didn't want to do this, but she really needed his help. "Where are we going?"

"I thought we'd go to the Hillside Café. If anyone sees us, we'll say we're two friends grabbing a cup of coffee."

If she didn't think he was right, she would have walked away. Okay, she probably wouldn't have, but she would have put up a fuss. The café was only two blocks from the police station, and she was grateful when he said little on their short walk.

Once inside, she slid into a booth near the back, and Brent sat next to her instead of across from her. Really? While she needed her personal space, she also needed Brent—or rather what Brent had to offer.

Instead of commenting, she moved toward the wall to put more distance between them and twisted toward him. "Tell me what you know," she said in as professional a voice as she could muster.

"Two teens died of a drug overdose last night."

"Oh, no. That is horrible. But while it's terribly tragic, what is there to investigate?" Wendy stilled, recalling the story she'd investigated of a truck driver who was thought to have died from an overdose when in reality he'd been poisoned. She'd spent weeks trying to learn who'd killed him, but that had resulted in a dead end. "Was it Crenathum?"

"Yes, it was. I thought you might be interested."

"There might be a story if the boys were also poisoned," she said.

"Like the truck driver?"

"Yes."

"We haven't received the autopsy reports back. For now, it looks like a drug overdose."

She huffed out a sigh. "What can I possibly do? Other than do a human-interest story on the teens."

"Detective Caspian wants to find the pusher, and you're so good with getting people to talk, I thought this might be up your alley."

Wendy would pretty much do anything to get the story. She'd yet to go undercover as a drug dealer though. "I asked questions a few months ago about who had supplied the truck driver with drugs, but I got nowhere. It was before anyone was aware he'd died from rat poison."

The waitress stopped by, and they both ordered coffee. Not that she really was in the mood for some right now, but she wanted to make it look like they were at the café to socialize.

"Do you have any actual leads who might have sold the teens these drugs?" she asked, keeping her voice to a near whisper. Capturing a big-time drug dealer might be newsworthy, but only if it wasn't just some two-bit local pusher.

Brent wove his fingers together. "No."

Okay, this had been a mistake. "What do you think I can do then?"

He pulled out a piece of paper from his pocket. "Here are the names of the two high school boys. This information will be released to the papers today. I don't know who was at the Evans' party last night when the two teens died, but if you ask around at their high school, you might get someone to talk. The boys came from wealthy families and participated on several sports teams. If they are as popular as I think they are, everyone at school will know who was there."

Wendy had to admit this intrigued her. "Don't the parents know?"

He shook his head. "Mike Evans' parents were away for the weekend and never suspected their son would throw a party. I listed the contact information for both parents in case you can charm them into talking to you. They've been resistant about sharing with us."

"Why? Don't they want to know who sold their kid drugs?"

"Yes, but they fear every paper will sensationalize their children's deaths."

Ouch. Her paper wouldn't do that. Others however might. Wendy folded the paper and stuffed it in her purse. "I appreciate this."

"Let me know what you learn."

"I will."

Wendy had to admit it was a smart move on Brent's part to include her. She could talk to school kids about the boys without attracting too much attention. Not only that, kids were more likely to speak to a journalist than a cop.

Before she went that route though, she wanted to speak with the parents of the Evans boy. They might not know who was at the party, but they should be able to list a few of his closest friends. If they were leery of journalists, she'd just have to convince them she wouldn't publish anything without their permission. Surely, they'd want the drug dealer caught.

After she and Brent finished their coffee, they went their separate ways. Once back at her apartment, Wendy called the Evans' home and was pleased when someone picked up.

"Hello?" The voice was female and sounded mature.

"Mrs. Evans?"

"I'm not making a statement. I'm sorry."

Oh, crap. "Wait, please. I want to help find out who did this as much as you do."

"Who is this?"

"My name is Wendy Oprander. I am working on an article for the Edendale Herald, but I won't mention your son's name unless you want me to." Wendy spoke as quickly as possible, hoping the grieving mother wouldn't hang up on her.

"I'm sorry, but my husband advised me to say nothing to anyone." Her tone came out colder this time, but it also sounded tortured. Her husband was a lawyer, so it made sense she'd respond that way.

"Why is that?" Wendy asked with as much sympathy as possible. Wendy could guess, but she wanted to keep the woman talking.

"I'm sorry, I can't help you."

"Please, Mrs. Evans. Just a few questions? I want to help."

She sniffled. "Do you have children, Ms. Oprander?" Mrs. Evans asked.

"No."

"When you do, you'll understand how horrible it is to not only lose a child but to have their discretions thrown in our faces."

Wendy was losing this woman. "Like I said, I won't print anything until you read the article first and approve it. I promise."

Wendy couldn't remember ever offering this to anyone before, but this woman's grief affected her.

"Why do you want to do this? Did you know my son?"

"No." This article wasn't just for the money or the potential job anymore. Wendy believed in justice. "I don't want what happened to your child to happen to anyone else's. Everyone involved in the drug distribution needs to be caught and locked up."

The woman's chuckle came out bitter. "And some female journalist can do that?"

Wendy's back bristled, but she tamped down her frustration. "I exposed a slave ring and helped bring down their leader last month."

Silence. "What do you need to know?"

The relief almost made her sigh out loud. "Can you tell me who was at the party or the name of someone who might know who was there?"

"I can't say for sure but ask Sherry Knowlton. That's Mike's girlfriend. She could tell you."

That piece of information was a huge win. "Thank you so much."

"Please help bring my son's killer to justice."

Mrs. Evans' plea choked Wendy up. "I promise to do everything I can."

What had started out as a paid job just turned into a cause.

"I'D LIKE TO take a trip to Thedia," Logan said.

Stone's eyes widened. "That's a long haul. What's there?"

Logan explained about the two teens who'd overdosed. "Someone is supplying this province with drugs, and we need to find out who it is."

"Why this case? I mean two teen deaths is sad, but what's so special about this one?"

"One of the boy's fathers—John Evans—has done a lot of pro bono work for the precinct. Chief Wilson wants to solve this case for him. Anderson is making it a priority too."

"And he doesn't have the computer expertise that you do to get into the needed records, I presume?"

Stone always caught on fast. "Correct. He wants me to look into some bank records and cell phone calls the boys might have made."

Stone leaned back. "That's right up your alley."

"It is."

"I'm sure you know that kids at parties do stupid stuff. I trust they were human?" his cousin asked.

"Yes. What is important here is that Anderson asked us to figure out who sold the drugs to those kids and find him. And that is what I intend to do. So are you up for the trip?"

"Do dragons fly?"

Logan actually laughed. It didn't matter he'd heard that expression since birth. He always enjoyed Stone's positive attitude. "Come on. Since I don't know how long we'll be staying, we should put a change of clothes in a pack."

"Sounds good. I'll meet you back here in thirty."

"I'll be ready. But first, I'll call Griffin to let him know what we're up to." His brother might wonder where his business staff had disappeared to when he came back to the office.

WENDY'S ATTEMPT TO learn something at the high school about the party where the boys had died had been a bust. She'd arrived at Edendale Prep School right before school let out since she thought that would be the optimum time to talk to Mike's girlfriend. When Wendy asked at the receptionist's desk for the whereabouts of Sherry Knowlton, she learned the girl had called in sick today, which made sense.

Not one to give up, Wendy decided to find someone else to talk to—someone who looked like they could have attended the upscale party. It would probably be a student who was fairly popular and well-dressed—or at least a kid who looked like they put effort into their appearance. She based that conclusion on the fact that the Evans and Sanderson families were well off.

When the kids piled out of the front door after the end-of-day bell, no one struck her as the hard-partying type. Wendy was about to head back to where she'd parked when she spotted a very pretty girl laughing, only the cheer didn't reach her eyes. For some reason, Wendy believed she would somehow be connected to Mike and Tom.

Wendy practically stepped in front of the girl in order to get her attention. "Excuse me."

Thankfully, the teen stopped and didn't look like she was about to blow her off. "Yes?"

"I'm Wendy Oprander, a writer for the Edendale Herald."

The girl's eyes widened. "Really? I plan to major in journalism next year in college."

What luck. Wendy certainly hadn't expected such a positive reaction to her profession, but she'd go with it. While her job wasn't glamorous, this girl seemed to think it was. "That is awesome. Then you'll understand that as a journalist, I need to ask questions. Do you have a moment to answer a few?"

The teen looked around. "Sure, but what's this about?"

"Let's talk someplace other than the main walkway."

Once they were away from the crowds, Wendy pulled out a tablet from her purse, ready to take notes. "Let's start with your name."

"Melanie Whittaker." She clasped her hands in front of her. "Is this about Mike and Tom?" Her voice caught, a sure sign this was an emotional topic.

"Yes. Were you at the party last night?"

She shook her head. "Tom and I dated for a bit, but a few months ago he got so full of himself that I broke things off. I stopped hanging out with anyone from our group after that."

That was disappointing as far as collecting intel for her story went. "I see. Did something happen to cause Tom to change?"

Wendy recalled that senior year was a time for searching for one's independence—especially if the family was demanding. Wendy wondered if Tom had used drugs to achieve this freedom.

"He got into the best school in the province—Hanfield University. That's what changed him."

Wendy whistled. It was for the elite of the elite. "That's impressive. Tom should have been proud of his accomplishment."

"He was, mainly because he never did well in school. Mike, who was his best friend, had been a shoe-in. Tom never got an A in his life, yet both of them received scholarships to play ball."

Something didn't add up. "If Tom wasn't strong academically, do you think he would have done okay at Hanfield? It is rigorous."

"Honestly? No. I mean, he had two great tutors this year, one for math and science and another for history and writing, but unless Mr. Quigley and Mr. Hammersmith went to the university with him, there was no way Tom would pass his classes."

"If Tom seemed so confident, he must have had a plan," Wendy said. From the way Melanie was picking at her nails, she was conflicted talking ill of the dead.

Melanie inhaled. "He just said he had everything handled."

"What did that mean?" Wendy asked, though she could come up with a few ideas. One involved paying off someone at the university, though that was a reach.

"I don't know. I just didn't like how once Tom was accepted, he changed into a different person."

"Do you think it was drug related?" It was a tough question to ask, but the answer might help point her in the right direction.

"No. That's the one thing that I believe wasn't involved. Tom was an athlete. When we were together, he never touched the stuff. I can tell you I was totally shocked when I found out he died from an overdose. I might believe he experimented with drugs, but not that he would take so much that he'd die. Both he and Mike were good kids."

That was a shame. "Could you give me the names of some other students who could have gone to the party? They might be able to shed more light on the boys' frame of mind."

Melanie lifted her chin. "Why do you want to write a story about them? I mean their poor parents have been through enough."

Wendy appreciated the girl's defense of Tom's memory. She liked her. "I'm actually doing an exposé on the person responsible for pushing the drugs. I told Mike's mom that I won't use any names if she doesn't want me to."

Melanie grabbed Wendy's arm. "Does that mean you know who

the dealer is? If you do, why isn't he in jail?"

Wendy held up a hand. "Whoa. No. I'm trying to help find out who this person, or persons, is. I'm only looking for clues to give to the police."

"Oh. Okay. Have you spoken to Mike's girlfriend, Sherry?"

"Not yet. She's out sick today. Can you think of who else might have been at the party?"

Melanie gave her the names of ten students. "I'm only guessing here, even though we were really tight at one time. In fact, we all went skiing in Thedia right before Tom and I broke up. His parents have a cabin there, and Tom told everyone that they could stay there for free."

The poor girl was a bundle of nerves. Wendy made a show of jotting down the information, even though it didn't seem relevant. "I appreciate your help."

Melanie's shoulders slumped. "I don't see how I helped, but I hope you do find this dealer."

After taking down Melanie's email address, Wendy left, her mind spinning.

Armed with a list of names to check out, she had the next few days cut out for her.

Chapter Three

WITH STONE ON his heels, Logan strode into the office building at the mines and slapped a notebook on his desk. "That was a bust."

"I wouldn't say that. I thought it was a nice change of pace seeing Thedia Province." Stone dropped his backpack on the sofa on the other side of the room. "Besides, we got the names of everyone who sells a large number of mushrooms as well as the names of the pharmaceutical companies who produce Trilox."

"I probably could have learned who sold that stuff with a few phone calls," Logan said.

He wasn't ready to admit that his lack of cheer was because his mind wasn't totally on this search, and that bothered him.

Stone chuckled. "Did you think someone was going to give us the name of all the drug dealers who pedal the stuff out of their province?"

"No. I don't know what I expected. I've looked through the bank records of suspected drug dealers in Avonbelle and couldn't find anything incriminating."

"You'll figure something out eventually." Stone slid a hip on the edge of Logan's desk. "I can tell something else is bugging you. What is it?"

"Nothing. I'm good."

"I'm calling bullshit."

Despite all of Stone's light-hearted attitude, the man was clever and astute. "Fine. I think Wendy Oprander is my mate, but she won't give me the time of day."

Stone chuckled. "Wendy? As in the girl who was held captive for a week by Malpan?"

Stone had been one of the Guardians who'd helped save the slaves in the mine. "The one and only."

His cousin sobered. "Maybe she's not ready to have a mate. I mean, I know I'm not. You have a lot of years left to enjoy each other. Wendy is a wolf shifter, so she'll come around eventually. I don't see the need to rush."

Sometimes Logan wanted to strangle Stone. "It's not as if my dragon is giving me much choice."

Stone winced. "That bad, huh?"

"It's becoming more and more distracting by the minute." Stone was probably not the best choice of confidant, but it wasn't as if he could confide in Griffin. Hell, his brother was mated to Wendy's cousin Danita. Any talk of mates would surely get back to Wendy, and Logan wanted to be the one to tell her that they belonged together—or at least tell her he wanted to give it a shot.

I won't let you fail when you do, his dragon said.

As if his animal had the power over Wendy. "Right now, I need to figure out something about this case. I don't need to be obsessing over a woman."

"Amen to that." Stone smiled. "You want to know what I think?"

Logan didn't like his cousin's tone. "No."

"I'm going to tell you anyway. You need to call her and ask her out. Get her out of your system."

"For starters, I have asked her out a couple of times, but she keeps turning me down. As for getting her out of my system, it doesn't work like that. Wendy is my mate. She is part of my being." Sheesh. "For a shifter, you should know better."

"Maybe I do. I still say you should ask her out again. You can wear her down. As soon as she agrees, you'll get your mojo back."

Mojo? Who says that anymore? It didn't matter. Stone might actually be on to something. "What if she turns me down again?"

"Don't be such a wuss. You're the charismatic Logan Caspian. I've seen you in action. You can be persuasive when you put your mind to it. Just don't push too hard. You've got this."

He hoped that was true, but if she said no again, he wasn't sure how he'd respond. Be angry? Resigned? Or more anxious? He prayed it wasn't all three. "I'll think about it."

"When was the last time you spoke with her? And I don't mean on the phone. Face to face."

"I don't know. Maybe three weeks ago."

"Right after her capture?"

"Not right after. I gave her some time to get over it."

Stone leaned closer. "Get over it? I've never known you to be so out of touch. A woman doesn't get over an assault like that. Ever. You need to show her some sympathy. We've all been in tough situations before. Draw on those memories and let her know that things will work out. Eventually."

This coming from playboy Stone? "That's what you would do?"

"Hell, yeah. I'd even take her flowers or something to show her I care. If nothing else, suggest she go to a spa for some rest and relaxation, but whatever you do, don't suggest she seek help. Wendy is well aware that therapy helped Danita. Let her cousin be the one to bring up the topic of getting some mental health help."

As much as he didn't want to admit his cousin might be right, Stone brought up some good points.

Logan searched his mind for what he and Wendy had talked about the last time he called her. "I believe I was sympathetic when we spoke. I asked her how she was holding up, and Wendy said she was doing fine."

Stone shook his head and then pushed back his chair. "You bought that line?" He huffed. "Here, I thought you had your shit together. You need to try harder to find out how she's really doing. A strong woman like Wendy won't admit she needs support."

"What if she won't talk to me?"

Stone held up his palms. "Who are you? I've never known you to be such a basket case. Knock on her door, cuz. If she is your mate, she'll know it as well as you do. She's just scared, I bet."

That was what his dragon had told him. "I appreciate the advice."

Stone stood. "I have work to do. If you need me to do anything, just give a holler."

"I will. And thanks."

Stone nodded and left.

It took Logan all of fifteen minutes to finally decide he should call her again. He would start by asking her about her trip to the police station. That was non-threatening.

Don't do that, his dragon chimed. *She'll think you're a stalker.*

You're right. If I say I saw her outside the police station, she'll ask why I was there. If I tell her I'm working on a case with my cousin Anderson, she'll ask what case it is. Knowing her, the nosy journalist will want to investigate the death of the two teens, and I can't let that happen.

The last time Wendy had investigated a big story, she'd poked the bear—or dark Fey in this case—and ended up in a cage at the bottom of a mine. Had it not been for her cousin's premonitions, Wendy might have died underground. Logan shivered at that thought. Even his own cousin Tory would have died at Malpan's hand if another Fey hadn't interfered.

Decision made. Logan would act as if everything was normal and then ask her out. She'd already finished her story on Malpan and probably another one too, so she had no excuse not to socialize. Pleased with his decision, he dialed her number.

WENDY'S CELL CHIMED. She picked it up and checked the caller ID. It was Logan. Again. She wasn't sure why she'd programmed in his number after he'd called the first time, but part of her wanted to stay connected. She told herself it was because her cousin was mated to his brother. "Hey, Logan. What's up?"

Wendy was pleased she kept her tone friendly. Considering her pulse was fluttering, she'd expected to sound breathless.

"I'm calling to check up on you."

"Check up on me?" She liked that he cared, but the implication was that she hadn't recovered from her capture, and that bugged her a little. Okay, it bugged her more than a little, though it was possible the stress of earning a full-time position at the newspaper was getting to her.

"I mean, I hadn't heard back from you, and I was worried," Logan said.

"Did I promise to call you?" He wasn't making any sense. She would have remembered if she had.

"Not exactly. You said you were too busy to talk the last time I called because you were working on your latest article. I believe you've published that Malpan piece, so I thought you'd be free to go out to dinner."

Whoa. Not where she thought he was coming from. Her heart lurched at the idea of a date though. The lustful and lonely part of her wanted to scream yes, but if she became distracted by the hunky Logan Caspian, she'd never meet her deadline for this next piece. Knowing her, she'd ask him for help with this drug case, and he'd throw a fit—assuming he was anything like his brother Griffin.

From what she'd learned about Logan, he would claim chasing after a drug dealer was too dangerous. And yes, it probably was, but she was a journalist. She'd also promised both herself and Danita that she would be more careful this time. She'd learned her lesson with Malpan.

"I really appreciate the invitation, but to be honest, I'm working on another article. If I don't finish this next piece soon, I might end up on the street." Crap. That sounded bad, but there was a lot of truth to it.

"Excuse me?"

"I meant that the editor at the paper is breathing down my neck to give him another newsworthy article. If I do, he'll offer me a full-time position and that, Logan Caspian, is my life-long dream."

"Oh."

"How about a rain check?" she asked before he could come up with another reason they should go out.

"Sure, darling, but if you need help with your story, will you promise to ask me?"

Darling? She didn't know if she liked the affectionate name or not.

Stop analyzing everything, her wolf said. *Enjoy it.*

If she really needed his help, she would ask. "I can do that."

"What's this big breaking story you're working on?" he asked.

Damn. "I'm not at liberty to discuss it." Silence. This wasn't going as planned. "I meant I'm trying to figure out which story I want to tackle next. I've had a few ideas and just need to do a bit more research to decide which one would be the best." She really only had one lead, but if a better one came along, she might change her mind.

No, you won't. You made a promise, and the Wendy Oprander I know, would never do anything but give it her all.

Why did her wolf suddenly decide to become so moral? And so chatty?

"I see," Logan said.

Damn. Now she'd hurt his feelings. "We'll go out to lunch just as soon as I clear up this story. I promise."

"Sounds good. Don't get into any trouble, you hear?"

She liked the sudden cheer in his voice. "I won't."

As soon as she hung up, she questioned whether she should have said yes. The stress release might have been a good thing for her muse. Wendy had only spent a short time with Logan when she'd asked for his help in locating the men who'd been held captive in the mine, and their time together had been fun. She'd loved the dragon flight with him so much that at the time she was almost willing to believe he was her mate. But could she make that decision after just being held captive? No. In the end, it was for the best that she'd said no.

No, it's not, her wolf shot back. *You'll never know if he is your mate—which I can assure you he is—unless you go out with him.*

I said I will. Just not now. So back off.

Her wolf growled. Whatever. She needed to focus on this article, which meant she wanted to speak to the kids whose names were on the list that Melanie gave her. While the teen wasn't positive all of the people had attended the party, some surely would have. Interviewing kids seemed safe enough. It wasn't as if she would be interviewing suspected drug dealers.

Finding their cell numbers would be hard, but contacting them via social media would be a breeze.

She'd just started her investigation when her cell rang again. Thinking it was Logan calling back, her pulse soared. He probably wanted to push a little harder for them to go out.

Her smile disappeared when she saw it wasn't him. Rather it showed an unknown caller. "Hello?"

"Ms. Oprander?" the stranger asked.

"Yes."

"This is Phil Landry from the Thedia Provincial newspaper."

Her gut clenched. Could this be the man Stanton Everhart had mentioned? "How can I help you?"

"You can help me by coming to Thedia Province so we can discuss your possible full-time employment with our paper. I was highly impressed with your piece on the Malpan slave ring. Great work. We here at the newspaper could use someone like you."

She didn't know what to say. Wendy had longed to hear such words of praise her whole life. "Thank you, but I'm in the middle of working on a big piece here, and I'm not sure I can get away." In all honesty, she needed to be paid for the piece first so she could afford the airfare and hotel bill. "When I'm finished with it, I'd love to meet with you."

Or would she? She wasn't sure she wanted to leave Edendale

where the weather was balmy and where her cousin lived. And then there was Logan, though Wendy wasn't sure if they were mates. Her mom had died when Wendy was too young to understand what sex and mating meant, and her alcoholic dad sure wasn't about to talk about stuff like that.

Stop it. She was doing it again. Why was she trying to talk herself out of considering Logan as a potential mate? Didn't she want to see if what she had felt might be a real connection between them? Or did she want Logan to be just another man?

"I'm afraid the offer is only open for another few days. I need a journalist now, one who will go after the hard stories. Let me know if you are interested. I'd be happy to pay for your ticket, hotel, and meals for the inconvenience."

Wow. That offer tempted her. "That's really generous. Thank you. I'll let you know. Soon."

"I hope to hear from you."

Mr. Landry hung up. Damn. Had she made another mistake by not jumping on his offer? Maybe, maybe not. If she were able to write this story about the two teen deaths, she could work full-time at the Edendale Herald instead. Then she wouldn't need to move to Thedia. However, the Thedia offer wasn't contingent on her writing anything. As much as she wanted to cling to that idea, Wendy wanted to see this story to the end. The parents of those teens deserved closure.

With an even stronger determination, she pushed aside the euphoria from the job offer. She then searched for, found, and contacted a few of the students on the list of potential partygoers. She didn't want to say too much on social media, but she hoped they'd meet her in person.

Only one person responded. The young lady said she'd talk to Wendy, but only over the phone. She asked for Wendy's number and said she'd call her when school was out. It was the best Wendy could hope for.

For the remainder of the afternoon, Wendy researched the drug

Crenathum and where it might come from. When her cell rang at four thirty, her nerves flared. "Wendy Oprander speaking."

"Ms. Oprander, this is Charlotte. You contacted me earlier today about Mike's party."

"Oh, yes. Thank you so much for getting back to me. What can you tell me about it? Remember, I won't print any names unless you give me permission."

"I appreciate that, but I wasn't in the room with them when they took the drug."

"That's okay. By any chance, do you know where Mike or Tom got the Crenathum? I'm only concerned about bringing the dealer to justice."

"I wish I did. I don't do drugs, so I wasn't told anything about that."

Wendy was good at reading people, but she couldn't quite decide if Charlotte was telling the truth or not. "Did they say anything about meeting someone earlier that day or the perhaps the day before?"

"No." She inhaled. "Wait. This probably means nothing, but Tom had a math tutor, a Mr. Quigley. I saw them talking together in the parking lot the day before the party. I doubt Tom was talking about drugs with him though."

No, but maybe Mr. Quigley was the one selling Tom the drugs. "Is Mr. Quigley a teacher at your school?"

"No."

"Do you know where I could find him?" Wendy asked.

"No, but I bet Tom's mom knows. She would have been the one to pay him to tutor Tom."

"Good point. I appreciate you sharing everything with me, Charlotte. If you happen to hear anything, can you call me? Remember, I won't mention your name."

"Sure."

Wendy hung up, her mind spinning. During her research on Crenathum, it appeared as if it was mostly processed in Thedia. Her former boyfriend, Deke Darnell, lived there. Not that he did drugs, but perhaps he could ask around. Doing so herself could be dangerous.

But first, she needed to call Tom's mom and ask for Mr. Quigley's number. Wendy hesitated to make the call since speaking with Mike's mom had been hard enough. Her grief had torn up Wendy's insides and reminded her of her own loss when her mother had passed, but Wendy couldn't let her issues get in the way. This was about finding an evil person. She could do this.

She dialed the number and waited. The phone rang ten times. Either Tom's mom was avoiding all calls, or she'd left her phone at home when she went out. Darn. When it went to voicemail, Wendy told her who she was and why she needed to speak with her. Wendy disconnected, planning to call again as soon as she returned from Thedia—assuming she decided to go.

Chapter Four

CONSIDERING THE NEWSPAPER in Thedia was picking up the tab for her trip, Wendy saw no reason not to listen to what Phil Landry had to say. She called him to let him know she would hop on a plane the next day. His offer might even be something she could live with. While she and her cousin Danita were close, once Danita had moved out of the apartment on the floor below hers and into her mate's place, the two of them hadn't seen nearly as much of each other. Knowing Danita was safe and happy was good enough for her.

As for missing Logan Caspian? She barely knew the man.

Whose fault is that? her wolf asked.

Okay, I'll admit it. It's mine. I haven't gone out with him, because Logan unnerves me. Do you remember when he asked me if I'd ever flown with a dragon before, and I told him no?

Yes, but I figured this powerful being overwhelmed you with so much lust that you couldn't think straight.

Finally, she understood. *Yes. Just a day or two before that, his own brother had flown me from the mines to Edendale. How could I forget that ride?*

Even if that hadn't happened, she and Deke dated for months, and he'd flown her many, many places. Clearly, she wasn't in her right mind when she was around Logan.

I have one word for you: mate.

The last thing Wendy needed was to continue this conversation. Right now, she wanted to do some research on this newspaper and learn what the surrounding area had to offer. Tomorrow, she'd call Danita and let her cousin know that she was about to fly to Thedia for a job offer. Wendy propped her feet up on the table and leaned back, trying to figure the best way to break the news to her.

"THEY'RE WILLING TO offer you a job based on one article you wrote?" Danita asked after Wendy explained everything the next morning. She wished Danita didn't sound as if it was too good to be true.

"It was a great article, if I do say so myself. I think since I was held captive during part of the time, it added a lot of authenticity."

Danita sighed. "I really am happy for you. How long will you be gone?"

"I plan to return in two or three days. I'll fly in later today, talk to Mr. Landry tomorrow, and then fly home."

"You did say Thedia, right?"

"Yes." Where Deke Darnell now lived. Danita was well aware of how much Deke Darnell had hurt Wendy when he'd walked out on her and never called again. His reason was that his dad had been injured in a car wreck. What was a good son supposed to do? Put sex above his father's well-being? Maybe not, but he shouldn't have ghosted her afterward. Sheesh. "I know it's cold there, and I might hate the place, but I owe it to myself to check it out."

"Are you going to contact Deke?" Danita's words came out metered—or should she say laced with disapproval?

Danita wasn't the type to let it drop. "If I do, it will be to see how his dad is doing." That wasn't the real reason, but if she revealed she was working on a story about the teens who'd overdosed, Danita would try to talk Wendy out of going.

"Uh-huh. You still like him, don't you?"

"I had feelings for him, but that is in the past. I doubt I can forgive him for never contacting me again. He should have at least texted me to let me know his dad was okay." In truth, the moment she met Logan, she realized that what she and Deke had was merely lust. "Look, I have to finish packing. I'm flying out in a couple of hours. I'll call you when I return. Hugs to Griffin."

"Be safe."

From her cousin's wistful tone, she was referring to staying safe emotionally. "I will."

Once Wendy finished packing, she took a shuttle to the airport. When she stepped up to the airline counter, she held her breath, hoping a ticket was waiting for her. Score! It was. Go Thedia Provincial. She liked a paper with class. Not that the Edendale Herald wasn't a nice place to work—when they were willing to published her material—but she didn't recall them springing for anything, even if it was for a story. To be fair to them, she was merely a contractor.

During the short flight, she studied her notes about the deaths of the two teens and wrote down the facts as well as her thoughts in a coherent fashion. No guilty party jumped out at her, but hopefully Deke could fill in some blanks.

After she landed and checked into her hotel, she gave him a call. Despite having lived in Edendale for four months, Deke had kept his Thedia number. She couldn't imagine what his cell phone bill had been like during that time, considering the cost of roaming charges nowadays.

"Wendy? Is that really you?" Deke asked.

She was thrilled he answered and actually sounded pleased. "Sure is." She told him that she was interviewing at the Thedia Provincial.

"That's great. It's what you've always wanted."

"It is. Apparently, Mr. Landry read a piece I did and was impressed."

"Good for you. I always knew you'd be a success someday."

He did? That was news to her. Wendy waited for Deke to suggest they get together, but apparently, he was waiting for her to make the first move. Being aggressive was not an issue for her however. "I have a favor to ask."

"What is it?" Wendy couldn't tell by his tone if he was hesitant or excited.

"Do you think we could meet tomorrow morning? It won't take long. I just want to ask you a question or two about a case I'm working on."

He chuckled. "I see some things haven't changed. Sure. What about Ripley's? It's a breakfast restaurant on Altuna Street."

That shouldn't be hard to find. "Perfect. How about ten?" Her appointment with Mr. Landry was at one, so she'd have plenty of time to make the interview after seeing Deke.

"Great. I'll see you there."

When she disconnected, she worked hard to push aside all emotions about what tomorrow would bring. To keep busy, she hung up her dress she planned to wear to the meeting with Landry and then hopped into the shower. Flying always made her feel grungy.

As she washed, her mind whirled. If she ended up taking this job, leaving everything familiar behind would be hard, but for her career, she could do it. Just when she thought maybe she could make the change, the image of Logan's face popped into her head. Did they have a real connection? She thought so, but Wendy wanted to wait until after this whole drug issue was solved to find out.

WHEN WENDY ENTERED the restaurant the next morning and spotted Deke, she was just about to smile when she noticed the beautiful brunette sitting next to him. Not to worry. This wasn't a date. Wendy had only claimed the meeting would take a few minutes. This woman could be a coworker for all Wendy knew.

Refusing to assume the worst, she painted on a smile as she moved toward him. "Deke."

Wendy then turned toward the mystery woman, held out her hand, and introduced herself.

The woman shook hers. "Nice to meet you. I'm Becky, Deke's mate. He said you two had met in Edendale."

Becky was his mate? That was fast, but the way she rattled off the fact that Deke and Wendy had merely met in Edendale implied this woman had no idea what had gone on between them. However, since what had happened was in the past, Wendy let it drop.

"Yes, we did. He helped me with a little investigation. That's why I called him today. I wanted to discuss another article I want to write." She faced Deke. "If this is a bad time, we can just email."

He pulled out a chair. "No. Becky and I have no secrets from each other."

She was about to say that he and his mate had a few, but then thought better of it. "Great."

"First, tell me about this job offer," Deke said.

She wasn't there for small talk. "I really don't know much, but I'll find out soon enough. Hey, listen. I'm working on an article about two teens back home who overdosed on Crenathum. Have you heard of that drug?" She believed everyone knew of it, but it didn't hurt to ask.

"I hadn't heard about the deaths, but I do know about Crenathum. I've never used it myself, but it can have some bad side effects. How can I help?"

"It is my understanding that most of the Crenathum is manufactured here due to the area's unique weather conditions. I was hoping you might have heard rumors about who might be making the drugs and then transporting them across province lines."

His eyes widened. "Me? No. I wish I could help, but it's not something I'm involved in. Word to the wise, I think you'd be better off investigating something less dangerous."

Out of habit, Wendy lifted her chin. "I can take care of myself."

One brow rose. "A wolf shifter doesn't have a fighting chance against a dragon, assuming one is involved in dealing this drug. In case you don't know, Thedia is crawling with dragons—more so than any other province. Our kind likes the cold."

She hadn't considered that. "I don't plan on approaching one. I merely want to learn something and then hand the information over to the cops—on the condition they give me an exclusive interview of course."

Deke nodded. "Of course. That is wise, but even asking questions can get you into trouble."

Her former boyfriend had no idea the lengths she'd gone to for her last story, nor how she'd almost died. "I appreciate the warning."

The waitress stopped by with a carafe of coffee, which Wendy gladly accepted. She had, however, lost her appetite. As Deke and his mate ordered, Wendy enjoyed her hot brew.

"For you?" the server asked.

"Nothing, thank you."

"You don't want breakfast?" Deke asked.

That had been her plan before he came with Becky. "I'm too nervous to eat, but thanks." As quickly as she could, Wendy drank most of her coffee and then pushed back her chair. "If you hear anything, please drop me a line." Wendy slipped Deke her business card in case he'd lost her email address or phone number. Wendy then faced Becky and smiled. "Nice to meet you."

"You too." This time, Becky's comment was filled with pleasure.

Wendy snapped her fingers before standing. "I almost forgot to ask. How is your dad?"

"My father?"

"You had to leave Edendale because he'd been in a car wreck."

"Oh, yes. The car wreck. It wasn't as severe as we first thought. His dragon healed him pretty quickly. Thanks for asking."

If his dad had healed that fast, why not return to Edendale if only to say goodbye? If nothing else, Deke could have called to tell her his father was fine. Deke was an ass. She should be happy he'd ended it. "I'm glad."

Wendy couldn't wait to get out of there. Not that she wanted to spend an hour reminiscing with Deke about the good times, but if they had, it would have been super uncomfortable in front of his mate.

With the promise that Deke would contact her should he learn something, Wendy left. The distance from her hotel to the restaurant had been less than a mile, so she decided to walk back. Because she hadn't anticipated having so much extra time, Wendy stopped several times to peruse many of the store windows and liked what she saw.

There were a few negatives to the town however. While Sawmill, the capital of Thedia Providence, was nice, it was at best half the size of Edendale, and Wendy was a big city girl at heart. That aside, she promised herself she'd keep an open mind.

Once she made it to her hotel, she headed straight to the restaurant to do further research. Since she had almost two hours to kill, she ordered breakfast. She then studied her surroundings. The clientele looked like what she'd typically see in Edendale, but for some reason, she had an uneasy feeling someone was watching her. It could have been because Deke made the comment about how it could be bad for her health to ask a lot of questions. For now, she'd push aside her drug related research and focus on staying calm while getting ready to ask questions and provide answers to Mr. Landry.

When it was time to go, the clerk at the front desk gave her directions to the newspaper office. Thankfully, it was only a short walk. Even though it was brisk outside, Wendy wanted the exercise. The sun was shining, and the rather dark clouds were far off in the distance.

Wendy arrived early to her interview. Better early than late as her mom used to preach. After waiting for almost a half hour in the lobby, a tall woman with short, curly hair approached her. "Mr. Landry will see you now."

Finally. The woman escorted Wendy down a hallway to an open door that led to an office. The nameplate next to the door read: Mr. Landry, Editor In Chief. He stood and smiled. Landry was a large man, and because his voice shook over the phone, she was expecting him to be a lot older, but the opposite was true. He was at most forty. Perhaps it was also because her boss at the Edendale Herald was ancient that she expected Mr. Landry to be too. The second similarity was that both this editor and her boss were humans.

Mr. Landry walked around his desk and held out his hand. "I hope you didn't wait too long. I needed to make sure tomorrow's paper was good to go. Have a seat."

"Not at all." Wendy would have said that even if she'd been asked to wait for hours.

Sitting on her hands to keep from fidgeting wouldn't have looked good, so she clasped them on her lap and pretended the cool-headed Logan Caspian was beside her. She inhaled and smiled, ready to be interviewed.

"I'm really curious about your piece on Malpan. How did you figure out he was involved in slave trading?"

Saying it involved a little bit of luck wouldn't sound good, so she picked the parts that showed she was resourceful and smart. Naturally, she left out some of the sketchier aspects of her investigation. Because she suspected he'd ask her this question, Wendy was well prepared to answer.

"I'm impressed with your ingenuity. Are you working on any other stories that I might be interested in?"

"Just investigating the death of two teens. I doubt it would be of interest to the Thedia readers."

Chapter Five

"KNOCK, KNOCK."

Logan looked up from his desk and smiled. It was his sister Greer. "This is a surprise. To what do I owe the honor?"

Greer ran the jewelry store with their cousin Tory in the building situated at the base of the SinCas building in town. Not only did she sell the goods, both she and Tory helped design the gems that the Sinclairs mined.

His sister pulled over a chair and sat down. "Mom is worried about you."

That was the last thing he expected her to say. "Why? Other than a quick trip to Thedia, I haven't left the office in what seems like forever."

"If that's the case, why haven't you answered her calls?"

"Shit. I saw she left a message, but I totally forgot to call her back."

"That's not like you."

"No, it's not." His pulse skyrocketed. "Did something happen? Is Dad okay?"

"Dad is fine. Mom is fine. It's just that she wanted to have a little dinner party next week for the family. Even though everyone seems to have settled into a routine after taking down that slave trader, we all have been lax about calling or stopping by."

Logan leaned back. "I'm guilty, but it's partly because Anderson has asked me to help with a new case."

That wasn't the whole truth since there had been a few weeks' gap between closing the Malpan case and this new one, but he needed some excuse. Actually, it was all Wendy's fault. If she hadn't walked into his life, he'd be on track.

"I hadn't heard about this new case. Anything interesting? Is it something the Guardians need to deal with?"

"I'm not sure." He told her about the two teens who'd overdosed. "I don't think I'd be involved if both of the parents weren't prominent in the community."

"Teens can be careless, but if you can help the cops find the drug dealer, it could save other lives."

"I agree." His voice trailed off mostly because he was thinking of someone else whose life could be in danger—as in right now. He was sure it was nothing, but when Logan had decided to take a different approach with Wendy and call her once more, her phone kept going to voicemail. It was as if either her phone wasn't recharged or she wasn't able to get to her phone. He didn't want to think she'd been kidnapped again. That would be like lightning striking the same person twice.

A hand waved in front of his face. "Tarradon to Logan."

He jerked his attention back to his sister. "Sorry. I was thinking about something."

A small smile lifted her lips. "From the way streaks of teal were slicing through your eyes, it's about a woman." She leaned forward. "Spill it. I haven't had any juicy gossip in a while."

"It's Wendy."

Her brows lifted. "Wendy, as in Danita's cousin?"

"Yes." He didn't know why everyone acted so surprised.

"I didn't know you were seeing her."

"I'm not," he said. "Though it hasn't been because of lack of effort on my part. I swear when she came by the office after her capture, we had a connection. I felt it, and I *know* she did too."

"A connection? As in maybe you've found your mate type of connection?"

His family would find out sooner or later. Whether he could convince Wendy of the fact was anyone's guess. "Yes."

Her smile lit up her face. "I'm thrilled for you. What does Wendy have to say about this revelation?"

He glanced at the ceiling in an effort to figure out how to phrase his failure. "She won't go out with me, so I've not had the chance to discuss it with her." Surprisingly, saying the words out loud hadn't been that hard.

His classy sister whistled—something he couldn't recall her ever doing before. "You need to step up your game, brother."

From her tone she was teasing, but Greer was right. "I'm trying. I've been calling her, but it only goes to voicemail."

"Could she be avoiding you?" Greer snapped her fingers, pulled out her phone, and swiped a number.

"What are you doing? I don't need any help. I can figure this out by myself."

"I'm calling Danita. If anyone knows what Wendy is up to, it's her." Greer pushed back her chair and stepped into the hallway.

That wasn't good. What was she planning? Greer didn't return for a good ten minutes, tempting him to listen in on the conversation, but out of respect, he didn't. When her laugh filtered into his office, Logan finally relaxed.

Greer waltzed back into the office and returned her phone to her purse. "All is well. Wendy was offered a full-time job in Thedia, and she went there for an interview. She should return tomorrow."

"How is that good? She is my mate, damn it. What if she takes the job?"

Greer waved a hand. "Wendy won't do that. She'd never leave Danita."

How could she be so sure? Apparently, Wendy didn't think they could be mates, or she would have conferred with him first. Right? This bit of information however created a good reason for Logan to find her—before she accepted the job.

"What else did her chatty cousin say?" Greer pressed her lips together. He pulled out his phone, ready to call Danita's mate if need be. "Griffin can get his mate to talk."

"Okay, okay. You'll find out soon enough. Before Wendy met you, she dated a guy who has since moved to Thedia."

His fists clenched. "What happened between them?" He could only hope the guy cheated on her or something. Then she'd never be tempted to look him up.

Greer shrugged. "I didn't get all of the details, but his name is Deke Darnell. In order to learn more about the real reason for her trip, I suggested to Danita that she and I, along with a few friends, invite Wendy to a girls' night out as soon as she returns. I'm sure we can drag all the juicy details out of her over some drinks."

"I like that idea. The more friends she has here, the less likely she'll be to relocate. If the topic comes up, find out why she won't go out with me—or answer my calls."

"That's not how these get-togethers work. It's not an inquisition. If Wendy happens to bring up your name, we can ask her."

"Fine. By any chance do you know what town in Thedia Providence she's in right now?"

Greer dipped her chin. "Don't tell me you plan to fly there and confront her."

"Not confront. Merely observe."

His sister crossed her arms. "What do you hope to accomplish?"

He hadn't thought that far in advance. "I don't know."

"What happens when she finds out you are basically spying on her?"

Once more, he hadn't thought it through. "I'll figure it out if and when that happens."

Greer smiled and shook her head. "Oh, brother. You have it bad. I have to say I'm pleased. I never thought you'd find your mate, but if you are determined to be your pig-headed self, Wendy is in Sawmill where she is interviewing with the Thedia Provincial newspaper today. Where she is staying, I couldn't say."

Being excellent with computers, he could figure out the rest on his own. "That helps. Thank you."

"You can thank me by answering your stupid phone if Mom or

Dad calls."

Greer had taken time out of her day to fly to the office to have a chat with him. It was the least he could do. "I promise."

AFTER THE QUASI disastrous meeting with Deke—and his mate—followed by the very long interview with Mr. Landry, Wendy was emotionally spent. Wanting some time to think about her options, she ate at the hotel restaurant instead of exploring the city. The good meal, along with a few glasses of wine, helped calm her brain.

Then after a long soak in the tub to help her sleep, Wendy crawled into bed and turned on her phone for the first time since leaving Edendale. Wendy had shut it off, because she was out of range for her Avonbelle service provider, and those long-distance charges could be brutal. Wendy wouldn't have bothered checking it, but Danita or Deke could have called.

After a quick look, she saw she had missed a few messages. Four to be exact, and they all had come from Avonbelle—only not from Danita but rather from Logan. While Logan seemed to have gotten the hint that now was not the best time to date, he must have changed his mind. What could he possibly want that would require four attempts to contact her?

Oh shit. Had Danita leaked it to Griffin where Wendy was and why? She wouldn't be surprised if Griffin had called his brother and told him that Wendy was in Thedia. Thankfully, even Danita didn't know about the drug connection to this province. Or did she?

Considering the late hour, she wasn't about to call Logan back tonight. Most likely, he'd thought of some cool place to take her when she'd finished writing her article, and he was concerned when her cell kept going to voicemail. As soon as she was back in Avonbelle, she'd call him back.

Wendy swallowed her disappointment that Deke hadn't called by now to say that he'd contacted a few friends—possibly at the police department—to see what they knew about any drug trafficking ring. She told herself that he hadn't because he'd come up empty-handed.

It was just as well. Instead of worrying about some drug dealer, she needed to replay the newspaper interview to make sure she understood exactly what would be expected of her should she decide to take the job. While the offer was beyond anything she had hoped for, there was something strange about Mr. Landry, only she couldn't put her finger on it. Sure, he'd asked for a lot of details about her last exposé, but that was to be expected. He would want to see how resourceful she was. Something else had bugged her, only Wendy couldn't figure it out.

Right now, she needed to rest. Tomorrow, she'd fly home and then decide what her next course of action would be. Mr. Landry had given her a week to decide, but it shouldn't take her that long. Usually, she was able to figure things out after a good night's sleep.

Wendy closed her eyes and managed to shut off the rampant questions racing through her mind—that was until the image of Danita appeared. While her cousin had Griffin Caspian in her life now, she and Danita had a bond that would be frayed if she moved away. Could Wendy live with the guilt of knowing Danita had no direct family in town? Ugh. Now wasn't the time to contemplate that big decision though.

Just as she pushed her concern for Danita aside, Logan Caspian, who was too handsome for his own good, filled her thoughts. She could tell from their two face-to-face meetings, along with the tidbits of information Danita had told her, Logan's main characteristic was being tenacious. When he wanted to find an answer, he never let anything go. That was a good trait—unless it interfered with her life.

Sleep, her wolf said. *I want to dream about him.*

I'll sleep, but I can't afford to think about him, or I won't get any peace.

That's your loss.

Not that it would do any good, but Wendy slapped a pillow over her face, hoping her wolf would get the hint and leave her alone.

Luck must have been on her side, because she fell into a deep slumber. She couldn't say how long she was snuggled under the covers, but her arm twitched and then her leg spasmed, rousing her.

When Wendy pulled down the covers to cool off, the scent of smoke registered in her brain. As much as she wanted to ignore it, her animal took over, forcing her to sit up and assess the situation. The smoke made no sense. She was inside a hotel room. Sure, she'd flipped on the heater before she crawled into bed, but it wouldn't smell so pungent, would it?

Even though it was in the middle of the night, Wendy eased out of bed, and only then noticed the insidious smoke pouring in under the door. Oh, shit. With lightning reflexes, she rushed over to the entrance to see how bad it was in the hallway. No one was shouting orders or screaming, which meant she had to time to get out.

Needing to learn her options, she opened the door an inch. Whoa. That was a mistake. Not only did the handle burn her hand, the hallway was consumed in flames, blocking all escape routes. If she was on the fourth floor, what did the floors below her look like?

Sirens sounded from far away. Good. Help was on the way—at least she hoped they were coming because of the blaze.

Breaking the window from this height and jumping out really wasn't a good choice, but at some point, that might be her only one. Of course, she'd be in her wolf form. Humans were way too fragile for a four-story descent.

Think. There had to be something she could do. *Wolf? Help me.*

Get the hell out of there, her animal shot back.

No kidding. Any idea how?

Her animal didn't answer, but it felt as if her wolf was using its claws to scrape against her stomach lining.

While it was probably stupid to care about her possessions, Wendy snatched up the few toiletries from the bathroom and stuffed them in her backpack where her tablet and day clothes were already snug inside.

If she had any chance of avoiding burns during her escape, she needed to wear something over her pajamas.

After donning her coat and slipping on her shoes, Wendy grabbed a towel from the bathroom, wet it, and placed it over her nose. Screams sounded from underneath her room just as her metal door began to glow red. Decision made, exiting the window it was.

Wendy rushed across the room and fumbled with the latch to open it. After jostling the swollen wood for a minute, fresh air blew in. The bad news was that the window only partially opened. Damn. Red and yellow lights flashed where a lot of fire trucks were littering the street below.

Wanting to let them know that she was trapped inside, she leaned out the window. "Help! I'm up here."

There was so much commotion on the sidewalk that it didn't appear as if anyone had even heard her. Crap. The door hinges crackled, implying it might break any moment. With the cross-ventilation, the whole room could explode.

It was time to jump or burn to death. Okay, she had no choice anymore. It was only a matter of how long she should wait before taking the dive. The firefighters had placed ladders against the building to help those on floors two and three, but she saw no tall extension ladder that reached the fourth floor.

Several firemen were placing large blow up mattresses on the sidewalk below that were only now inflating—albeit slowly. Wendy leaned further out the window and waved. "I need to jump now!" she shouted.

Apparently, the screams from the other hotel guests drowned her out, because no one even looked up. It was time to shift. With as much of her body out of the window as possible, she transformed, working hard not to tumble before she succeeded. But before she had the chance to inhale and push off, an explosion from behind knocked her out of the window, sending her spiraling downward.

Wendy wasn't sure which deity she should pray to, but right now what she needed was a miracle.

Chapter Six

HOLY SHIT. WHEN Logan made the decision to check on Wendy in Thedia, he never expected to find her hanging out of a window in a hotel that was on fire. Had she not called out for help when she did, he might not have even spotted her.

Good thing it hadn't taken much sleuthing to find her hotel reservation at the Sawmill Vacation Resort, in part because it was the nearest hotel to the Thedia Provincial newspaper office. Danita mentioned that the paper was picking up the tab for Wendy's airfare, hotel, and food, so it made sense they'd want her close.

As pleased as he was that the paper was treating her fairly, it meant they really must want her if they were willing to foot the bill. Just as soon as he saved her, he would do what it took to convince her not to take the job.

Logan shifted and soared upward just as a powerful fireball shot through the room, jettisoning her into midair. His instincts exploded. With his quick reflexes, Logan managed to snatch her fifteen feet from the ground. Having her in her wolf form helped since he was able to grab her whole body with one claw. Cradling her with his other claw, Logan held on tight as he searched for a spot to land safely.

Wanting to be out of the way of the rescue workers and the commotion, he found a nearby field in a park and landed. When he released her, she collapsed onto the ground, her breathing coming hard and fast.

Logan shifted back, dropped to the ground next to her, and placed a gentle hand on her flank. His heart rate tripled at the lack of response. "Wendy?"

No answer. Her body was warm but not hot, making him think she hadn't been burned. "Wake up!" he pleaded.

When she whined, and then opened her eyes, his relief made him grunt. A few seconds later, her body shook, and fur flew. Wendy shifted into her human form but remained on the ground. It reminded him of the first time he'd seen her after she'd been removed from her prison cell in the underground mine—somewhat disoriented and slightly dirty.

She looked around. "What happened? What are *you* doing here?"

She had to be scared and confused, but answering her question about why he was there might not be in his best interest considering what had just happened. He didn't need to tell her why he'd followed her to Thedia either. That conversation would come later.

"That's not important at the moment," he said. "Are you okay? Were you burned?" He tucked a strand of hair behind her ear.

She slipped her backpack off her shoulders and stared straight ahead, as if she couldn't figure out how she'd ended up in the park. Nearly falling forty feet would disorient a person.

When she didn't answer, Logan reached out and pulled her to his chest.

It was several seconds before Wendy leaned back and looked up at him. "I'm fine, and no I wasn't burned. Just shaken a bit. I've never been blown out of a window before." Her voice had trailed off, implying she was still in shock.

He expected her to scoot backward, but instead she melted against him. Logan would hold her for as long as she wanted, but at some point, he needed to find a paramedic to check her out. She hadn't been in her wolf form long enough to fully heal, and wolf or not, inhaling smoke could do a lot of damage to a body.

Logan ran his palm over her head and then leaned back. "Let's get you checked out just to be sure there won't be any after-effects from all that smoke."

Wendy eased out of his grasp and stood. She brushed off a few leaves and small twigs and lifted her chin. "I'm good."

He bet her stubbornness had served her well in the past, but right now, he wished she'd do as he asked. Logan rose to his feet. "I'm just trying to help. There are ambulances nearby. It will only take a minute."

She placed a hand on his arm and squeezed. "Logan, while I appreciate the suggestion, I'm good. I swear."

"If you say so." The moment she showed any signs of distress though, he'd take her to a hospital whether she agreed or not. "Then how about we grab something to eat? I'm hungry, and I think you should drink something if you inhaled smoke."

"Fine, but how did I get here? All I remember was falling."

"I caught you and flew you to the park to make sure you were okay."

"Really?" As if she'd lost her mind for a moment, she stood on her toes and lightly kissed his cheek. "Thank you."

Her touch unnerved him. Wendy had actually kissed him. So what if it was as a thank you? A kiss was a kiss. He called that progress. "Let's find us some grub."

"Sounds good, but you never answered my question. How did you manage to be at my hotel halfway across Tarradon at the exact moment I was blown out of the window? And in the middle of the night?"

Logan forced a smile. "Good luck?"

She punched his arm, and then her lips actually curled upward. "I am so not buying that."

Relief slammed through him, because he could almost believe she was feeling better—at least physically.

"Once we find a place to eat, I'll tell you about it." Which meant he'd have to think of what to say.

He had flown to Thedia, so they had to hoof it. Not that they had much of a choice. There was no way a taxi was getting anywhere near the hotel area with all of the rescue vehicles blocking the way.

They walked south away from the commotion. At three in the

morning, it took some doing to find a coffee shop that was open. During their stroll, Logan studied Wendy's posture to make sure her breathing wasn't labored. She must have sensed the smoke quickly because she didn't seem to have been adversely affected, thank goodness.

Once inside the coffee shop, they slid into a booth across from each other. Only then did Logan notice she was wearing a coat over pajamas. At least she had been thinking clearly enough to protect herself. "Can you tell me what happened?" he asked.

She opened her mouth, but then quickly shut it, acting as if she wanted to grill him first. Thankfully, she didn't push it and answered. "There's not much to tell. I woke up in the middle of the night to find smoke billowing in under the door. After studying my limited options, I put on my shoes and coat, grabbed my stuff, opened the window, and then yelled for help."

"I appreciate the unemotional listing of the facts, but can you give me a few more details, such as the heat level, noises in the hallway, unusual sounds, and such." He held up a hand. "Pretend you are writing an article about it."

She flashed him a smile. "You sound like my editor."

"Thank you."

Wendy started again, describing how she roused from a deep sleep rather disoriented. "I think it was my wolf who made me get out of bed. Only then did I realize something wasn't right."

"Good. Go on."

"There was smoke, of course, but when I grabbed the door handle and tugged, it was really hot. Wanting to see if there was a viable escape route, I opened it an inch or two but quickly realized that fire was blocking my way."

"Flames on the fourth floor probably meant the fire started there. Did you notice if the floor in your room was hot?"

She glanced to her right. "No. I have to admit I wasn't in an investigative mode at that moment. I was more in a save-my-life-mode."

Logan could fill in the rest of the blanks. "You figured you would sustain fewer injuries if your body was covered."

"Yes, and then I rushed to the window, only to find the sash was painted shut. I had to force the window open."

"I'm not surprised. The building looks old."

"When I finally got it open, there wasn't much space to crawl out. I did yell for help, but because of all of the commotion, no one heard me."

"I did."

Wendy reached across the booth and placed her hand over his, and her warmth seeped deep into his soul. "I owe you for that. I will never be able to repay you."

He smiled. "How about a proper dinner date once we get back home?"

She grinned. "Deal, but it still begs the question: What were you doing in Thedia in front of my hotel at three in the morning?"

"In due time." He smiled. "Finish your story first."

"That's about it. I looked down, wondering how many bones I'd break when I jumped. The firemen were blowing up those big air mattresses, but they were only partially inflated. While I believed my wolf would heal me after my fall, I had no idea how long it would take to recover."

"I'm glad you didn't have to find out."

"Me too."

The waitress stopped by and took their order. They both asked for a coffee and a pastry. "By the way, how did the interview go?" he asked, trying to keep his voice neutral and off the topic of why he was flying by her hotel.

"Danita told you, didn't she?" Wendy asked.

She had perfected the art of not answering his questions—kind of like him. "Actually, it was Greer who asked Danita about you. You weren't returning my calls, and I became worried."

Her eyes widened. "Because I got into trouble the last time, you thought I'd run into trouble again?"

He lifted one shoulder. "It was a reasonable assumption."

"You might be right," she said. "I'd turned off my phone, because I didn't want any roaming charges."

That made total sense. He should have thought of that. "Tell me. Are you considering taking the job?"

Since he almost lost Wendy tonight, Logan needed to know what his chances were of the two of them spending enough time together for her to realize they were mates. He didn't relish the idea of moving to Thedia, though he would if he had to. Not only would it make running the family's mining business more difficult, it would inhibit his ability to be an effective Guardian.

"I was considering it, but I'm not sure I want to leave Edendale. Danita and I are close."

He mentally pumped a fist. *As will the two of us be after our date.* "I see. So, you're going to turn down the offer?"

"I think so."

Something in her tone implied another issue was rattling around in her head. "You only came for an interview, right?" Logan would never ask if she was there to rekindle something with her former boyfriend.

"Of course, why?"

As much as he didn't want to ask about the drug story, he couldn't help himself. "With the recent news of the deaths of the two teens, I thought you might have come here for a story."

"Story? What are you talking about?"

From her lack of eye contact, that was one of the reasons she was there. "I think you know. Tell me this. Weren't you tempted at least a little bit to investigate?" He hoped he wasn't giving her any ideas. "Drugs? Crenathum? Sound familiar?"

Their server arrived at that moment and set down their coffee and pastries. Instead of answering his question, Wendy stuffed one end of her sugar donut in her mouth. That was okay. He could wait her out.

Logan patiently sipped his hot brew while she finished eating.

"What was the question?" she asked with fake innocence.

She was stalling. There was more to her visit than an interview. He was certain. "Spill."

Wendy placed both palms flat on the table and leaned back. "I still don't know what you are talking about."

Logan almost chuckled at her weak attempt to put him off. "Wendy, you are a journalist. Two kids dying from drugs might not normally have caught your attention, but didn't you work on a piece that involved another death by drugs a few months ago?" Technically, it had been rat poisoning but why mention that?

Tension ripped across her shoulders as her brows pinched together. "You talked to Stanton Everhart?"

"I didn't need to. You might think I'm just a pencil pusher at a mine, but trust me, I'm a lot more." He'd learned about that investigation and her involvement from Anderson.

"Now you're a journalist too?"

She didn't have to act so shocked. "I don't write down my stories, if that is what you're asking, but I do investigate. I'm good at it too, and I often lend a hand when my cousin Anderson Caspian needs help."

"Shit. I forgot that you two are related. So now what? You're on this case too?"

"Too?"

Wendy hissed in a breath. "Okay, fine. You're right. I did come to Thedia for another reason." She told him how desperate she was for another lead. "I learned about their deaths and wanted to investigate. We need to stop these pushers."

"I agree, but why did you need to travel all the way to Thedia to investigate? Was it the mushroom connection?" Or because her former boyfriend was here?

She inhaled. "I came for the interview but then realized I might find answers about who was dealing the drugs. The mushrooms used to make Crenathum—the drug the boys overdosed on—are only grown in a cold climate. Thedia was as good a place as any to start looking. I also happen to have a friend here who I contacted. I asked him to ask around." She lifted her chin.

Logan worked hard not to let his eyes swirl red—a sure sign of anger and jealousy. "Was this contact your ex-boyfriend by any chance?" Damn, he hadn't planned for that to come out.

Wendy's mouth dropped. "Seriously? Danita and I will be having a discussion about crossing personal lines."

Logan held up a hand. "Danita didn't tell me. My sister and I were both worried, and Greer wormed the information out of Danita. Even you have to admit that dealing with bad people can backfire."

"True, which is why I asked someone else to ask the questions instead of me—namely Deke."

He had to hand it to her. She had learned her lesson but depending on how this ex-boyfriend carried out the favor, someone—as in some drug dealer—might have learned about a nosy reporter from Avonbelle. Not that Logan believed the fire at the hotel was anything other than an accident, but he planned to ask their Avonbelle arson investigator, Josh Gerrard, to give his opinion on how the fire started. He might not have any jurisdiction in Thedia, but Josh could get in and out without anyone the wiser.

"I'm glad. Does that mean you're returning home tomorrow? I mean today?" It was almost four in the morning.

"I had planned to, but I'll need a shower somewhere. I can't exactly go on a plane wearing pajamas and smelling like smoke."

He loved her positive attitude. Most women would be in a catatonic state right now after a near-death experience. "I'm heading back to Edendale right after I finish eating. You want a lift?"

She smiled, and his dragon sat up and took notice. Hallelujah. "I thought you'd never ask." She picked up her coffee, blew on it, and then drank it down.

LOGAN STILL HADN'T explained to Wendy why he was outside her hotel at three in the morning, but right now she had more important things to think about—like getting home, taking a shower, and then crawling into bed—her bed, to be exact. Tomorrow would be soon enough to ask him more questions. Even if he had told her his reasons right now, she wasn't sure she'd remember it in the morning. The reality of what happened still hadn't fully sunk in yet.

One good thing to come out of this whole experience was that if Wendy became inspired, she might write about her harrowing, near-death experience and how to deal with the aftermath of the life changing event. Her piece wouldn't expose or take down a hardened criminal, but a good human—or rather shifter—interest story always brought in readers.

After her mom had died, Wendy had to learn a lot about coping mechanisms. Her father's answer was to drink, whereas Wendy became more determined than ever to right some wrongs. While she couldn't prevent people from dying from diseases, she could adopt a positive attitude about what to do when bad things happened.

"Take my hand," Logan said, as they were about to cross the street.

Normally, Wendy would have questioned his motives, but she could use the comfort. He only let go once they were safely across the street to the park. A gust of chilled wind blasted her, causing Wendy to clasp her coat tighter. As a wolf shifter, she usually didn't feel the cold, but her body must be off-kilter right now.

Logan wrapped an arm around her shoulder and pulled her close. Their bodies seemed to align perfectly, and his warmth seeped into her, allowing her to breathe a little easier. "Don't need you to catch a cold," he said as he smiled down at her.

Aw. He was so sweet. She leaned her head against his shoulder. "Thanks."

Once they reached the field in the middle of the park, Logan stepped away from her and shifted. The first time she'd met him, Wendy had opted to have him fly her to town instead of driving in a car with him, because she thought he was hot. If she remembered correctly, he didn't try to impress her with some acrobatic moves, and she appreciated that. If he did anything like that on this flight, she might puke. Her head was pounding, and her stomach was rolling. Too much had happened in the last hour that she had yet to deal with.

Logan gently took hold of her and flew upward. All during the flight, her mind spun. The more she thought about it, the more Wendy realized that she needed answers on how the fire had started. She wasn't usually the paranoid type, but she had the sense someone might want her out of the way. The big question was who and why?

Chapter Seven

WENDY JERKED AWAKE to the sound of her phone ringing. When she opened her eyes to sunshine streaming in her bedroom window, she let out a breath. For those first few seconds, she'd been convinced she was still in the hotel room with smoke pouring in under the door, and then the ground below mocking her.

After she wet her mouth in order to talk, Wendy lifted her phone and then shook her head to clear her mind. The caller ID said it was the Thedia Police. After a brief conversation, she told them that she was fine. When they asked how she'd escaped, she told them as soon as she smelled the smoke, she'd called her boyfriend. As she jumped out of the window, he swooped in and saved her. That little exaggeration would save answering a lot of questions.

"I'm glad you are okay, Ms. Oprander."

"Me too."

She disconnected. Less than thirty seconds after she dropped back onto the pillow, her phone rang again. Really? She'd so wanted to sleep in. This time, the call was from Danita. Was she wondering about the interview, her contact with Deke, or had she heard about the fire? Only one way to find out—by answering the damn phone.

"Hey there," Wendy said with as much cheer as possible. She scooted back on the bed and leaned against the headboard.

"How are you? Griffin told me there had been a fire at your hotel last night—or rather early this morning. Logan told him that if he hadn't been flying by that you would have had to jump four stories."

"Yes, Logan saved me from many possible broken bones."

"I want to hear everything—the interview, Deke, the fire, and Logan."

Whoa. That was a lot of information to absorb. "Which do you want to hear about first?"

"All of it, but I know Greer wants to hear it too. I'm getting together with her at Wings tonight, along with a few other friends. Can you join us? You can tell us all about it."

"I'm a little tired."

"You have all day to recover. Besides, it will do you good to get out and have some fun."

Danita might be right. In the presence of Greer, Danita didn't dare ask about her true feelings for Logan. Even if she did, Wendy couldn't say since even she didn't understand them yet.

I know what you're feeling, her wolf shouted. *Logan is the one for you.*

Just because Logan might turn her on didn't mean he was her mate, though after last night's epic save, she was beginning to believe he was. *We'll see. Now leave me alone.*

"Wendy?" Danita asked. "Are you sure you're okay?"

Crap. Spacing out wasn't a good sign. "Yes, I'd love to meet up with you guys. Where and what time?" Or had her cousin already told her? Maybe this whole thing with the interview, the hotel catching on fire, and Logan saving her had affected her more than she wanted to believe.

It was being in Logan's grasp for so long that has your libido out of control.

Okay, I'm not reading any more romance novels unless I know you are sound asleep, she told her wolf.

"I said tonight at Wing's. We're meeting at seven." Danita sounded a bit agitated with her.

"I'll be there." Wendy swiped off her phone and collapsed back onto the bed. She needed some control in her life or she'd never write that exposé or tell about the fire episode.

She had only a few days to consider the job offer in Thedia. The amazing up-front bonus would allow her to rent a really nice place, but was that what was really important in life?

If you take the job, what about Logan? her wolf asked.

If he really wants to date me, he can fly the ninety minutes to see me, right?

Aren't we selfish today?

You're right. I'm sorry.

If she did move to Sawmill, she'd be giving up too much, and Wendy wasn't sure she was ready for that.

"YOU'RE SAYING YOU believe the fire in Thedia was arson?" Josh Gerrard asked over the phone.

Logan hoped he wasn't asking his friend to spend time on something that was the result of someone being careless, but he had to know for sure if someone was targeting Wendy. Logan believed he and Stone had stayed under the radar when they asked around about the drug dealers in Thedia. But Wendy? Who's to say? Bottom line was that she was his mate, and he couldn't be too cautious.

"Possibly." He told Josh about Wendy's new focus. "Her questions could have set off a few alarms. We both know that drug dealers would just as soon eliminate the problem than deal with them in a quieter manner."

"Tell me about it. What did the arson investigator in Thedia say?"

"I called him this morning, but he wouldn't, or rather couldn't, tell me much. He was still investigating."

"He's probably telling the truth. The process takes time. Not everyone has my innate talent to detect chemicals."

Josh wasn't bragging. The dragon shifter had an amazing ability. "I know, which is why I've called you. I wouldn't ask you to do work outside of your job or your jurisdiction, but this is—"

"No need to explain. I know that Magnolia and her sisters help the Guardians any time they can. Am I to assume Wendy is your mate?"

"Yes, only she won't admit it. I just need time to convince her, which means I can't afford to have a target on her back."

"How well I know what denial can do to a soul." Josh laughed. Apparently, Magnolia, one of the Four Sisters, was as stubborn as Wendy was when it came to admitting she and Josh were mates. "Tell me a bit more what we are dealing with."

"All I know is that she smelled smoke, and when she opened her room door, the hallway was on fire. She had to jump out of the window on the fourth floor. Had I not flown there to make sure she stayed out of trouble, she might have been seriously injured."

"Say no more," Josh said. "In fact, I just teleported to the hotel. It is not in the best of shape."

He'd forgotten about Josh's ability to teleport. Once the arson investigator mated with Magnolia, he'd told the Guardians about this talent. "Thank you. Can you tell anything?" Logan asked.

"Give me a sec. Okay, I'm on the fourth floor. Part of the roof is gone."

Logan's gut churned at the thought his mate might have burned to death. "That's terrible."

"I agree. Okay, it looks as if the fire was started on this floor. From the amount of damage, I can tell their fire department responded quickly." Logan could hear Josh inhale. "An accelerant was definitely used to start the fire. Do you know if Wendy was in room 421?"

"No, but I can text her. I do know she jumped from the fourth floor, somewhere in the middle of the building."

"That's where 421 is located. Do ask her, because I found accelerant splashed all over the carpet in front of that room and nowhere else."

"Oh, shit."

"My thoughts exactly," Josh said.

They discussed a few other possibilities, but if she had been in room 421, Logan had to convince Wendy to stop her investigation. "I owe you one," Logan said.

Josh chuckled. "I'll remember that."

As soon as he disconnected, Logan was more determined than ever to keep Wendy safe. Frustration gnawed at him. So far, Josh hadn't mentioned anything that pointed to the identity of the arsonist, but whoever was responsible, Logan was convinced Wendy had been the target, even if she was a room or two away.

The best way to keep her safe was to find the arsonist and get him to confess that he had targeted her. It made sense that someone in Thedia had overheard her asking her ex-boyfriend about drug dealers. And the best way to find this person was to look into who had the most to gain by not having Wendy publish her exposé. Logan had investigated enough cases not to limit his search to Edendale.

His first thought had been that the dealer was someone who was on the Hanfield University waiting list and who also went to Edendale Prep. With these two kids gone, he might have thought he could take their place. A reach for sure, but one that was possible. If that were the case though, how did the fire play into all of this? Or didn't it? Logan found it difficult to believe a teen would have the connections or the money to hire an arsonist to target Wendy, unless an adult was involved. Even if the teen was able to pull it off, how would he know she'd asked questions that day?

In the end, Logan decided to stop pursuing that line of questioning and look into known arsonists in Thedia. He was halfway through this search when his cell chimed, indicating a text. He swiped his finger across the screen. His pulse rose when he noted it was from Wendy. All the message said was: Room 421.

Well shit. It was always possible she wasn't the target, but it seemed highly likely that she was. With this new information, Logan needed to make sure she understood what was at stake. To hell with her insisting he wait until she contacted him. Her life could be on the line, and he needed to take control. Besides, she had agreed to dinner at some point.

Logan dialed her number, but it went to voicemail. Again! Ten Denlars says she was avoiding him. "Wendy, call me. It's about the fire. It wasn't an accident."

That should get her attention, or so he hoped.

"I CAN'T BELIEVE you were trapped in a burning building," Nan Masters said.

Nan was Greer's mate's sister, but Wendy had the sense she was rather sheltered, despite owning a store that sold spa items.

"It was terrifying. I'm just thankful that Logan was there to grab me in midair."

"How lucky was that? Why was he there?" Ivy Woodson asked. "Thedia is a long way from home, even if you fly."

Thank you, Ivy, for asking that question. She must have read Wendy's mind. She had never met this woman before, but the very pregnant lady was mated to Poppy's mate's work partner. Poppy was one of those very special Four Sisters who ran their own pottery shop on the edge of town.

"I don't know, but I suspect my cousin's big mouth had something to do with why Logan happened to be there at three in the morning," Wendy said.

"I'm sorry, Wendy," Danita said. "We were all worried about you."

"It's okay. I should never have mentioned that I went to Thedia for two reasons."

"Two reasons?" Danita asked.

"I told you. One was for the interview and the other was to ask you-know-who for some help." Oh, crap. Wendy meant to say she was there to ask Deke about his dad's health.

"Ask for help?" her cousin asked. "About what? I thought you just wanted to touch base with Deke to see how his father was doing."

Her and her big mouth. Wendy had told so many half-truths that she couldn't keep her stories straight. Since Logan was now aware of her hidden agenda, eventually so would Danita. "It's a long story."

Danita held up her glass. "I have time." She looked around. "Right, girls?"

They all murmured their interest.

Wendy inhaled. "Okay. Here's what happened. It all started with the death of the two teens right here in Avonbelle."

All of the women nodded, clearly having read about the sad tale. "The high school athletes who overdosed, right?" Marianna asked.

Wendy hadn't met this woman either, but she was not only a lawyer in town, she was also Rafe Tremont's sister, the man who had mated with Primrose, another one of the Four Sisters. "Yes."

Marianna leaned forward. "Not that I know the specifics, but there was something about that whole event that sounded suspicious to me. All young kids do stupid things, but two kids who were just accepted to the top school in Avonbelle to play sports usually aren't so careless as to overdose. At least in my experience they don't."

"That might be true," Wendy said, "but I suspect they didn't realize how potent that drug could be."

"Then the dealer who sold them the drugs should have warned them." Marianna picked up her drink and chugged half of it.

That wasn't how the world worked, unfortunately. Something must have happened to Marianna to have caused her to react so strongly but now wasn't the time to ask. "It was probably harder for the boys' bodies to metabolize the drug since they were human. A shifter could have handled it better."

"Maybe," Marianna said, her tone implying she was willing to drop that line of questioning for now.

"What is your connection to them?" Nan seemed a little uncomfortable with the whole drug issue.

"I never met the boys. Truth is, I was offered a full-time position at the Edendale Herald under the condition I write another big story like the one I did on Malpan. I thought a story about the inflow of drugs into our province would be a good one to tell." She held up a hand. "Don't worry. If I do unearth any evidence, I'll turn it over to the police. They can be the ones to catch the drug trafficker, not me. I'm writing the story in the hopes that some lives might be saved if this dealer is off the street."

The women all talked at once. The words noble, sad, and dangerous were being thrown out just as the server refreshed their drinks and brought an additional round of snacks. Because Ivy was pregnant, she refrained from indulging in any alcohol.

"You said you went to Thedia because you were offered a job," Nan said. "Are you going to take it?"

Wendy didn't glance at Danita, mostly because she could only imagine the look on her cousin's face. "I'm not sure. They gave me a week to make my decision. Whether I can get this story or find another big one will factor into whether I stay or go at this point."

Danita's hand clasped hers. "You'll think of something good. Does Logan know you might be moving?"

"He knows that I don't want to take the job if I can help it."

"I bet he was relieved when you told him," Danita said.

Wendy stilled. "Did he say something to you?" Her pulse beat hard, though she wasn't sure what she wanted Danita to say.

"Logan didn't say anything," Danita said. "I just think the two of you would do well together. Besides, if you dated my mate's brother, we would be like sisters-in-law." Danita smiled.

"That would be wonderful."

Thankfully, the chatter turned to Ivy's impending birth, and Wendy had to work hard not to feel a bit left out. She wanted to settle down and have a family, but the timing wasn't right for that either.

Then you need to get a different job, her wolf said.

They'd been over this before. *It's all I know how to do, and it's what I enjoy.*

Enjoy Logan. I bet he could find something to keep you busy.

The image of lying in bed with Logan all day shot into her mind, but Wendy pushed it aside. Even if she suddenly won the lottery, she wouldn't stop working. She enjoyed the thrill of uncovering facts that would lead to taking down someone who deserved it.

Logan or no Logan, Wendy would always want to work.

Chapter Eight

LOGAN COULD BE patient. Or so he wanted to believe. He tapped his fingers on his desk, wondering why Wendy hadn't called him back last night. Hell, he'd dangled the news about the fire being something other than a careless event, and yet she hadn't taken the bait. Something seemed off. Wendy, the journalist, should have been interested enough to call him. Or had he misjudged her desire to find the truth?

It was always possible she'd put her phone on silent when she went out with his sister and some friends last night, but shouldn't Wendy at least have looked at it this morning to see if she had any messages?

It was possible that she had a hangover and couldn't even think about talking to anyone. Decision made. If she didn't contact him by later today, he'd stop over at her place. She owed him a dinner date, and he planned to collect.

Thankfully, Greer promised to let him know if Wendy planned to do something dangerous, or if she happened to mention her interest in him, and so far, his sister hadn't contacted him.

Right now though, Logan needed to concentrate on this drug dealer case. It made sense that the sooner the guy was caught, the sooner Wendy could write her story about the trafficker. Once she did, he'd help her celebrate at the best restaurant in town.

With a renewed desire to stop this dealer, Logan went to work searching the truck manifests of those entering the province. While he didn't expect to find a truckload full of drug packets or anything incriminating, it would be easy to hide the drugs in something like boxes of food or containers of medical supplies, so he focused on trucks carrying that kind of cargo. He also wanted to compare the weight manifests from one stop to another in case the dealer pulled over somewhere, received the drugs, and then hid them inside the truck. The problem was that the driver would know the weights would be different at the next weigh station. To make things worse, it could take months to figure out who was doing the transporting.

After an hour of research, his cell rang, and his pulse spiked. Damn. It was only Anderson.

"Hey, you got something?" Logan asked, hoping by some miracle the case had been solved.

"Yes and no. We have no clue as to the identity of the dealer, but the autopsy came back from the kids. We have a problem."

Anderson's ominous tone made Logan still. "What kind of problem?"

"The boys didn't die from an overdose. The drugs were laced with poison. That is what killed them."

Logan shoved his keyboard off to the side in frustration. That put a whole different spin on the case. Not that the drug dealer didn't need to be caught, but a murderer needed to be caught pronto. "I can't believe this is happening again. What poison was it this time?"

"The same as with the truck driver—rat poison, like the kind that can be found in any hardware store."

"Damn. Who would want to poison two popular kids?"

"That's what I would like to know," Anderson said. "Mind if I stop over? I have a few ideas."

"I'm at my mine office."

"See you in a few." His cousin then hung up.

Logan's mind shot back to Yancy. It was the story Wendy had worked on months ago. When the cops failed to turn up any suspects though, she'd moved on. It might be a coincidence, but it seemed like the two cases could be related.

Wendy, Wendy. She always seemed to insert herself into dangerous cases. If she learned of this new development, it would be just the kind of angle that would appeal to her. However, he was most definitely not going to tell her about it. Knowing her, she would run to every hardware store trying to figure out who'd bought rat poison in the last month. If people learned of her interest, no telling who might try to stop her.

As soon as he and Anderson finished their brainstorming session, Logan planned to make sure Wendy understood the dangers of her investigation. If she refused to listen, he might have to camp outside her apartment and tail her. If she spotted him, it might kill any chance of them actually going out on their date, but he had to chance it. He couldn't live with himself if someone harmed her, and he could have prevented it from happening.

The door to his office opened, and his cousin walked in. "I thought we'd have more privacy here," Anderson said.

"Definitely. Have a seat. Before we start, I need to tell you what happened in Thedia."

"I'm listening."

Logan told him how Wendy had asked her ex-boyfriend to look into any drug dealers who were known to transport across province lines. "That night, Wendy's hotel was set on fire. At first, I thought she was just in the wrong place on the wrong day, but it turns out the arsonist started the blaze by dousing the area in front of her door."

Anderson whistled. "How do you know that? I didn't think the arson investigator would be willing to share that information with you."

"He didn't. I asked Josh to look into it."

"Smart. Did you warn Wendy that she needs to be careful and stop investigating this case?"

"I plan to," Logan said. "But it will be like asking her not to breathe."

Anderson's huff and smile were brief. "Are you certain Wendy only spoke to her ex-boyfriend during the trip? She might have mentioned her thoughts to others.”

“I don’t know. It wasn’t a topic I discussed with her, but I intend to.”

“Do you know her ex-boyfriend’s name?” Anderson asked.

“Deke Darnell. He’s now my top suspect.”

Anderson held up a hand. “Easy there. The friend could have done as Wendy asked. His questions might have resulted in some criminal going to the source.”

“You could be right. I guess I just don’t like the idea that she would turn to him for help,” Logan mumbled. He had offered to be a part of her investigation, but she never took him up on it.

Anderson smiled. “Instead of you? Is there something I should know?”

Well crap. He might as well hire a sky writer to announce it since he’d already told quite a few people—everyone but Wendy that is. “Wendy is my mate, but we’ve yet to go out on a date.” Since his sister hadn’t called to discuss what happened at the bar last night, he had to assume his name wasn’t mentioned. Logan wasn’t sure if he should be happy, or if he should be insulted.

Anderson smiled. “Good for you. Make sure she understands that no story is worth her life. She’ll just have to find a different topic.”

Spoken like a true protective dragon. “I couldn’t agree more. Clearly, we need to learn who killed the kids, or she’ll never let it go. If we do that, we might find the connection to the drug dealer. For that to happen quickly, we need to enlist more Guardians.”

“I agree.”

“You have some ideas?” Logan asked.

“I do.”

WENDY WAS AT her computer the morning after her fun night out, working on her piece about being trapped in a hotel room that was on fire, when her cell rang. She assumed it was Danita wanting to see if she had a hangover—which she did not. When Wendy lifted the cell and spotted Logan's number, her hand froze as her heart raced.

"Hello?"

"It's Logan."

"Hi."

"Do you have time to do lunch? There is something I want to catch you up on."

"Did something happen?" He sounded worried.

"Did you listen to my most recent voicemail by any chance?"

"About what room I was in at the hotel? Yes. I answered it."

"I was referring to my voicemail about the fire."

Her heart dropped to her stomach. "No. I'm sorry. Last night, I was busy working on my story, and then I was getting ready to meet your sister and some friends. I turned my cell on silent, and I didn't turn the ringer on until a moment ago. What happened?"

"I would rather tell you in person."

Her stomach spun. "Okay. Where do you want to meet?"

"How about I pick you up at your apartment at noon?"

She owed Logan so much, which meant she didn't need to inconvenience him. She was sure he was busy. "How about if I just meet you at the restaurant?"

"Sure. The Highlander's Steakhouse?"

That was really expensive. Knowing Logan, he'd insist on paying, and it was she who should pay. "What about the Hillside Café?"

"Works for me. See you there at noon."

Logan disconnected before she had the chance to question him further. That was just as well. She had less than an hour to get ready, and Wendy's questions could wait. Besides, seeing his expression in person was a lot better than hearing his voice over the phone. She'd be better at detecting the truth that way.

While this wasn't their official date, Wendy wanted to shower and put on a little makeup. The last time he'd seen her, she had been a hot, smoky mess.

But first, she checked her phone to listen to the voicemail. Her stomach seized when he said the fire hadn't been an accident. Now, she couldn't wait to hear more.

Get moving. We don't want to be late, her wolf said with too much cheer in her voice.

I'm hurrying.

Wendy showered quickly and then carefully applied some light makeup. Next, she picked out something simple to wear. For some reason—fear maybe—she wanted Logan to think this was what she wore around the house. It wasn't true, since she mostly lounged in her pajamas when she was writing, but he didn't need to know that intimate detail of her everyday life. And only she'd know she had on her best underwear beneath her short-sleeve shirt and jeans.

Because the restaurant wasn't far from her apartment, Wendy opted to walk. If she had driven, no telling how far away she'd have to park. She swore Edendale was growing by the day.

Despite her best estimate though, she walked in five minutes late. She glanced around the busy place but failed to spot Logan. That seemed odd. Of all the people, she would have thought he would have been early, if only to grab a seat.

Just as the hostess showed her to one of the last empty tables, Logan rushed in.

"Sorry, I was late. I got a last-minute phone call."

Wendy could relate. "No problem."

He slid in the booth across from her. "How are you feeling?"

"About what? Almost dying or possibly drinking and eating too much at last night's girls' get together?"

He laughed and her stomach fluttered. "I'd love to hear about your night out, but I was more curious about your mental state. I know I would still be shaken if I woke up in the middle of the night to a smoke-filled room."

"Thanks for reminding me." She held up a hand and chuckled. "I'm fine, but I appreciate you asking." Wendy didn't even have to think about her response. It was her standard refrain. The truth didn't enter into the equation.

"I'm happy to hear that. I hope you are being cautious now and not asking a lot of questions."

She was a journalist. Wendy was about to say that he had no right to tell her what to do, but then she remembered Deke had been the one who always tried to control her actions—not Logan. "Questions about what?"

"Remember I asked you what room you were in at the hotel?"

"Yes. What about it?"

"The investigator concluded that the fire was arson. In fact, he found accelerant right in front of your door and no place else."

She shook her head, not wanting to believe what he was saying. "I told no one where I was staying. I couldn't be the target."

"I figured it out. It would have been easy to either follow you to your room or ask at the front desk which room was yours."

"The hotel was classy. They wouldn't just give out that information. How did you figure out where I was staying?" She'd taken an airplane to Thedia. As a dragon shifter, he wouldn't have been able to follow her.

"It was the closest hotel to the newspaper office where you had your interview. I wouldn't be surprised if someone went to the desk, claimed to be from the newspaper, and told the clerk that he had a job offer for you or something."

"That would work?" What was she saying? She'd used a line like that before, and it had gained her entry.

"Sad to say, yes. Hotels aren't always careful about what kind of information they give out."

Her mind spun. "If Deke had been asking questions about drugs, maybe the dealer figured something out. It's possible he mentioned I was a reporter doing an exposé on the drug trade. Deke could have believed he was speaking to a cop, but that cop could have been dirty."

"Wendy, it doesn't really matter right now how they found out where you were staying. The bottom line is that they found you. You were lucky you woke up when you did."

"I know." She snapped her fingers. "Mr. Landry."

"Who's he?"

"The editor of Thedia Provincial. He was the one who interviewed me for the job. He supplied my airline tickets and my hotel room. If anyone knew where I would be staying, it would be him."

"Or his secretary. I seriously doubt a busy man like Landry would make the arrangements."

She sighed. "You're right."

"How sure are you of this Deke fellow?" Logan asked.

She didn't like what he was implying, but she could understand why he asked. "Deke is a decent guy, though he sucked as a boyfriend."

"Would you mind if I do a little background check on him?"

At first, Wendy wanted to say that she did mind, but in truth Deke had deserted her. What kind of man does that? "Sure. Go ahead. His name is Deke Darnell. His father owns a large furniture manufacturing company that Deke works at. While he never said if he would take over once his father retired, it was kind of implied." She had no idea why she offered all of that information, except that she wanted to let Logan know that Deke wasn't hard up for cash.

"How did you meet him?" Logan asked in a neutral tone.

This was not where she wanted to go, but she had nothing to hide. "I met him at a bar."

"In Edendale or Thedia?"

"Edendale."

"How long did you date?"

Wendy leaned back in her seat. "Why the interrogation? I'm not dating him anymore, nor am I interested. For your information, he has a mate now."

"Is that so?"

"Yes." Wendy couldn't figure out what he was getting at.

"Is he a wolf shifter too?"

"No, a dragon shifter." Wendy didn't know why he cared.

"Look, if you're thinking Deke was involved in setting my room on fire, he wouldn't need to use accelerant, now would he?"

"No. I'm not thinking he was involved, but rather someone he spoke to realized you were asking too many questions." Logan leaned forward. "There's something else I need to tell you."

"What is that?"

The waitress stopped by to ask what they wanted to drink, and if they were ready to order. Wendy hadn't even picked up the menu. "Coffee. I need time to decide what to have."

The waitress looked toward the line of people waiting for a seat. "Sure. Wave when you know what you want." She faced Logan. "And for you?"

"I'll also have a coffee, black, and a number six special."

"You've got it, sugar." The woman's smile could have melted the sun.

Wendy refused to address the streak of jealousy shooting through her. She reached out and touched him, in part to get his attention, and in part to be connected to him for a moment. "You said there was something else you needed to tell me. What is it?"

"It's not important."

She was good at reading people. "It must be, or you wouldn't have brought it up."

He sat back and let out an audible exhale. "Fine. I shouldn't tell you, because I fear you'll stick your nose where it doesn't belong, but you'll find out eventually."

As a journalist, her nose belonged in a lot of places. "What is it?"

Chapter Nine

LOGAN WASN'T SURE why he hesitated, since his goal was to convince Wendy that she was way in over her head. "The two boys?"

"What about them?"

"They didn't die from an overdose."

She shook her head. "I don't believe you. You can't scare me off that easily."

"I never thought I could. I just needed you to truly understand what kind of person we're dealing with. Pushing drugs is one thing. Murder is another."

"They were murdered?"

"Yes. Someone poisoned them," he said.

"Holy shit! When did you find this out?"

"My cousin showed me the autopsy report right before I came here. The boys had Crenathum in their systems, but it wasn't a lethal amount."

"Who would want to kill two teenagers? Those two were headed for the most prestigious school in the province."

"I know. It's a terrible shame."

Wendy leaned forward. "What should we do?"

She was something else. "*We* need to let *me* investigate."

"You're telling me to back off?"

This time he cupped her hand and squeezed it. "Yes."

Wendy slipped her hand from his. "That's rich. Obviously, you look like you could handle yourself, but come on—you are a businessman, not a trained investigator."

While he probably should reveal he was a Guardian, one of the protectors of the realm, now was not the time or place. Only when they were close to mating would he reveal that piece of information. "Even though you might be trained how to dig deep, I doubt you'd do well in a fight—especially if dragons are involved."

She looked away for a moment and then pinned him with a glare. "If everyone lived a life of fear, we'd have no press."

Shit. He hadn't meant to put down her profession. "I agree there are a lot of cops who aren't dragon shifters, and they do well in a fight, but they are trained like I am." Logan never kept it a secret that he too had some skills.

"Were you in the military or something?"

"Or something. I don't like to advertise that information, but I do keep up on the newest fighting techniques. It helps me stay out of trouble." Logan smiled, hoping to disarm her.

"Oh."

"I know you want to help, and I appreciate that. I'm hoping we can pool our resources that we've already collected. Together we might be able to give my cousin the evidence he needs to arrest this killer."

She ran her fingers down the napkin-covered silverware. "That sounds tempting. Tell me what you know?"

Logan couldn't believe how excited he was just thinking about the two of them discussing what they'd each uncovered. However, if Wendy intended to interview a suspect or informant of any kind, she'd have to pass her plans by him first. And that was something he doubted she'd agree to.

"I found out that the boys had been given rat poisoning, just like the truck driver from Thedia."

Her eyes widened, and then she blew out a breath. "I remember when everyone thought he'd just overdosed. I investigated that case but came up empty. Do you think these two cases are connected? I mean death by rat poisoning, coupled with Crenathum, can't be that common."

"I agree. And both were made to look like overdoses. The question is what would two kids from Edendale have in common with someone from halfway across Tarradon? Ted Yancy didn't even live in Avonbelle Province. He was delivering his cargo from Thedia."

She inhaled. "This probably means nothing, but did you know that Tom, one of the boys who died, and his family used to live in Thedia? Right outside of Sawmill to be exact."

How had he missed that? "No. How did you find out?"

A glint flashed in her eye. "I spoke to a student at the school—a former girlfriend of his."

"Former?"

Wendy told him about the interview with Mike's mom, and how she'd mentioned her son's girlfriend. "Mrs. Evans thought Sherry might know who was at the party, but when I went to the school to speak with her, she was absent that day. While there, I ran into a girl by the name of Melanie Whittaker. By chance, she used to be Tom's girlfriend."

"I have to say, I'm impressed."

Wendy smiled, and his cock hardened.

"It took some doing to get her to talk at first, but I promised that I was only interested in learning the identity of the drug dealer."

Logan was doubly impressed with her ingenuity. "Clever. Did you learn anything else?"

"Your turn," she said smugly.

He inhaled, not surprised at her request. Wendy was a cautious woman, and he liked that about her. "All right. Like you, my cousin Stone and I figured that the drugs were most likely coming from Thedia due to the cold climate. We tracked down some of the names of people who sell the mushrooms, as well as contacted the pharmaceutical companies who make Trilox. That's the—"

"Yes, I know. It's the opiate needed to blend with the mushrooms, along with a few other ingredients, to make the drug."

Wendy was on top of things. "Yes. Anyway, we got nowhere, though we too asked some friends to check things out."

"When were you in Thedia?"

"A day or two before you."

"Then it's possible you and your cousin and not me put these men on high alert. When I showed up and asked around, they became worried."

He liked her logic. "It's a possibility."

"Why did you return to Thedia the night of the fire? Had you found out something else?" Wendy asked.

"I told you. When I called and you didn't answer, I became worried. I mentioned it to Greer who called Danita. She told Greer that you might have turned off your phone because you were in another province. Putting the journalistic pieces together, I thought you might be investigating the same drug trail."

"Danita didn't tell Greer I was there to interview for a job?"

"She did."

"Did you think I just told my cousin a lie so she wouldn't worry?"

The thought had crossed his mind, but it would be stupid on his part to say so. "I totally believed you had been offered a job, especially after that brilliant article you wrote." That was the truth.

She smiled and lust filled him. "You read it?"

"I did. I had to see if you got the facts right." He winked, hoping she understood that he was kidding. The fact he'd read the article was true.

The server came by, and she ordered. "So now what?" Wendy asked.

"What do you mean?"

"You said we could work together. Where do we go from here?"

A plan fell into place. "How about stopping over at my office tomorrow? We can make a list of everything we've learned so far. I believe that if we share our resources, the path will become clear."

"Fair enough."

"Say at ten?" That way, they could take a break in town and have another lunch date.

While Logan was interested in picking her brain about the case, he really just wanted to spend time with her.

"Sounds good."

Logan sipped his coffee, happy the logistics of his plan were out of the way. "When you aren't working, what do you like to do?" he asked.

She lowered her chin. "This doesn't count as a real date, you know."

Logan held up his hands. "Absolutely, because if it were, I would have picked you up at your house carrying a bouquet of flowers, and we would be having dinner together in a fancy restaurant and not lunch at a café."

She laughed, just as he'd hoped. "Do you really arrive with flowers in hand on a first date?"

Logan wanted there to be no secrets between them. "Not unless it's for a special lady."

"Logan Caspian. Be good. I do want to go out to dinner with you, but I have to write this story first."

She didn't have time to go out with him, and yet she could spend the evening with her girlfriends? Besides, she was nowhere close to writing an exposé on the deaths of the teens. Something else was going on, but he didn't want to pressure her just yet for the truth.

"Fine, no dating until after your article is finished. I too have a business to run, and I don't have time to do my work, crack a drug ring, solve a murder case, and date you at the same time."

He couldn't be sure, but he thought from her heavy exhale that she was disappointed. At least, she didn't call him out on his lie.

The food arrived shortly after, and he was careful not to ask any more personal questions—just those related to the case. When she asked about him, he shared as much as he could.

As they left the café, Wendy turned left to return home. Normally, Logan would have escorted her to her apartment to make sure no one was following her, but he suspected she'd balk. It didn't matter.

He planned to watch her another way.

"Tomorrow then," he said over his shoulder.

Wendy's eyebrows raised, implying she was surprised he wasn't walking in her direction. The SinCas building was to the right, so she'd know something was up if he turned left and walked with her.

"Tomorrow." She then took off.

Logan needed to do some reconnaissance on Wendy. Hopefully he could catch sight of her from the air. This might not be Thedia, but if someone murdered two innocent boys here, the drug cartel's tentacles probably extended this far.

To be honest, after learning how the teens died, he wasn't sure the drug cartel was involved in their murders. The teens could have purchased the stuff from some local dealer and used the drug without prompting. The poison could have been a separate issue all together. The uncertainty of it all served to drive him harder.

Once Logan reached the roof top, he took off. The problem with this method of surveillance was that he needed to be low enough to watch Wendy but high enough not to be spotted. He wouldn't put it past her to check the sky for him since she might suspect it would be something he would do—and she'd be right.

Once he caught sight of her and confirmed that she entered her building, he continued toward the mine. Upon arrival, he landed, shifted, and then headed straight to his office. He'd just sat down when Stone came in. "Where have you been?"

His comment wasn't accusatory but rather contained interest mixed with a hint of humor.

"I asked Wendy out to lunch. I wanted to let her know that she was possibly the target of the fire at her hotel." He told him what Josh had learned.

Stone pulled up a chair. His cousin loved this kind of sleuthing. "Why would anyone want her dead?"

Logan filled him in with his best guess. Because Logan appreciated Stone's keen mind, he also explained what Wendy had learned from speaking with the boys' mothers, as well as what Tom's ex-girlfriend had told her.

"What's your next step?" Stone asked.

"I want to do a deep dive on Wendy's ex-boyfriend."

"You think he'd try to kill her?"

"I don't know. That's why I need to investigate."

"Can I help?"

"For now, make sure the mine runs smoothly while I'm looking into this. I can't let anyone else harm Wendy."

Stone pushed back his chair. "You've got it."

Once Stone left, Logan began his work. He wanted to be armed with facts when Wendy showed up tomorrow. It shouldn't be hard to find rudimentary information about Deke Darnell, especially if his father owned a furniture company.

The image of hiding drugs in empty drawers and transporting the furniture across province lines flashed in his head. It was a reach, but it was a place to start. The first thing was to find the name of the father's company.

Chapter Ten

W ENDY WAS SO confused. While she'd told Logan that she didn't want to date because she needed to work on this article, that was only partially true. It was that she needed to keep some distance. Why? Logan unnerved her every time he was near, or more precisely, he set her body on fire. He also made her lose all common sense. She blamed that for the reason why her muse had abandoned her.

What was worse, for most of their lunch, she found herself just staring at him, fascinated how several times his eyes would have glorious swirls of teal in them. Studying him like that had been so unprofessional, but she couldn't help it. The man seemed to have put a spell on her soul. But did that mean Logan was her mate?

Yes! Her wolf chimed in.

Mom, why did you have to die before you had the chance to give me the full lecture on mates? Sure, her friends had tried to fill her in, but a mother's perspective would have been better. Wendy had heard enough to know that if Logan wasn't her fated mate, his reaction at least meant he was highly attracted to her. The problem was that she wanted more than just sex. Just not right now.

A small smile lifted her lips when she remembered how she'd caught him staring at her after he'd asked her a personal question— something about what she wanted out of life. She swore he was holding his breath, urging her to tell him she wanted him.

I want him, chimed her wolf. *Don't you?*

I can't afford to think about it. Remember, the only way to stay in Edendale is to write some awe-inspiring exposé. I can't be daydreaming about Logan Caspian.

Wendy sat up straighter. If she wanted to show Logan that she could be a team player, she needed to go through her notes and write them down in a clear and concise manner. This would include her impression of each person she'd spoken to—like whether a person was nervous, if they made eye contact or not, or if they sounded sincere. Hopefully, that would help Logan figure out who to keep investigating.

With a plan in mind, she pulled a notepad from her desk drawer and got to work. Wendy wasn't sure how long she'd been at her desk when her cell rang. Again! Her pulse shot up, thinking it might be Logan. It wasn't. It was Danita. Most likely, her cousin had found out that Wendy had met with Logan for lunch, which meant that nothing Wendy could say would convince Danita that it hadn't been a real date.

"Hey, what's up?" Wendy asked.

"I called to find out about your date."

News traveled way too fast. "It wasn't exactly a date."

Danita chuckled. "Sure, it wasn't. Did you enjoy yourself, or was Logan an insufferable ass?"

As much as she wanted to complain about him, she didn't want to lie. "He was a perfect gentleman."

"When are you going to see him again?"

"Tomorrow morning. We are going over our case notes at his office."

Danita said nothing for a minute. "Really? Logan didn't try to convince you to drop this enquiry and find something else to write about?"

"He did more or less, but I think he understands that I need to do this."

"He really is going to let you put yourself in danger like that?"

Now her cousin sounded like him. "I think Logan understands that he can't tell me what to do. We're meeting tomorrow to compare notes. That's all. If I find anything, he can talk to anyone who's sketchy. I'm not going up against a dragon shifter. That would be insane."

"Good for you. But Wendy?"

Uh-oh. She knew that tone. "Yes?"

"I know Deke hurt you by dropping out of your life unexpectedly, but Logan isn't like that."

Wendy wanted to believe that, but she had been burned before. "I know. Look, I need to prepare for our meeting."

"You mean your date." Danita chuckled.

"Sure." There was no use arguing. "Talk to you later."

BECAUSE WENDY WANTED to keep what was between them professional, she dressed in a skirt and heels and arrived on time. No one was manning the front desk of the mining office, so she headed down the hallway to Logan's office.

His door being ajar implied he was waiting for her. Before she had the chance to even greet him, he looked up and smiled. Swirls of teal slashed through his eyes, and a few pulses of sapphire lit up the skin at his throat where he'd left his white shirt unbuttoned. Her traitorous heart jackknifed, and her wolf whined at the glorious sight. Holy crap, he just might be her mate. Yikes.

Logan pushed away from his desk and came around to the front. As he neared, her body quivered. "Hi," she said, trying to be friendly but not act as if she was having a hard time breathing around him, which she was.

"Glad you could make it," he said as he gathered her into a hug.

While Wendy understood she should move back, she liked the way his arms enveloped her and made her feel warm and tingly.

"Hey, have a seat," he said. "Can I get you some coffee, tea, juice, or water? We have a well-stocked breakroom." He grinned and then winked.

More heart pounding happened. It was her wolf who was doing

this, she was sure.

He asked you a question, her wolf said.

"Coffee would be great. Black. Thanks." Wendy smiled but her stupid lips quivered in the process.

He ran a hand down her shoulder before stepping toward the door. As much as she wanted to ignore his fine ass, she couldn't.

As soon as Logan disappeared down the hallway, Wendy looked around his office. It was neat, yet comfortable. The furniture seemed a bit worn, like real work was conducted here. When he returned, Logan was carrying two coffee mugs with steam rolling off the top, which he set on the desk. "Better let it cool."

She appreciated how considerate he was.

Needing to focus on the job and not on the hunky man in front of her, Wendy pulled out her notepad. "Did you find out anything significant since yesterday?" she asked, trying to get her head in the game.

A strange look crossed his face. "I don't know how significant it was, but I learned that Ted Yancy was a driver for Sawmill Furniture."

She'd uncovered that tidbit months ago. "I know."

"Do you know who owns Sawmill Furniture?"

"Deke's father. I looked into him. Just so you know, the incident was before I met Deke. The driver might have worked for Deke's dad, but that didn't mean his father had anything to do with the man's death."

"I agree. In light of the death of the teens though, I want to do a little more digging."

"Fine by me. Do you have anything that indicates the deaths are linked?"

"No, which was why I spoke with Anderson this morning. I asked him to check if there were any other deaths in the recent past in which someone had Crenathum and rat poison in their system. He found nothing."

She had to think about that. "I can see it is possible the same person murdered the driver as well as the boys, though I can't imagine why."

"Neither can I for now."

Needing a moment to think, Wendy reached over to his desk, lifted her cup, and blew across the still hot surface. When it had cooled a bit, she sipped the hot brew. "Then let's prove it."

Logan smiled. "I plan to. With your help, naturally," he said.

Wendy prided herself on being open-minded, and she didn't want him to think that she was prejudiced, especially with her having dated Deke. "Then let's get to work."

"Good. I've set up a computer on the table if you want to use it." He nodded to her tablet. "Or you can use your own." He gave her the Internet password so she could do her searches.

"Thank you."

"Do you know the name of Deke's mate?" he asked once she was set up.

Clearly Logan had no other clues if he wanted her name. "Becky. I don't know her last name."

"What does she look like?"

She was beautiful, exotic, and a shifter. "Brown hair, green eyes, and model thin."

"Thanks."

"Why?" Wendy really wanted to know how his mind worked.

Logan leaned back from his desk. "When I research, I like to paint an entire picture of the people involved. Even the smallest detail can help."

She couldn't argue with that. "Good to know. Did your cop cousin teach you to do that?"

"Anderson certainly helped."

Logan returned to viewing his computer. The chair at the table he'd set up for her faced him, and the arrangement wasn't going to help with her concentration. It did have one benefit though. She could study Logan. If he found some juicy piece of information, she doubted he'd be able to hide it.

Get to work! she told herself. As much as she'd like to watch him, analyzing his strengths and weaknesses, she had a job to do.

Wendy lowered her gaze to the laptop. The first order of business was to look for photos of the two dead teens in the Edendale Prep High School's online yearbook. Why? Wendy wanted to know who both Mike and Tom hung out with. While it was a long shot, it was possible one of their acquaintances might be the killer or at the very least be able to point her in the right direction. As she did her search, she sipped her coffee.

"Did you know that Deke has a criminal record?" Logan blurted, interrupting her concentration. From the smug look on his face, he was happy to have found something wrong with her former boyfriend.

Wendy's fingers stilled, and she forced herself to keep a blank face. "No, but I can't imagine it was for anything serious. As a young dragon shifter, he probably wasn't the most well-behaved, especially since his father was wealthy and was often at work instead of playing with his son." Deke complained how his dad wasn't around much during his childhood.

"You're right. It was never for anything serious. In fact, he never even spent a night in jail. Rather, he was fined for his transgressions."

Which his father probably paid. "What were the offenses?"

"Deke was brought in a few times for disturbing the peace and getting into fights."

That wasn't so bad. "How long ago was that?"

"Enough time for him to have grown up."

She appreciated that Logan was willing to be fair. However, it bothered her a bit that Deke had never mentioned his less than perfect past. "For all of his flaws, I never thought he was the type who looked for trouble. His father was quite powerful in the province. If Deke messed up, it would have reflected poorly on his dad. From what I recall, his father ran for city council a time or two, but I'm not sure if he ever won."

"Would you say they were close?"

She wasn't sure what he was getting at, but she'd answer honestly. "I had the sense there was some resentment between them."

"Good insight. I'll check it out. What angle are you working on?"

She told him about trying to find who the boys hung out with. "One of their friends might have been jealous of their success and wanted them gone. According to Tom's former girlfriend, Tom struggled in school. I think she was surprised he got into Hanfield."

"A person with a higher scholastic ranking might believe he or she should have been the one to get into that school."

"That's what I was thinking. Even if this person didn't harm either boy, I might be able to figure out who was at the party that night." Melanie's list had basically been a bust. "If their friends had been doing drugs, it probably wouldn't have been their first time. They might even know who sold them the drugs."

"Great job. Keep working on that." Logan smiled, and Wendy held in a sigh at how handsome he looked.

Pride filled her. More than anything, she wanted him to respect her abilities.

Wendy returned to her search of the online yearbook. Whenever the same student appeared with either Mike or Tom more than a few times, she made a note of his or her name. After a while her eyes began to blur. Just as she was about to get up and refresh her coffee, an image caught her eye, but she had to blink a few times to prevent her imagination from running rampant. It was a photo of Tom with a man in the school parking lot. And the man looked a lot like Deke. It couldn't be him though, because there was a sign in the background announcing an ongoing play in town during the time she thought Deke was back in Thedia. If the photo hadn't been so blurry, she would have asked if maybe Logan could enlarge it.

Most likely, it only looked like Deke, because they'd just been talking about him. She pushed it aside and continued making her list.

"Coffee?" Logan asked.

Oh, crap. She hadn't even noticed Logan had left his desk and was standing next to her with a coffee pot. "Yes, thank you. You read my mind. I was about to get some."

He filled her mug and then leaned over her shoulder. His alluring lemony scent had her wolf scratching. She worked hard to push aside the lust.

"You find anything?" he asked.

"I think so." She showed him her list of student names. "I will contact them to see if they were at the party." She could only hope she had better luck than her first try.

Logan tapped the image on the screen of Tom and the man. "Who is he?"

"I don't know. Tom had two tutors. It could be a teacher or either Mr. Quigley or Mr. Hammersmith. They both worked with Tom."

"How about we print the image and show it around the school?" Logan asked.

"It's kind of blurry."

"Agreed, but someone might recognize him."

"You really think it's important?"

"I'm not sure, but all adults are suspect. While it is possible the drug dealer was a fellow student, I want to cover my bases in case it wasn't."

"I thought we were trying to find a murderer, not a drug dealer," she said.

"Who's to say they aren't one and the same?" He then cocked a brow. If his eyes hadn't been twinkling, Wendy might have felt he was testing her.

"They definitely could be." She sighed. "I swear, the more I dig, the more loose ends I uncover. Soon I'll be buried in them." Her stomach grumbled, and she sipped her coffee.

Logan chuckled. "It always seems like that." He snapped his fingers. "I have an idea."

She looked up. "What is it?"

"Before we check out the photo at the school, how about we catch some lunch and then take a little trip?"

That was the last thing she expected him to say. "Where to?"

"It might be time to get some help from a person who seems to *know* things."

"That's a little cryptic. Who is this person?"

"Do you remember Kenton and Bevon from the mining incident?"

"Remember them? I could never forget Kenton. He saved me from that terrible Malpan."

"True. If you didn't know, Kenton and Bevon have a few other siblings who also have abilities. I'm not sure I would call them psychic, but they have powers. They've given advice to Burk, Griffin, Nessa, and several other members of my family at one time or another."

"Do you think Kenton will be there? I'd love to thank him."

"No guarantees, but it will be fun to see the eternal flame again even if he's not."

"That's pretty far away." She'd read about the flame in school but spending all that time driving for a short visit never seemed worthwhile.

"Not for a dragon shifter."

"We'll fly then?"

"If you're up for it."

She smiled, and his nails extended, not to mention something else grew right before her eyes. "For sure."

Logan cleared his throat. "You can leave your purse and tablet here. You don't need to be carrying anything during our hike through the forest." He held up a palm. "But first, lunch is on me."

"I appreciate that."

Once outside, Logan stepped back and shifted. Sunlight bounced off his sapphire and black scales, and she had to swallow a sigh. He was truly magnificent, so powerful and hot—no pun intended.

His mouth parted slightly, and Wendy could have sworn he was smiling, though she didn't know if dragons could smile. He moved closer, reached out, and gently picked her up. After he interlaced his talons to provide a comfortable resting spot, he soared upward. Wind whipped through her hair, and the air cooled the higher they traveled. His heat seemed to alter something inside her. It was as if they were connected on an elemental level.

Mate, mate, her wolf shouted.

I'm beginning to think you are right.

Hallelujah.

The trip to town was unfortunately short-lived. She might have been disappointed had she not known that after lunch, they'd be going far across the realm, and she could once again be pressed against his body, able to feel his soaring strength. Their destination in town was the SinCas building where he landed on the roof. Logan set her down and then shifted.

"You good?" he asked, sounding so sincere, she wanted to remind him she was anything but fragile.

Wendy stepped close and ran her hand down his arm. "Very good."

With a palm to her back, he walked her over to a metal door that led to a downward flight of stairs. She didn't ask which restaurant they were going to, because she didn't honestly care.

Wendy wasn't sure when exactly her attitude about being with him had changed, but after seeing Logan work on the case that she wanted to solve, it had created a bond between them—and it was time to see where it could lead.

Chapter Eleven

L UNCH WITH WENDY had been hard to get through, mostly because every time Logan looked at her, he wanted her so bad that he was tempted to tell her they were mates.

She knows we are, his dragon chimed in.

I wish she would act like she knew.

Wendy was currently in his grasp high above the fertile plains and hills of Tarradon. Clearly, it would take all of his control just to fly to the middle of the realm with her so close to his heart. And those damn flames inside his body kept erupting with a need to make her his own. But he would practice patience even if it killed him.

Stop being so dramatic. Enjoy her while you can.

His damn dragon needed to shut up. It didn't matter that his animal might be right for a change.

Logan didn't fly to the middle of the realm often, which might be why he was in awe of the spectacular scenery, and he hoped Wendy appreciated the view too. To her credit, she didn't squirm. Even her grip on his talons was light. Logan supposed having dated a dragon shifter before helped her get over her fear of flying.

Eventually, the edge of the forest appeared, and he slowly made his way to the ground. Once he landed, he gently placed Wendy down. As he stepped back to shift, she stretched, implying the flight must have been hard on her body. Not moving for that long would have been difficult—not that he had that kind of first-hand experience.

He had considered meeting Fay by himself, but Wendy needed to hear what she or any of the siblings had to say—assuming they were around.

Logan recalled the trouble his brother Griffin had when he'd tried to learn the fate of their cousin Tory after Kenton Forrester had transported her to his realm. Griffin had waited hours for one of them to show up at the eternal flame. Only when he'd exited the forest ready to take flight did Fay Forrester make an appearance. All she would say was that everything would be okay, and thankfully, she'd been right.

Before Logan had decided to take this trip, he had considered seeking out the Four Sisters for their help, but they only performed their magic when a mate was in trouble. His wasn't, and he planned to do everything in his power to keep it that way.

"It's about a twenty-minute walk. Are you up for that?" he asked.

She smiled, forcing him to block out her allure. He had a mission to complete.

"Lead the way."

Logan pointed to the wide opening in the trees. "It's just down this path."

She walked by his side, oohing and aahing whenever the light streamed through the leaves. Wendy grabbed his arm to stop him. She then looked upward and spun around, her eyes wide. "Can you feel the magic?"

Logan took a moment to absorb the atmosphere. "Not so much for me, but if the Feys and Fairies live nearby, it probably is all around us."

He only saw a wide dirt path and tall trees on either side. If she was able to spot magic, maybe Wendy was part white lighter. It was possible she was like her white lighter cousin, Danita, though if she were, Wendy would have been aware of her abilities. Then again, Danita didn't know she could stop time until after she'd been captured.

Logan had lived long enough to know anything was possible in Tarradon, but now wasn't the time to explore that concept. They needed to reach the eternal flame first.

They were halfway there when Wendy tripped. His fast reflexes allowed him to catch her by the waist. "You good?" he asked.

She straightened and then faced him. "Yes. Thank you. I really need to watch where I'm going. I owe you enough." She smiled, and Logan wanted to kiss her, if only to drink in her joy—but he didn't. Hopefully, that would come later.

During the final leg of their trek, he told her about his family's former interactions with the Fairies and Feys.

"Do you think one of these people will know who killed the teens—teens who live in a different province?" she asked.

"I don't think that's an issue for the Forresters. Are they omniscient, you might ask? I couldn't say. What I do know is that they come from a different realm, though I don't need to tell you. You were the one who saw Kenton create a portal to Feyrion."

"I saw a portal, though I can't vouch for where it went."

He could understand her hesitation to draw that conclusion. "My relatives were told there are additional portals near the eternal flame, but they never saw one in action like you did."

"You know, I never had the chance to ask why your family was at those mines to save the slaves."

He'd wondered when she'd ask. Logan debated telling her about them being Guardians, but he wanted the timing to be right. "Our sales of copper had plummeted dramatically for two months straight. When we heard there might be a competing mine using forced labor, we had to investigate." That was no lie.

"I see. I'm glad you were able to shut it down."

"Me too." He needed to clear up one more thing before they met with the Forresters. "When we get there, I'd like to do the talking." Wendy stopped and spun to face him, probably ready to give him a lecture on them being equals. He rushed on. "It's only because the Forresters have interacted with my family that they might trust me."

Her lips pressed together, and then she inhaled. "You're probably right."

A flicker of light caught his attention, and Logan leaned close. "I think we're near."

Wendy straightened, but her shoulders looked stiff. He guessed it was because she understood how big this could be for them. When they stepped into the open area, it was as he'd feared. While he spotted the large cement bowl with the lit eternal flame to the side of the fountain, no one was there. Damn.

"Let's check out the fountain and make a wish," he said. Considering the metal pipe sticking out of the rock face was the water source, she might not call it a fountain.

"This isn't a social visit," she whispered.

"I've been told it's how we contact the Forresters."

"Oh."

"As long as we're tossing in a coin, you can make a real wish." Logan flashed her a smile, hoping to relax her.

Wendy looked up at him. "All I'll wish for is to find the SOB who killed those two innocent boys."

Logan wanted that too, but he had hoped she'd wish for the two of them to be mates as well as solve a crime. If Wendy were willing to join forces, Logan believed they'd be unstoppable.

Facing the rock wall, Logan dug his hand into his jeans pocket, pulled out a coin, and handed it to Wendy. "Close your eyes and toss it in." This making a wish in a fountain thing was an Earth tradition, but he liked it nonetheless.

When their fingers touched, Logan swore his dragon might shift without permission. Without questioning him further, Wendy tossed it in the shallow pool. When she opened her eyes, she faced him. "Now what?"

"Hello, Logan," said a feminine voice behind him.

The coin trick worked! He hadn't really believed it would. As he spun around, his pulse dropped, and Logan tried not to show his disappointment that this wasn't Fay Forrester. "How did you know my name?"

The small woman with the long brown hair imperceptibly shook her head. She walked toward them and held out her hand to Wendy.

"I'm Meena Forrester. You must be Wendy."

"How——?" Wendy started to say before Meena cut her off.

"Know who you are? Easy. I'm not from around here."

He would rather have answers than enigmatic phrases, but the fact was, a Forrester was here, and that was good enough for him. "Thank you for coming," he said.

"I sensed you two were troubled."

That was an understatement. "Yes. Two innocent teens were drugged and poisoned in Edendale. We were hoping you could give us some guidance that would help us find the responsible party. We're rather directionless right now."

Wendy placed a hand on his arm, indicating she wanted to be the one to plead with this woman. "The families of these young men need answers," Wendy said.

Meena's lips formed a peaceful expression. "Let's see what the pool can tell us."

Griffin had *gone to the pool* and had been shown something he described as a movie of what had happened to his mate. With a hand to Wendy's back, Logan turned her around to face the stone wall.

"Thank you," he said to Meena.

The Fairy said nothing for a moment, almost as if she needed some time to conjure up an image. She then waved her hand over the water, and what looked like a video appeared on the surface. Even though Griffin had warned him, Logan was still impressed. The movie was of a man dressed in a business suit, his hands held out in front of him, seemingly needing to keep someone at bay.

Wendy sucked in a breath and grabbed his wrist. He pulled her close to show they were in this together.

"I'm sorry, Mr. Darnell," said a male voice out of view. "If you don't come up with the money in three business days, we'll be forced to act."

What did that mean? Because the wind was blowing across the surface, the image wasn't totally clear. From his research, this was indeed Robert Darnell. What was for sure, was that Darnell was inside a fairly large building. People were milling about in the background, but they appeared to be oblivious to the discussion. Logan didn't see anyone pointing a gun at Darnell or any kind of weapon for that matter. If that person had been there to harm him, others would have noticed—or at least he hoped they would have.

"I will get you the money. I promise, but I need more time," Darnell pleaded.

"Three days," the man on the other side of the desk said.

Then the image disappeared. Damn. What he wouldn't have given to have seen the face of the person interacting with Darnell.

Wendy looked up at him and then back at Meena. "Who was Mr. Darnell speaking to?" she asked.

"I'm not sure, but I do know that the lack of funds and subsequent action caused Mr. Darnell to seek revenge," Meena said.

"What kind of revenge?" Logan asked.

"That's all I know," she replied.

Or was it all she was willing to share? "Thank you for showing this to us." To be honest, Logan wasn't sure how this really helped.

"You're welcome, but you two need to be careful."

"What do you mean?" he asked. Logan needed to make sure coming here hadn't put his mate in any more danger.

"Darkness is descending."

Before either one of them could question her further, she literally disintegrated before his eyes. While he had seen Fay change into what looked like points of light, against the background of the shaded trees, Meena's transformation was downright eerie.

Wendy spun around. "Where did she go?"

"She kind of shifted and flew away." He should have warned Wendy that was how the Fairies made their exit.

"That was creepy."

Logan laughed. "Tell me about it. Ready to go?"

"If we have time, I'd love to check out the eternal flame. I've never been, and I'd hate to have come this far and not see it."

He smiled, really appreciating how resilient his mate was. It was an admirable trait. "Absolutely."

Together, they walked over to the flame. As Wendy ran her fingers over the engraved words on the plaque, he waited for her to ask about Meena's warning or the meaning of the watery video—one that seemed to have been conjured up by the Fairy herself. If that didn't shock her, Wendy had to at least wonder what the man speaking with Mr. Darnell was referring to. Logan sure was interested. Was Darnell involved in some kind of drug deal? Or was he merely negotiating a business deal?

"It's mesmerizing," Wendy said, her voice sounding far off.

She was probably trying to lose herself in the flames as a way of coping. Logan could relate. Moving behind her, he gently clasped her shoulders and turned her around. "Talk to me."

"What do you mean? There's nothing to talk about."

He raised his brows. "I know denial when I hear it. If you're scared, it's totally understandable. Just so you know, everything the Forresters have told my family has come true, which means we need to be careful."

Wendy stepped out of his grasp and crossed her arms—a sure sign she believed Meena. "How did she know that trouble was brewing?"

That was what bothered her? Hell, Logan was still freaking out from seeing a movie appear in a pool of water. "And yet she does. I'm just happy Meena was nice enough to show up and warn us."

Wendy stilled. "Is she a goddess or something?"

The Four Sisters of Fate could teleport, and he suspected they were goddesses, but he didn't need to tell her that now. "I don't know. She's a Fairy, but I'm not that knowledgeable about what she can and can't do. You saw her create the image in the water. What did you make of it?" He wanted to redirect the conversation.

"I don't know."

"Me neither. I need to wrap my head around all of it. We should get back. Now that I know Darnell is somehow mixed up in this, I'm hoping a little research will reveal something. About the only concrete thing Meena said was that Darnell was out for revenge," Logan said. "I wish I knew against whom."

"Taking revenge doesn't necessarily mean he's a killer."

"I agree." As they headed down the path, Logan's mind sorted through the scene a few more times. "Did you see anything in that swirling pool of water that would indicate where the discussion took place?" He might have missed something.

"Given Mr. Darnell's nice suit and the fact an edge of a polished desk was showing, I didn't get the sense it was some drug deal gone bad. If that were the case, the man talking would have had armed guards standing by."

"I had thought that at first too, but armed guards wouldn't do a lot of good against a dragon shifter."

"True. A bullet won't kill my kind either unless it goes through the heart. What about a dragon? Can a bullet to the heart kill one?" she asked.

"No. There is only one spot on a dragon that makes us vulnerable. It's a soft spot right about here." He pressed slightly between his rib cage and the bottom of his heart. "Fortunately, no one in my family has ever been shot there. Other than that, ripping out a dragon's heart is the only way to go."

"I'll keep that in mind." She smiled, and his libido went wild, sending enough hormones through his body to drown him.

Not wanting Wendy to realize how much she affected him, Logan averted his gaze and fisted his hands. Regardless of how much he redirected his thoughts, the glowing scales on his arms couldn't be covered up. When he looked over at her, he noted her hands were in a loose fist too. Dare he hope it was to prevent him from seeing her sharpened nails? He could only hope.

What worried Logan now was that if Deke's dad had been involved in anyone's death that she would hold it against Logan for finding out. Clearly, he had his work cut out for him.

Chapter Twelve

LOGAN KEPT TALKING about the image in the pool and what it could mean. Normally, Wendy wanted to know his thoughts, but at the moment, she needed some quiet time to figure it all out—or as much of it as she could get. Was Logan trying to convince himself that Mr. Darnell was behind everything or was he attempting to convince her? Hell, maybe it was a little bit of both.

Even she had to admit that Meena was very believable when she implied Mr. Darnell was out for revenge—but why was he? Because someone demanded he pay back money he owed? If Wendy hadn't seen Meena's two brothers create a portal and throw Malpan into it, she might not have believed the Fairy woman possessed such powers—but clearly she did. Creating a video on the surface of the water was almost impossible to comprehend.

"I'm leaning more toward Meena being able to read people's minds," Logan said. Where did that comment come from? Wendy must have tuned out for a few minutes.

"You're probably right."

"Regardless of how she came in possession of the information though, we need to do more research and stay safe while we do it," he said.

"I agree." Staying out of trouble though didn't mean she'd stop looking into the meaning of Meena's video.

"Ready for your flight back?" Logan asked as they exited the dense forest.

"I'm not walking."

He smiled, and she allowed herself to let out a small swoon.

Logan's hazel eyes transformed into something that was otherworldly, and those flashing blue scales totally excited her.

Logan shifted into his glorious dragon form. This time, she approached him, and a second later they were airborne. She might have enjoyed the trip back to Edendale more if she hadn't kept going over what Meena had showed them. It sure looked like Darnell was somehow involved in something bad. Why else would Meena show them that scene if he weren't?

They'd been flying a half hour when Wendy remembered that the man on the other side of the desk called Deke's dad, Mr. Darnell. That sounded like a business transaction to her, not some drug deal—or had she watched too many movies and read too many books about the mean drug lords?

Not only that, Darnell was a big businessman. It made sense he'd be at a bank and that he might be behind in his payments. That meant Logan should be able to find information to confirm it.

Before she could finish going over her crazy theories, they arrived at the mine. Logan set her down, stepped back, and shifted.

"I'm good," she said before he could ask if she was okay. The long trip left her a little stiff, but the ride was magical at times—when she let herself enjoy the scenery.

Logan smiled again. "You know me well."

Not really, but now she wished she did. Logan kept studying her, probably to see if she would fall apart. Wendy wouldn't. It wasn't who she was. "You going to stare or are we going to get to work?"

This time he grinned, and Wendy had to turn away, fearing her eyes were flashing amber. Not that she didn't want Logan to know how much she desired him, but they had work to do.

Back in his office, she decided to do a little search on Mr. Darnell and then research Tom's dad, Charles Sanderson. If Darnell owned Sawmill Furniture and other companies, maybe he was strapped for cash at some point in his career and was in need of a loan. For now, she wanted to go with the business-gone-bad scenario. She wasn't ready to accuse Deke's dad of any wrongdoing, despite having a son who would walk out on a woman without so much as a goodbye.

For the next few hours, Logan kept his head down and worked, giving her time to concentrate. Normally, Wendy thrived on doing research, but today, she was mostly frustrated. When she was unable to make any more progress, she pushed back her chair. "I think I'll head home."

Logan looked up. "You're finished?"

"Not by a long shot, but today has been a bit stressful. I need a break."

He opened his mouth, but then quickly shut it. "I get it. Thanks for coming with me to meet Meena."

"I'm glad I did, but now my mind is spinning in so many directions, I need to take a bath, have a glass of wine, and just relax. I'm hoping the pieces will come together once I sleep on it."

Logan stood and came around his desk. He clasped her shoulders, causing heat to race down her body. "You will heed Meena's warning, right?"

"Me? She could have been referring to you. Someone might not have appreciated you looking into their affairs."

Logan didn't break eye contact. "I can handle myself. Don't forget no one tried to burn down the hotel I was in. If my memory serves me right, Meena said the two of us needed to be careful, not just one of us."

She stood up straighter. Wendy wasn't totally convinced the fire was meant to harm her, though she wasn't stupid enough to think it wasn't possible. "That may be, but you needn't worry. I too can handle myself. You've never seen my wolf teeth. Not only that, I'm fast and agile." She smiled at him, but naturally her wolf teeth didn't show.

"That's good to know. How about we head to the high school tomorrow to see if anyone recognizes the man in the photo?"

"Sounds like a plan. Is ten a.m. good for you?" she asked, wanting to be the initiator this time.

"Absolutely."

"Okay, I'll see you here tomorrow."

Logan leaned over and kissed the top of her head. "Rest."

Oh, my goddess! She loved his little touches. It made her want him all the more. Maybe she had been too aggressive in telling him they were merely co-workers. Perhaps tomorrow she'd suggest they go out on the promised dinner date.

FOR THE FIFTH time the next morning, Logan checked his watch. Wendy was forty-five minutes late to their ten a.m. meeting. Even though this wasn't some job where she had to be on time, he was worried nonetheless. Most likely, she'd learned something while researching last night and wanted to run down a lead. If he hadn't been so smothering in his need to protect her, she might have called to let him know.

But he was her mate, damn it, and a Guardian. As such, it was his job to make sure she was safe. Even if she'd balk at the intrusion, Logan needed to hear her voice at least. He picked up his cell and called her.

"This is Wendy Oprander. I'm unable to come to the phone. Please leave a number, and I'll call you back."

"Wendy, it's me. I thought you said we'd meet at the office at ten. I'm hoping I misheard you. Call me, okay?"

Logan disconnected, not pleased with the pleading nature of his message. He never acted weak, but Wendy had gotten under his skin. He'd give her fifteen minutes and then try again.

Hold up. What was he thinking? He was Logan Caspian, computer expert extraordinaire. All he had to do was ping her phone to find her location. His hormones must be blocking his brain function. Unless it was urgent, he didn't invade someone's privacy, but after Meena's warning, he couldn't help himself.

It only took a few minutes to locate her cell. She was home—or at least her phone was—and Logan breathed a sigh of relief. She was probably so engrossed in what she was doing that she lost track of time. He wouldn't be surprised if she'd put her ringer on silent like she had a time or two before. He'd let her work for a little while longer before calling her a third time. If she didn't answer, he'd have to go over there.

He tried to busy himself for a bit, but all attempts to focus failed. Eventually, his nerves got the best of him. Logan dialed her number again and heard the same voicemail. To hell with it. It was time to head on over to her place.

Before he took off, he stopped in Stone's office and told him he was stopping over at Wendy's.

"You're worried, aren't you?" Stone asked.

He'd told Stone about Meena's prophecy. "I'm telling myself I'm not, but what if someone came into her apartment like they did the last time?"

A few months back, Malpan's men had charged into her place, stabbed Wendy with a sedative, and then carted her off to a prison cell. The image caused a rush of injustice and anger to burn in his gut once more.

"Go. I'll call if anything groundbreaking occurs."

His cousin was the best. "Appreciate it."

Logan rushed down the hallway, and once outside, he shifted and then soared upward. The higher he flew the more concerned he became.

There is nothing to worry about. There is nothing to worry about. Too bad that mantra didn't help as much as he'd hoped.

Once in town, Logan landed on top of the SinCas building and then raced down one flight to take the elevator to the bottom floor. Every time he didn't stop and say hi to his siblings and cousins, guilt attacked him. Today though, he couldn't afford to. All he could do was promise he'd make it up to them soon.

After exiting the building, he jogged toward Wendy's apartment building. Once he arrived, he took the steps two at a time until he reached the third floor. At her door he knocked, but she didn't answer.

"Wendy? It's Logan."

He didn't need to press his ear to the door to recognize that nothing was moving inside. Damn. In case, she was still asleep or was listening to music using earphones, he knocked again.

Still no answer. When he pressed his palms to the door, his body tingled, indicating his mate was near. He wished he could figure out what kind of game she was playing. Surely, she sensed he was on the other side of the door. They were mates after all.

He jiggled the door handle and found it open. What the hell? When he pushed it open, he froze. It took him a good second or two before his body could even move. Wendy was sprawled on the floor, her cheek pressed against the carpet, and her eyes closed. He rushed over to her, dropped to his knees, and shook her shoulder. "Wendy? Can you hear me?"

Her breathing was ragged and her skin pale. Why hadn't her wolf healed her? Both Greer and Declan were healers. Since they'd know what to do, he called his sister. When he'd passed the SinCas jewelry store on his way out of the building, Tory was manning the store, which meant Greer would be free.

"Hey, Log. What's up?"

"I just found Wendy unconscious on her apartment floor. Can you come over and do your magic?"

"What happened?"

"I don't know. I just arrived at her place."

"Just hang tight. I'll be right there."

He didn't know if Greer had ever visited Wendy at her place. "She's in the same apartment building as where Danita used to live. It's apartment 308."

"Got it. I'll contact Declan in case he's better suited to heal her. Is she bleeding anywhere?" Her high heels clicked on the steps going up to the rooftop.

Shit. He hadn't even thought to look. "Let me see."

"Check her whole body."

He wasn't about to undress her, but he did do a visual sweep. Seeing nothing that resembled any kind of injury, he rolled her onto her other side. "No. Nothing."

"Good. Stay with her. I'll be there shortly."

Like he was going to leave his mate? When he disconnected, he pressed two fingers to her neck though he wasn't sure why. Her chest was rising and falling slowly, meaning she had a pulse, faint though it was.

"Come on, Wendy, wake up for me."

Only she didn't move—or moan. Logan looked around the apartment to see if there was any evidence of a struggle, but everything appeared to be in order. Even her laptop was undisturbed on the table. If she'd fainted from lack of food or something, her wolf would have stepped in and cured her.

The next few minutes waiting for Greer or Declan were the longest he'd ever spent. Feeling helpless was foreign to him, and he didn't like it one bit.

As if Greer had the ability to teleport, his sister appeared by his side. "Logan, scoot over. Let me see what I can do."

"Is Declan coming?"

"He'll be here as soon as he can. How about getting a cold compress for her?"

Happy to have something to do, Logan jumped up and rushed into the kitchen. He suspected it was to get him out of the way while his sister administered her healing powers, but he wasn't about to question her.

Before he was able to retrieve the cold cloth though, Declan arrived, and Logan gave himself permission to relax for the first time since he'd found his mate. At least she was now in good hands.

With the cold compress in hand, Logan strode out of the kitchen half expecting to see Wendy in her wolf form to finish the healing process.

What he found instead were two very worried faces. Both Greer and Declan were on the floor conversing. He handed the cloth to Greer and then squatted next to them. "What's wrong with her?"

His sister reached out and clasped his hand. "We can't be sure, but given her lack of response and the aura surrounding her, we both think she might have been poisoned," Greer said.

Logan's world spun. All he could think of was the two dead teens. True, they were human, and Wendy was not, but she might have ingested more than they had. "We have to do something."

Declan stood. "We've done what we can. Wendy should be fine in an hour or so, but we want the medic to take some blood samples just to be sure."

The doctors at the Sinclair mine were trained for every contingency. "I'll take her there now."

"Be prepared if she happens to wake up mid-flight," Declan said.

"I will. Thanks. How about you call the doctor and fill him in?"

"We will. Go," Greer said. "We'll pack her laptop and clothes too in case she needs to spend the night."

Without any more delay, Logan lifted Wendy, who seemed to weigh nothing. With her in his arms, he rushed into the hallway and then took the stairs up one flight to the rooftop.

Inhaling, he shifted and took off. *Please let her be okay.* He wasn't really the praying type, but this was his mate. Logan would do whatever it took to make sure she healed.

Chapter Thirteen

LOGAN HATED NOT knowing who had tried to poison Wendy. Most likely the attack was meant as a warning to keep her from researching the death of the two teens. While Logan was no expert in wolf anatomy, he'd never heard of a wolf shifter being poisoned to death. That meant either the person didn't know she was a shifter, or it was just to let Wendy know the next step would be fatal. Speculating however would get him nowhere. Research was his friend.

As Logan headed to the Sinclair mines' underground safehouse with an unconscious Wendy in his grasp, he constantly checked the surrounding airspace to make certain that Deke Darnell—or any other dragon—wasn't following him. Not that he would know what Deke's dragon looked like, but if anyone else approached, Logan would be hard-pressed to do battle while holding her.

When the mines came into view, he relaxed a bit. Logan adjusted his altitude and landed as close to the front entrance as possible. Thank goodness, one of the medical staff members was there to help open the doors and guide him inside.

"Put her on the gurney," the attendant said. "The doctor is waiting for her."

Not wanting to let her out of his sight, he followed the attendant who pushed Wendy down the long corridor. As they neared the medical room, the doctor stepped into the hallway.

He faced Logan. "Greer called me, but can you tell me what happened exactly?"

Wendy groaned, opened her eyes, and gave Logan a small smile.

"Where am I?"

"You're in a safe place now. I found you passed out and brought you here. This good doctor wants to check you out," Logan said, thrilled that she would be okay as Declan had said.

"K." She smiled and then nodded off to asleep again.

"Why don't you wheel her into the room?" the doctor said to the attendant before returning his attention back to Logan "Go on."

"I stopped by her apartment a short while ago and found her on the floor. Wendy had been working on a story involving the death of two teens." Logan explained that it could be rat poisoning based solely on the fact that it was what was found to have killed those kids.

"Did you see a box of poison?" the doctor asked.

"No, but those two boys died from a mixture of Crenathum and rat poisoning."

"I'll test her blood. Why don't you get something to drink and give me some space?"

Apparently, healers didn't like anyone hovering. "Sure thing. Can I bring you anything?"

"No, but when Greer and Declan arrive, send them in."

Logan wanted to say he was Wendy's mate, but the doctor and he didn't need to be wasting time arguing. "Sure."

Instead of grabbing his drink, Logan returned to the entrance to wait for his sister and cousin. Hopefully, they found what had caused Wendy's collapse.

It wasn't long before Logan spotted two specks of black in the air. They landed a few seconds later, and Greer rushed up to him. "Is she okay?"

"Yes. She woke up but was a little disoriented. I didn't get a chance to ask her any questions though. She's with the doctor. Did you find the source of the poison?" he asked.

Declan handed him Wendy's tablet and shook his head. "No, and we looked."

"Damn. The doctor wants to talk to you both. I'm going to call

Camden to see if he can test the food in the house."

"Good idea. While we don't know what kind of poison it was, I sensed some kind of evil lingering in her body," Greer said.

He could only hope some dark Fey hadn't come back to take revenge for her exposing Malpan. Logan shook his head. He couldn't think that way, or it would drive him crazy.

Logan followed Greer and Declan inside. While he wanted to track down the person who did this, he didn't want to leave Wendy in her time of need. If her apartment complex had security cameras, he would have requested the footage of who came and went into her place. The fact her front door was open when he arrived really bothered him. He hoped Wendy hadn't been careless and left her door unlocked.

In front of the doctor's office, Greer gave him Wendy's satchel. "She'll want this when she's feeling better," his sister said. "Here are her keys too. We found them on the table. Don't worry, we locked her front door when we left."

"Thanks."

Declan knocked on the closed medical room door, pushed it open, and then stepped inside. Logan wouldn't do any good waiting there, so he headed down the hallway to find an unoccupied room for his mate. The nicest rooms were the suites at the end.

He placed her case near the entrance and her tablet on the desk across from the bed. When Wendy was well again, she'd ask about it for sure. He couldn't remember a time when she didn't have it with her.

In need of something to perk him up, he went to the kitchen. Once Logan poured himself a cup of rather cold coffee, he called Camden at the lab.

"Hey, big brother. What's up?"

"I guess you haven't heard."

"Heard what?"

Logan wasn't sure where to begin. Since his chemistry-genius brother needed to understand the history of what happened, Logan started with the deaths of the two teens, the death of the truck driver a few months back, and then how Wendy had been targeted twice now. "She's definitely stepped on some toes."

"I'd say."

"If the driver of the furniture truck from Thedia hadn't died of the same lethal combination of Crenathum and rat poisoning as had the two teens, I'm not sure I would have believed she was poisoned. Greer and Declan sensed she had been, but the doctor is doing tests now."

"What do you need me to do?"

"Can you find the source of the poison at her place?" Logan asked.

"I can look. Do you have the key to her apartment?"

"Yes, but you'll have to pick up the key from the safehouse. I'll meet you out front."

"I'm on my way," Camden said.

"I'll owe you big time."

Camden worked in the SinCas lab mostly designing and setting gems into jewelry pieces, but his real specialty was building and embedding tracking devices into rings and necklaces, as well as being able to determine the chemical composition of anything and everything. Whereas Stone loved to be outside flying around searching for clues, Camden would rather stay cooped up in his lab being creative.

Let's hope both of their talents could help save Wendy.

A QUICK CRAMP shot across her abdomen, jarring her back to awareness. What was going on? Wendy tried to open her eyes, but it was as if her muscles had gone on vacation. Out of nowhere, soothing waves of pleasure washed over her, helping to reassure her that things would be okay.

A soft, warm hand clasped hers. "I think she's coming out of it."

It was a woman's voice, but Wendy couldn't tell who it belonged to. She tried to say something, but her lips appeared to be stuck together.

"Logan, try holding her hand," said the woman.

Logan? Yes. Everything would be okay. She was sure of it now.

"Wake up again, Wendy. You did it before."

She remembered seeing Logan's face, which meant she must have passed out again.

Warmth and strength seeped through to her from his gentle grip. Even if the woman hadn't said Logan's name, Wendy would have known it was him. The connection between them pumped up her heart, and it was as if he was transferring his health into her.

Her eyes popped open all by themselves, and then his face loomed over hers.

"Welcome back," Logan said with a smile.

Her mind spun but came up empty. "Did I fall asleep again?"

"You did."

"What happened?" she asked.

"I'm not quite sure." He explained about finding her on the floor in her apartment and how Greer and Declan helped heal her. "I know you have a lot of questions. I do too. Bottom line is that we believe someone poisoned you."

All of a sudden reality flooded in, and her stomach churned. "Poisoned? How is that possible? I was by myself ever since I left you, though you might be right. My stomach isn't totally back to normal."

He patted her hand. "How about resting, and when you are feeling better, we'll figure it out, okay?"

"I'm already feeling better. I don't even need to shift to finish healing."

Logan dipped his chin. "Wendy."

"Okay, I'll shift for a bit, and when I'm good, I'll rest even more."

Logan let go of her hand. He nodded to the others, and they all exited the room.

When she awoke the next time, the lights were out. While she couldn't tell how long she'd slept, she felt a lot better. All she needed was a moment to assess what happened. She shifted back into her human form, and just as she swung her legs over the edge of the bed, her stomach grumbled. Considering she'd been poisoned, she was a bit surprised she'd want food—but she did. *Thank you, my wolf.*

You're welcome.

Wanting to see this safe place, she located the light switch by the door and flicked it on. Nice! Was this Logan's house per chance? No. It couldn't be. Even if he'd called someone to make a house call, he wouldn't have an exam room.

The room was quite large. One wall was covered by a closed drape, and in the corner sat a small sofa, two chairs, and a table. Across from that was a desk, and on it was her tablet. Excitement raced through her. How thoughtful of Logan to bring it here.

To the left of the door sat her satchel. When Wendy opened it, she found several changes of clothes, including underwear. Heat flushed her face thinking about Logan going through drawers. She didn't know why she was embarrassed. He must have realized she'd want something to change into and had acted accordingly. Or had Greer gathered her stuff? She and Declan had helped heal her, so Greer might have grabbed a few things for her to wear.

Across from the covered wall was a door that led to a luxurious bathroom. Wow. Not only did it have a large shower, there was a soaker tub too. After what she'd been through, Wendy decided to enjoy the luxury. It would help her heal more fully, both physically as well as mentally.

Almost giddy, she dragged her case with her clean clothes into the bathroom and then stripped. While she believed she and Logan belonged together, Wendy closed the bathroom door, convinced that Logan never slept. Dragons, she'd been told, didn't need much rest. Knowing him, he'd hear that she was up and want to talk to her. It didn't matter it was in the middle of the night.

Hoping she could have another few hours to reflect on who might have tried to poison her, Wendy drew a bath. While luxuriating in the tub, someone knocked on the bathroom door. *Called it!* "Yes?"

She knew it was Logan from the way pulses of pleasure were rippling over her skin.

"Are you okay?" Logan asked.

At least this time she understood why he'd ask. "I'm good."

"I'd like to talk to you."

The clock on the nightstand had said it was only two. "Give me a sec to get out of the tub. I just need to dry off and change."

"Okay. Take your time."

Logan must have learned something if he felt it that important to talk to her in the middle of the night. Wendy climbed out of the tub and drained the water. As she ran her towel over her body, she stared at the mirror and cringed. Maybe it was the rather dim light over the sink, but her skin looked almost gray. She felt okay, so why did she look so bad? Sheesh.

As quickly as she could, she tossed on some clothes and then brushed her teeth since the metallic taste in her mouth was rather disgusting. When she opened the door, she almost expected to see an empty room. Most men wouldn't have been so patient but apparently Logan was.

He jumped up from the chair and rushed over to her. Clasping her shoulders, he studied her. "How are you feeling? And don't just say okay. I want the truth."

"I was a little weak, but the rest did wonders. I'm fine, really.

He smiled briefly. "Good. Are you hungry?"

She didn't have to think about that. "Surprisingly yes. You said I was poisoned, but it must be out of my system, or I wouldn't be."

"Great. Then follow me."

"In the middle of the night?"

He smiled. "It's two in the afternoon. You've slept a lot."

That made no sense. "But the room is so dark."

"We're underground. There is no light streaming in because we have no windows down here."

"Is this some kind of bunker?"

"Yes, but we have good medical facilities here, as well as food and a few other surprises, which was why I brought you here. It takes time, but you get used to its little quirks."

Get used to it? She didn't plan to stay that long. Shivers tripped up her spine at that thought. "You said someone tried to poison me. Isn't it remotely possibly that I ate something that gave me food poisoning?"

Logan faced her and cupped one of her cheeks. "Highly unlikely. Or do you remember throwing up?"

"No, but my wolf might have counteracted it."

He lowered his arm. "I suppose, but considering the hallway in front of your hotel room was doused with accelerant right after you asked your friend to look into some drug deals, coupled with the poisoning, I'm thinking someone wants you scared off. I asked my brother Camden to locate the source of the poison so we can be sure."

"I appreciate that." She hadn't even realized he had a brother named Camden. "How many kids are in your family?"

He smiled. "Let's get you some food, and I'll tell you all about them."

Chapter Fourteen

"I PROBABLY SHOULD write all those names down," Wendy said after Logan listed his immediate and extended family.

He chuckled. "We're basically one big family. Mom and Stone's mother are sisters. One married a Caspian and the other a Sinclair, but I swear half the time I was growing up, I slept at my cousin's house. We really think of each other as brothers and sisters."

Wendy smiled. "That sounds like a wonderful childhood."

Logan returned her smile. "It was great, though it had its challenges." Soon he'd tell her about being a Guardian and all that it entailed. Now that she'd eaten and seemed more rested, it was time to broach the more sensitive topic. Logan inhaled. "Considering these two recent attempts on your life, I don't think your apartment is the safest place to be."

She instantly shook her head. "I can't move. I can barely afford this apartment."

"What I'm suggesting is that you move in with me—strictly for your safety, of course."

You think you'd get a wink of sleep with Wendy in the spare bedroom? his dragon asked.

Shut up. This is about her, not us, you horny animal.

Wendy stilled. "That is so sweet of you, but we aren't even positive I was poisoned on purpose."

She was the most stubborn woman alive. "I'm really worried about you, Wendy. What harm can it do? You'll have your own room, and you won't even know I'm there. Hell, I spend most of my life at the office."

Wendy lifted her chin. "I don't think that would work. For starters, you distract me too much."

For real? "How?"

"You're very protective of me."

"I am. So?"

"That means you might tell me it's not safe to ask questions and then suggest I stay inside." She raised her brows as her lips curled upward—lips he wanted to kiss. "Right?"

He chuckled. It was true that Logan would suggest she stay inside his condo, but then he might have to leave. Being in the same room with her would distract him too. "Guilty as charged, but come on, a female wolf roaming the world where dragons and bears exist isn't safe." She was his mate, damn it. At least when they mated, she'd become a dragon shifter. Even then, he'd have to make sure she was trained to fight before he stopped worrying.

She ran a hand down his arm. "I appreciate how you always want to protect me—and too often have saved my life—but I've lived on my own for years, and I'm still alive." She glanced down for a moment. "Though I guess I haven't done a very good job of taking care of myself recently, have I?"

It's time. Tell her you two are mates, his dragon urged.

I *agree*. "No, you haven't. Wendy, I don't want to argue with you, but you need to understand something."

"What?"

His damn cell rang. "Crap." It was Camden, hopefully with the results of the apartment search, but damn, his timing sucked. Logan wasn't sure if the information would help or hurt his cause that Wendy move into his place, but he needed to find out. "Give me a sec, okay?"

Wendy picked up her glass of water and sipped it, her gaze never leaving his face.

"You got something?" he asked his brother.

"Yes. I tested the half empty glass of sweet tea she was drinking. Guess what? It was laced with rat poisoning."

Shit. "I appreciate the info."

"I can show you the printout of the spectrometer readings if you like."

Good old Camden. He was thorough if nothing else. "Maybe later."

"How is Wendy doing?" Camden asked.

"Good. She's sitting here with me right now having a bite."

"Glad to hear it. I'll return her apartment key to the bunker in a few minutes."

"That would be great." Logan disconnected and set the phone down.

"Who was that?" she asked.

Logan debated telling her about the poison, but he wanted to finish his conversation about them being mates first. "My brother."

He had several, so she wouldn't know it was Camden.

"Which one?"

Damn. Journalists never let anything go. "Camden."

"What did he want?"

"To see how you were doing."

Wendy leaned forward and squinted her eyes. "I think you're lying."

She didn't say it as an accusation as much as with intrigue. "Why would you say that?" he asked.

Wendy slowly reached out and ran her hand around his head but never touched him. "I'm not sure, but I saw a gray halo right above your head when you told me what Camden said, but now it's gone."

"A gray halo?" Maybe the poison had affected her brain. "And you think that means I lied or something?" He'd never heard of anything like that before.

She sat back and looked a bit confused. "I don't know. The concept just entered my head." She waved a hand. "Never mind. My eyes might have been playing tricks on me. Did he say anything else?"

He hoped her eyes were the problem and not something more

serious. As much as he wanted to discuss their mating, that conversation would have to wait. He suspected she wouldn't let this topic go.

"If you want to know, Camden found rat poison in your iced tea."

She barked out a laugh. "That's absurd. How could it get there?"

"Someone had to have put it in there." Logan didn't know how else to explain it.

"I'm serious. I made that tea a day ago and had some right before I went over to your office the first time. I suffered no ill effects then."

He waited a beat to see if she could figure it out. When she said nothing, he offered his thoughts. "Tell me this. Was your door unlocked when you went home after our meeting?"

"Of course not. Why?"

"Because when I came to see why you hadn't shown up at the office yesterday, the door was unlocked."

Her brows pinched. "I mean, it's possible. I just shoved the key in the lock without testing the door." She wagged a finger at him. "But I would have locked my door once I entered. I'm a creature of habit."

He didn't want to think of a more likely scenario. "Did you drink any tea when you got home?"

"I had dinner and then poured myself a glass. So yes. I guess it's possible someone could have come in while I was at your office, doused my pitcher of tea, and then left. This person could have picked the lock but then wasn't able to relock it on his way out." She wrapped her arms around her body. "If that was what really happened, it's horrifying."

"When you arrived home, you would have entered and relocked the door," he said.

"Exactly, so how was it unlocked for you?"

"I'd be guessing," Logan said, "but after he doused your tea, you came home early and surprised him, forcing him to hide. Once you passed out, he left."

Wendy sucked in a breath and shifted her gaze to the side. "That's too scary to consider. I'll buy a better lock for sure."

A flimsy lock wouldn't keep her safe. "Before you decide how you want to handle this situation, there's something else I need to discuss with you."

She looked up at him. "I'm not moving in with you."

"So you've said. Do you know why I'm so focused on keeping you safe?"

She froze, her eyes going wide. Okay, that wasn't good. Damn it. He better not have screwed things up worse than they already were.

"Because you like me?" Her lips were a cross between a smile and a grimace.

He could see she was scared of that fact. "I do like you. A lot, and yes I might be a little bit of a control freak, but mostly it's because you are my...mate."

The air rushed out of his lungs from the relief at finally telling her.

"Your mate? How do you know?" she asked with caution.

He hadn't expected that question. "You don't feel an attraction between us—a draw, something you can't control?"

Wendy lifted her near empty glass to her lips again. "Maybe."

She did feel it! "Wendy, as your mate, I want to take care of you. No, I need to take care of you. Not only that, I think about you all the time. As in every minute of every day, in fact." Bringing his need for hot sex into the mix would only frighten her more.

"For real?"

"For real."

She chewed on her bottom lip. "Okay. I'll admit it. I feel those things too, but I also have a need to prove myself as a writer. I want to help others—like I did when I exposed Malpan."

Her plea rang true to him. "That doesn't have to stop, but it will if you're dead."

She said nothing for a moment. "I get it, but I wasn't raised to let someone take care of me. If it will make you feel better, I'll take self-defense lessons. Surely, you know someone who can teach me fighting skills."

He loved she wanted to be independent, but she didn't seem to understand the full riskiness of her situation. However, he was willing to take one step at a time. It was all about patience. "That works. We can start with fighting strategies—ones that would be universal for all shifters whether they be wolf or dragon."

"But not from you. All that touching might cause…"

She didn't finish her sentence. She didn't have to. Her eyes had turned amber, and her nails had sharpened. Logan wanted to save her the embarrassment of explaining further. "My cousin Thane trains me. I'll ask him to show you a few moves."

As if he'd popped a balloon, the air seemed to go out of her lungs. "Thank you."

Logan finished the rest of his sandwich. "If you are determined to stay where you are, let me at least install some security devices in your apartment."

Her lips twisted and then curled into a full-blown smile. "Deal."

"Great. With that out of the way, I'd like you to work at the office most days. We still need to go to the school to check out that photo you have of the man speaking with Tom, and it will be easier if you're already at the mines."

"Sure. That would be great."

Her quick agreement surprised him, but Logan was pleased with her concession. He wanted to come up with a few more things they could do together, but he believed it would be best to start out slow. Logan imagined sharing lunches, then dinner, and then afterwards…a little kissing. Who knows? She might want to move in all on her own.

Wendy polished off her food, and Logan was happy to see her appetite had returned. When she was done, Wendy carried the dishes to the sink and started to wash them.

"You can leave them," he said.

She spun around. "Don't tell me you have maid service here?"

He shrugged. "The perks of being a Caspian."

She stepped away. "Fine. Then how about we get to work?"

"Work?"

"It's what? Almost three in the afternoon. Maybe we can go to the school now and find out if the man in the photo is Mr. Quigley and where we can find him."

Given what just happened, he didn't really see how a name would help, but he was game. "You aren't worried there will be another attempt on your life?"

"It's possible, but you'll be by my side."

He wasn't just talking about the trip to the school. He was referring to her being alone at night, but as a businessman, he knew when to push and when to retreat. "I agree."

"And before you ask, between Greer, Declan, and the doctor, I'm fine."

He chuckled at her fierce independence. "Considering how your appetite seems to have returned, I believe you."

Just as they exited the kitchen, Camden came down the hallway most likely to return the apartment key. Logan introduced them.

While his brother was an incredibly talented scientist, he was still a man. His eyes sparkled as he discreetly checked her out. "Nice to meet you. I hope you are feeling better after being poisoned."

She smiled. "Much better, thanks to Logan for finding me, and some of your family members' healing talents. And to you for finding the poison at my place."

Camden smiled. "You're welcome."

Logan placed a hand on her back. "If you want to make it to the school before they close, you'll need to pack."

She stood on her toes and kissed his cheek. "Thank you, my savior."

Heat raced up his cheek. "You're welcome. Go grab your stuff."

As soon as she was out of sight, Camden smiled. "Nice!"

"Watch it, little brother."

Camden held up his hand. "I get it. She's yours."

"Damn right. Listen, Wendy and I are going to do a little sleuthing, but I need you to do me another favor."

"What is it?"

"After this second attempt on her life, I want her place to have full security, including cameras in the hallway. I'd do it, but I need to keep Wendy busy for a while. Take Stone if you want and then leave her apartment key on my desk at the mining office."

"You owe me." Camden chuckled.

"I suppose you'll be wanting more gadgets for your home office in return for this favor?" Camden had a full lab in the basement of his house and could rig up anything from hotwiring cars to making explosives. The man would be seriously dangerous if he were evil.

His brother grinned. "I'll make a list."

His brother was kidding—or so Logan hoped.

Chapter Fifteen

WENDY HOPED SHE had done the right thing in turning down Logan's offer to move in with him, but damn it, being around him—all day and all night—would drive her wolf crazy.

Now do you believe me about you two being mates? her wolf asked.

Yes, I do.

Please tell me you are happy you finally found him.

Wendy didn't need to think about it. *Yes, but I'm not mating until I'm ready.*

We'll see about that, her wolf said, acting as if that was a challenge.

Everything was changing so fast, and she attributed it to drinking that damned glass of tea. She was convinced something strange was happening to her body—or rather to her mind—because of the poisoning. Wendy hadn't felt well after a few sips, but she'd blown it off, mostly because she couldn't afford to be sick. The article wouldn't write itself.

She had finished the first half of the story about narrowly escaping the fire, when her stomach had cramped. As she pushed away from the table to go lie down for a few minutes, her knees buckled.

That was it! No other memories surfaced until she'd heard Greer's voice. By then, Greer and Declan had infused her with their healing powers. After that, Wendy told herself she was ready to move on, until she saw that gray halo around Logan's head. The weird part was that she'd never seen anything like it before. It had to be some residual effect from the poison, or else the healers had altered her in some way.

The halo could have been a sign Logan was her mate and not that he was lying, but wouldn't she have heard of such a thing before? Maybe Danita would know. It sounded like a white-lighter thing.

First though, Wendy needed to finish packing her things, making sure to put her tablet in between the layers of clothes to protect it. Once done, she left the bunker room more confused than ever. If there had been windows in her room, she might have agreed to stay. The room where he'd put her was quite large, and the entire underground complex seemed to contain everything anyone would need.

Logan was waiting for her in the hallway. "Ready?" he asked.

"Yes, but I should drop off my satchel at my apartment before we go to the school."

"Let's leave it at the office. We have to stop by there anyway to pick up the photo of the man."

That made sense. "Okay. We have to hurry. The school will be closing soon."

Once outside, Logan slipped the satchel from her fingers, and the brief brush of his fingers ignited something inside her, confirming that he really was her mate. The big question was what to do about it?

Before she could think of what to say or do, he'd shifted into his dragon form, and the bag disappeared. Logan beckoned her toward him, and Wendy went willingly. To think they were mates still boggled her mind. She mentally tested out a few scenarios of them kissing, them getting naked, and then making love.

"Wendy?"

She looked around. Holy shit. They'd already landed at the Caspian mine, and she didn't even remember him setting her down. "I'm good," came her usual refrain.

"You look…I don't know. Dazed."

"I was just thinking about that photo."

One brow rose. "Then let's get that picture and go."

After he placed her gear in his office, he retrieved the printed photo. In all honesty, she didn't think this lead would pan out, but at least she was able to spend time with Logan. It wouldn't take her more than a day to finish her current article and then a day to polish it. Once she submitted it to Mr. Everhart, she would start on the story of the teens' murders. Too bad, it had no ending yet.

"Here it is," Logan said. He folded the photo, stuffed it in his pocket, and motioned they leave.

This time Wendy was determined to pay more attention during the flight. While she did enjoy the view from above, they landed in the school parking lot all too soon. She liked being carried by Logan. The security alone helped calm her.

Logan set her down, shifted, and then glanced around at the near empty parking lot. "Let's hope some of the staff are here."

"They should be."

Inside, they were greeted by a receptionist. Just as Wendy was about to ask about the photo she'd found, Logan whipped it out of his pocket and placed the opened paper in front of the woman. "By any chance, do you recognize the man with Tom Sanderson?" he asked.

She picked up the photo and studied it. "Poor Tom. The man looks familiar, but I don't know his name."

"He's not a teacher here?" Wendy asked.

"No."

Darn. "Thank you."

Once they left, Logan turned to her. "What's next?"

She appreciated that he was willing to let her decide. "Let's see what Tom's mom knows. If this man was Tom's tutor, she would know."

"Tell me where she lives."

It would have been easier to find the house again if she were driving, but she gave him the best directions she could. The flight was so short, Logan wasn't able to fly very high before landing on the Sanderson's front lawn.

Once he shifted, she faced him. "How about staying here?" she asked. "If Tom's mom is anything like Mrs. Evans, she might be hesitant to speak to both of us."

"Sure thing."

Wendy smiled and squeezed his arm with affection. "Thank you."

"Any time."

Wendy walked up the path to the front door and knocked.

To her delight, Mrs. Sanderson answered quickly. "Yes?"

"Mrs. Sanderson. I'm Wendy Oprander. I left a message the other day about your son."

"Of course. You're the journalist trying to find Tom's killer. Come in. Did you find out something?"

"I'm not sure." Wendy held out the photo. "The picture is quite grainy. Do you recognize this man with your son?"

"It looks like Mr. Quigley, Tom's math tutor."

Yes! "By any chance do you have his phone number?"

"I think so. Don't tell me he had anything to do with Tom's death. My son spoke highly of him."

"I'm not sure. It could be something, or it could be nothing."

Tom's mom nodded. "Give me a second to find my phone." She located her purse, pulled out her cell, and found the number. "Here it is."

Wendy typed it into her phone. As a journalist, she often found people ignored her calls, so she wanted to be able to find him another way. "Thanks. In case I can't get a hold of him, do you by any chance have a check receipt for when you paid him?"

"I never paid him. He said he worked for some charity that tutored kids from all walks of life."

Wendy found it odd that a charity would tutor students who were well off rather than focusing on those in need, but what did she know? "That was nice of him."

"I thought so too."

"Do you by any chance remember the name of the tutoring

service where he worked?" Wendy asked.

"The Learning Center."

Wendy made a note. "That helps, thanks."

Wendy needed to wash away all doubts about the man's identity. She pulled out her phone, scrolled through some pictures, and found Deke's picture. "The photo I showed you doesn't have a lot of facial details. Could this be him too?"

"I think so. I mean, I only met the man once or twice. You could ask his former girlfriend, Melanie Whittaker. She was often with Tom when Mr. Quigley was tutoring him."

"Thanks. I'll do that."

As Wendy turned to leave, Mrs. Sanderson placed a hand on her arm. "Thank you for trying to help our family."

"You're welcome."

Heart pounding, Wendy couldn't wait to get out of there, though she had learned long ago that she couldn't run away from her demons. It appeared as if Deke was posing as Mr. Quigley. But why? Sure, her former boyfriend had the skills to tutor in math and science, but wouldn't he have told her? At the time the photo was taken, Deke lived in Thedia, or so she believed. Ugh. Things like this always drove her crazy.

When she reached Logan, he placed his hands on her shoulders. "What's wrong? You look like you received some bad news."

"I kind of did. I think you might be right."

His eyes widened. "About what?"

"Deke Darnell could be behind all of this. Why or how, I don't know."

"Hold on a minute. What led you to that conclusion?"

Wendy looked over her shoulder. Mrs. Sanderson was watching them through the window. "Let's go back to the office, and I'll tell you."

"Okay."

It would give Wendy a few minutes to sort through her thoughts. Logan swooped her up before she was even aware he'd shifted. She had to get her act together or chance losing it.

The trip back to the Caspian Mines didn't give her long enough to come up with a plan though. She must be missing some key fact, only she couldn't figure out what it was. She could only hope the level-headed Logan could help.

Once he landed and shifted, they went into his office. "Coffee?" he asked.

"I'd love some."

As soon as Logan disappeared Wendy retrieved her tablet from her suitcase and fired it up. He returned not only with coffee but with two cookies as well. Logan's abilities must extend to mind reading.

"It's all we had," he said apologetically.

"Are you kidding? This is great," she said. "Thanks."

Logan pulled a chair over to her table and looked her in the eyes. "Tell me everything."

She explained that Mrs. Sanderson had no problem identifying the man in the picture as her son's math tutor. "She gave me his phone number. I also asked whether she had a check receipt for when she paid him, and she told me he was a volunteer for some charity organization."

"Which one?"

"The Learning Center. I plan to give them a call to check it out."

"I'm not sure why you're pursuing this line of enquiry," Logan said.

"Mr. Quigley is Deke Darnell."

"Oh, shit."

Her thoughts exactly. The number Mrs. Sanderson had given her didn't match Deke's Thedia number however. Before she tried him directly, she called this center. When they answered, Wendy asked if a Mr. Quigley worked for them.

"I'm sorry, but no one by that name was ever a volunteer here, and I've worked at the center for over twenty years."

Her stomach soured. "Thank you." Wendy disconnected and

looked up at Logan. "If I call the number and Deke answers, I don't know what to say."

"Give it to me. I'll call him."

She told him the number. Logan called and waited. He shook his head. "It's been disconnected."

"Why am I not surprised? Maybe we should go to Thedia," Wendy said.

"Whoa. You want to confront Deke?"

"Yes. There might be an innocent explanation, not that I believe there will be."

"If he's guilty, he'll make up some story."

She sighed. "I know, but why would a wealthy playboy tutor a high school kid in Edendale? And before you say he wanted to give back to the community, not only was that not Deke's personality, he would have told me—bragged about it even. Helping others is a hot button for me. It would have endeared me to him even more." Logan's jaw hardened. "I just mean, if Deke was trying to impress me, that would have helped."

Logan crossed his arms over his chest, an action that implied he was anything but happy. "Then why do it behind your back?"

"I don't know, but before I go off half-cocked, I want absolute confirmation that Deke is this tutor. Mrs. Sanderson said that Tom's former girlfriend, Melanie, would be able to identify Mr. Quigley, since she was often around when Tom was being tutored."

"By all means, contact her."

Wendy sent Melanie a text with the photo she'd taken of Deke and then pressed send. "Okay, I asked Melanie if this was Tom's tutor, Mr. Quigley. Now we wait."

Less than sixty seconds later, her email chimed. Melanie had responded. "That was fast." Wendy's blood pressure soared as she read the message. "Deke and Mr. Quigley are one and the same. Damn." Wendy slumped against her seat. "What is Deke hiding?"

"Didn't you say the Sanderson's have a cabin in Thedia?"

"Yes, they used to live there. Melanie said a bunch of fellow students went there and used the cabin when they went skiing last winter."

Logan picked up a pencil and twirled it over his knuckles. "It is possible Deke met Tom while skiing. They could be friends, and he used an alias so his dad wouldn't know Deke was helping him."

"You're making excuses for him. I don't buy they'd be friends. There is too big of an age difference."

Logan leaned forward. "In an effort to be unbiased, is it possible that during the time the Sandersons lived in Thedia, they knew the Darnells through some business affiliation? Mr. Darnell is quite well connected, and Mr. Sanderson is a banker. It's not a stretch to think their paths had crossed."

His mind was a few steps ahead of hers, but she liked where he was going. "Agreed, but maybe not in a good way."

"You're probably right." Logan shot her a brief smile. "I have an idea. Give me a sec."

"Sure."

He rushed over to his computer and tapped away. In less than ten minutes, he leaned back in his seat and smiled. "Well, well, well. What do you know?"

Excitement raced through her. "What is it?"

Chapter Sixteen

LOGAN DIDN'T WANT to get Wendy's hopes up or have her jumping the gun and accuse any of the Darnells of something they didn't do, but he had to admit finding a possible connection between the two families gave him hope they were involved somehow.

"Mr. Sanderson worked at Thedia National Bank for ten years. He left two years ago and moved to Edendale where he now works at a different bank," Logan said.

"People change jobs all the time. Why are you smiling?"

"Guess who banks at Thedia National?" he asked.

She tilted her head. "I imagine you're going to say Robert Darnell, but that doesn't prove anything. Thedia National is a big bank. Lots of people do business there."

Logan walked around his desk and slipped a hip on the edge. "Hear me out. Remember the images we saw in the pool at the eternal flame?"

"Yes. It looked like Mr. Darnell could have been in an office of some kind."

"Right, like a glass-enclosed office in a bank. We don't know if he was speaking with Mr. Sanderson or not, but Darnell wasn't happy," he said.

"That was an understatement."

"Meena said Mr. Darnell was out for revenge."

"I remember." Wendy leaned back in her seat. "However, we have no idea when this confrontation took place. It could have been ten years ago."

Logan pressed his lips together. "You might be right, but why would Meena show us that image now?"

"The only way to truly know is to fly back to the forest and ask her, but I get the sense she wouldn't tell us anything more—assuming she knows something."

"I couldn't agree more. From what my family has said, the Fairies and Feys are aware of a lot, but they are bound by some pledge not to reveal more than is needed for our safety."

"What do you suggest?" she asked.

"How about we stop by Mr. Sanderson's Edendale bank and see if he'll speak with us? It's not as invasive as going to his home," Logan said.

Wendy pushed back her chair. "I'm game."

"First, I want to stop by the police department."

"Why?"

"If we're going to be asking questions, it would be very helpful if Anderson made us temporary deputies," Logan said. "He's done it before for me when I've needed to gather sensitive information. Afterward, we can go to the bank. If Sanderson tells us what I think he will, I will have to stop by my condo to pack a few things for when we go to Thedia."

She smiled briefly. "Really? You're willing to confront Deke Darnell?"

What Wendy said about Deke made sense. "I think I can handle him."

"Great. Let's go."

Logan so enjoyed how willing Wendy was to do whatever it took to make things right in the world. He escorted her outside, shifted, and then lifted her up as he took off. Because of the density of the city, one of his few options was to land on the SinCas building and walk from there. The police department wasn't that far and being granted deputy status only took a few minutes.

After Anderson explained the limits of their newfound power, they both signed some documents.

"Don't abuse your new authority," Anderson said with a glint in his eyes.

"We'll be respectful," Logan said.

"You better." This time his cousin smiled.

Armed with proper identification, they headed to the bank. During their short walk, they discussed their strategy on how to approach the topic of Mr. Sanderson's departure from Thedia.

"I think you should handle the inquisition," Wendy said.

That was a surprise. "I appreciate that and don't worry, I will be sensitive to the man's loss, I promise."

At the bank, Logan explained that they were working with the Avonbelle Province Police and had a few questions for Mr. Sanderson. Both of them were shown into his office right away. While researching Mr. Sanderson, Logan had seen a few pictures of the man, but it looked as if he'd aged ten years since they'd been taken.

Mr. Sanderson stood. "How can I help you? My assistant said this had something to do with my son's murder."

"Yes. Did you know a Robert Darnell when you lived in Thedia Province?"

The man's lips pinched. "I'm afraid so. Why?"

"He's a person of interest, which means we can't discuss the details, but the more information you can tell us about your relationship with him, the better."

"Did that son of a bitch have something to do with my son's death?"

That comment was telling. "We don't know yet. We were hoping you could fill us in," Logan said.

"What do you need to know?" The man's breathing had accelerated to a dangerous level.

"Why did you leave your job in Thedia?"

Mr. Sanderson waved a hand. "That's none of your business."

"It might be your son's business if your departure had anything to do with Darnell."

The man's mouth opened and then his chest deflated. "How did you know?"

"Call it a hunch."

The banker motioned they take a seat in front of his desk, while he dropped onto his chair. "Several years ago, Mr. Darnell came to the bank asking for a loan for one of his companies. We thought he was a good risk at the time and lent him the money." Mr. Sanderson dragged a hand down his jaw. "If you recall, we had a little downturn in the economy, and Darnell couldn't pay us back, so we had to foreclose on the property."

That aligned with the images Meena had shown them. "How did he react?"

"Poorly. He said I'd pay for not believing in him. A few days later, some reckless driver sideswiped my wife's car, forcing her to run into a metal guardrail. She broke a few ribs and sustained some cuts and bruises. The driver of the other car never even stopped."

"I'm sorry. Did you think Darnell was responsible?"

"I thought so, but I had no proof."

Logan glanced over at Wendy, but she'd schooled her features. He had to give her credit for remaining so calm. "Did the cops ever find out who was responsible for the accident?" Logan had to ask.

"Eventually. It was some punk, but we never could prove he had any connection to Darnell."

Logan might have to research that case. He would look for any kind of money trail between Darnell and the hit-and-run driver. "Was that why you quit your job and moved to Edendale?"

"Yes, but I didn't leave right away. There were two more incidents about three months apart that convinced me to go. Tom was on his way home from practice and was mugged. The man roughed him up pretty badly, but we never identified the guy. Then someone broke into our house while we were at work and stole some electronics. It was all replaceable, but my wife had a break down, and Tom's grades got steadily worse. We all feared something horrific would happen to one of us if we stayed."

"I am so sorry," Wendy said.

"Thank you."

"Could you have upset other people, enough for them to target you?" Logan asked.

Sanderson shook his head. "Doubtful. I mostly dealt with commercial loans. I never had any problems during my entire tenure at the bank, until Mr. Darnell."

Darnell seemed to be a key player. "What do you know about Tom's math and science tutor?" Logan asked.

"I never met him, why?"

"Just trying to put the pieces together." Logan stood and held out his hand. "You've been very helpful. Thank you."

"I hope you get the bastard who murdered my son."

"So do we."

Logan waited until they were outside the bank to discuss what happened. "What do you think?" he asked Wendy, respecting her take on things.

"The poor man is still afraid of Darnell and maybe rightfully so."

Logan placed a hand on the small of her back to help them weave their way through the crowded streets. "Many people make threats but never carry them out."

"That may be, but how do you explain Deke's presence as Tom's tutor?" she asked. "The fact he lied about being a volunteer implies something was going on. He could have been feeding information to his dad about the family's whereabouts."

"I agree that Deke looks involved. You said the two of you had already broken up when that picture was taken, right?"

"Yes, but it appears as if Deke tutored him while we were dating, yet he never said a word. He was hiding something. I can feel it."

"We should upload a photo of Tom and Mike onto your phone, so we can ask Deke when we see him." Logan would love to meet the guy and tear him limb for limb, but it might be because of jealousy and not because the guy was guilty of anything.

"Good idea. Deke aside, do we have anything that points to Mr. Darnell being a drug dealer?" she asked. "Or to being a murderer?"

"Not yet. I need to do a little more digging to see why Darnell had a sudden change of fortune after the bank foreclosed on his company. When I checked his financials for this month, the man seems to be very well off. I'm wondering if his newfound fortune could be a result of dealing in drugs."

"The timing works, I guess. When Deke moved to Edendale, he said his father was quite wealthy."

"Did Deke have a job in town here? Is that why he moved here?"

"Sort of. He worked part time for his dad, drumming up furniture business in Edendale. He also did some online stuff, like creating websites."

"He could have been helping to set up the dealers in our town."

She shivered. "If that is true, I can't believe I wouldn't have known."

"It is still possible Deke is a pawn in all of this." Not that he believed the guy was innocent. One doesn't grow up with a snake and end up clean. "Let's hope Anderson learns something. He'll be working with the Thedia police." They went back to the office, picked up her bag, and then headed over to Logan's condo. "This is where I live. Let me grab a few things for our trip."

He led her inside the building and took the elevator to the sixth floor.

"I wish my apartment had an elevator," she mumbled.

He found her comment endearing but sad at the same time. Thankfully, Logan never took things for granted, and always appreciated how lucky he was to have grown up in a loving family who wanted for nothing.

"You know the offer always stands to stay here." When Logan looked down at her and found her sucking on her bottom lip, his cock turned rigid. Crap. *Stand down*, he told his dragon.

We're about to go into your apartment with our mate. Did you forget there is a bed there?

His animal was insufferable, not that he could blame him. His poor dragon had been yapping about a mate for close to a hundred years. *No, but we have more pressing things to attend to.*

I'm not that patient.

No kidding, but Logan blocked that response from his animal.

She lifted up on her tiptoes and kissed his cheek. "Thank you for helping."

Once more, her touch set off a firestorm in his gut, and his need for her escalated. Shit. If Wendy didn't keep her distance, Logan wasn't sure what he might do. Part of him wanted to ask her to go back down to the lobby while he packed, but that might break any trust they had built between them.

"Not that I'm complaining, but what was that for?" he asked.

"For the offer to stay with you and for letting me go to Thedia with you even though I know you think it's dangerous."

"I need you." In more ways than one.

She smiled. "Good to know."

At his door, Logan leaned forward and placed his eye on the scanner. A second later, the latch popped open.

"Wow," Wendy said. "I've never seen one of those before."

"One can never be too safe."

When she stepped inside, Logan hadn't realized he was holding his breath, wanting her to like what she saw. Unlike some of his siblings and cousins, he had a flare for style. He felt the seafoam green sofa and navy blue and green striped chairs created a calming effect. The pictures on the walls of the mountains and seaside were painted by local artists. His condo was his happy place.

"I'll be back in a moment. Feel free to look around," he said.

Wendy's eyes went wide again. "I can't believe you live here. It's amazing."

Endorphins shot through his system. "Check out the view. It's even better."

As Logan entered his bedroom, her light footsteps implied she was doing as he suggested. He didn't expect to be in Thedia for long, but just in case they were, he packed for three days. Who knows? They might find something fun to do while there. Thedia would be colder than Avonbelle Province, so he tossed in a sweater—one that Wendy could cuddle in if need be. Though if she were anywhere near him, she wouldn't need much to stay warm.

That's what I'm talking about, his dragon chimed.

Ignoring the comment, he slung his backpack over his shoulder and left the room. Wendy was in the kitchen looking through his cabinets, and he couldn't be more pleased.

She turned back to face him. "You cook?"

He laughed. "I do. Does it ruin my image?"

She planted a hand on her hip. "No, but in all honesty, I didn't think you would know a sauté pan from a double boiler."

He didn't know what a double boiler was, but he wasn't going to admit that. "Are you ready to go?"

"Yes. Do you know where we are going to stay?"

He hoped in the same hotel room. "I figure we'll worry about that in an hour or two when we arrive." He snapped his fingers, and then pulled out his phone from his pocket. "That reminds me, I need to call Stone to let him know I won't be around for a few days."

The call didn't take long. When they were at the station, Anderson had promised to let the Thedia Province Police know that Logan and Wendy would be asking some questions. Because Logan was on official business, the cops shouldn't interfere much. Apparently, the two police departments had agreed to share the investigation until such time as it became evident that the teen deaths had nothing to do with any drug criminals from Thedia.

Logan stuffed his phone back in his pocket, hoping he wasn't forgetting anything. "Let's go."

Wendy threaded an arm through his and looked up at him. "Promise not to leave my side? I have this feeling something bad is going to happen."

Whoa. What had prompted her wave of concern? He patted her forearm. "You don't have to worry about a thing. I can protect you." To prove to her he would do everything in his power to keep her safe, he kissed the top of her head.

She smiled, and Logan nearly turned around and dragged her into the bedroom.

Chapter Seventeen

WENDY'S LAST TRIP from Thedia back home seemed to take longer than this trip. It could be because on the previous trip, she'd nearly burned to death and had barely escaped a painful fall. Not to mention that at the time, Wendy had been a little distracted. Looking back, she regretted not fully enjoying being in Logan's grasp.

When they arrived in Thedia, Logan landed in the same park where he'd flown her after rescuing her from the hotel fire—a hotel that was understandably closed for renovations. That meant they had to find another place to stay.

"We need to head this way," Logan said as he guided her down the paved path to the main sidewalk. His stride was quite purposeful.

"I assume you know where you're going?" she asked him.

"I do. I located a few hotels, but only one was to my liking."

Interesting. She hadn't realized he needed such high-end accommodations.

It didn't take long before they reached a very upscale hotel. "Does this look okay?" Logan asked.

Was he kidding? Wendy thought the hotel the newspaper editor had put her up in was grand, but this was way out of her league. "You paying?" She certainly couldn't afford it.

He ran a knuckle down her cheek. "Wendy, you are my mate. My goal is to provide you with whatever you desire."

Logan's words nearly melted her. She'd been on her own for so long she almost didn't know how to accept help from others. "That sounds too good to be true."

Logan smiled. "Come on. Let's hope they have a room."

A room, as in one they would share? Heat pooled between her thighs at that thought.

Say something about this awesome opportunity, her wolf urged.

"I didn't picture Thedia as a destination vacation except maybe in the winter." She wasn't the skiing type, but several of her friends were.

I meant something sexual. Sheesh.

"There is snow year-round in some parts of the province, so people can ski anytime they want."

As was his habit, Logan placed a hand on her lower back as they walked toward the desk counter, and that one touch made her already escalating lust shoot higher. "Oh, crap," she mumbled.

Logan stopped. "What is it?"

"I forgot to call Mr. Landry and tell him I'm not interested in the job." Actually, the expletive referred to the strong need to jump his bones right there in the lobby, but she wasn't about to say that out loud.

Logan smiled. "You sure? I for one am glad you want to stay in Edendale. What was the deciding factor?"

She shook her head. "Not even going there."

Most likely Logan wanted her to say that since they were mates that she could never leave him. That was true, but there was another reason. Wendy sensed an evil in this town and wanted nothing to do with it.

He held up a hand. "Your choice, but I bet I can worm it out of you at some point." He winked.

That made her chuckle. In truth, if they both were naked, she bet she'd tell him anything.

At the front desk, Logan asked for two rooms, and Wendy didn't know whether to appreciate his thoughtfulness or be disappointed that they'd be apart.

"I'm sorry, sir, but we only have one room left. What with one of the hotels having a devastating fire, we're near to full capacity."

Logan looked at her, his brows raised. "It's fine," she said with a straight face, though inside her heart was pounding with excitement. Would it be a little awkward? Perhaps, but she'd deal.

If Logan was trying to contain his excitement, his body was betraying him. Teal swirls merged with the greens and browns in his eyes, making him sexier than anything she'd ever seen. If he hadn't been wearing a light coat, she bet she'd see his blue scales flashing.

As it was, Wendy had to work not to let him see her sharpened teeth or nails. She couldn't prevent him from noticing that her eyes had turned amber already, indicating her wolf wanted a taste of his dragon.

Wendy had been in denial for too long. She wanted him. Plain and simple. She had thought sleeping with him would cloud her ability to think clearly. Now, she was convinced it would help.

The clerk slid the key card across the counter. "Room 204."

One plus of staying in this hotel was if she had to jump out the window, it wouldn't be a long drop to the ground.

"Let's put our stuff in the room and then grab something to eat."

"Sounds good." Wendy wouldn't be able to sleep unless they had a plan on how to find information about Deke and his dad. She almost laughed out loud. Who was she kidding? Being in the same room with Logan Caspian for the night would prevent her from sleeping a wink.

They took the elevator up one floor. When they entered the room, Wendy halted. One bed. One loveseat. Two chairs. Hmm. She should be thrilled not to have two beds, but now that she was actually in the room with Logan, her nerves flared up.

Having learned how not to react, she set her bag on the bed and faced him. "If we're going to be walking around at night, I think I should do a little layering. It's a bit brisk outside." Damn, she couldn't even make eye contact. That was so not like her.

Logan moved toward her after placing his backpack on the luggage stand. When he clasped her shoulders, heat swamped her body, and her breath nearly burst from her lungs.

"Wendy?" He turned her around. "What's wrong?"

He certainly seemed to be able to sense that her yearning was mixed with tension. "Nothing."

"I don't believe you, love," he said.

He lifted her chin, forcing her to look at him. Those teal colored eyes swimming with desire melted her. And the intense blue of his flashing scales near his throat nearly did her in. But it was the look of want and need aimed directly at her that broke her willpower.

Before she could respond, he leaned over and kissed her gently. From the tension in his fingers though, he wanted more. And so did she. When Wendy had finally decided it was time to explore this amazing man, she couldn't say. All she knew was that being with Logan felt right. Oh, so right.

As if her hands had a will of their own, she wrapped them around his waist, pressed her body against his, and parted her lips in invitation.

He groaned and then lifted his hands to cup her cheeks. When their tongues touched, a bolt of pleasure soared through her so fast she felt as if her toes weren't even touching the ground.

Logan broke the kiss. "I can't lie. I need you."

"Is that so?" she asked as she tilted her head. Wendy usually sucked at flirting, but with Logan it was easy.

"If you're hungry, we can eat first and then continue, but I have to tell you, my mind is not on food."

She laughed, probably from nerves, but it also contained a lot of joy. No one had ever been so desperate to be with her before. Maybe that was what being with a mate meant. "Me neither."

Wanting to participate in this soon-to-be monumental event, she shucked off her jacket and then kicked off her shoes. Logan did the same and then clasped her hands.

"Are you sure? Because once I start, I won't be able to stop."

She inhaled, sensing no reservation on her part. "I'm sure."

He dug a hand in his jeans pocket, withdrew a condom, and waved it.

"You were pretty confident," she said, barely able to contain a smile.

His grin came out lopsided. "I was hopeful. You seemed to be warming up to me."

She waited a beat before answering. "Okay, okay. You're right. How about showing me that I'm not wrong in wanting this?"

"I can think of nothing better." His teal eyes flashed once more as he tossed the condom on the nightstand. He then lifted her up and deposited her on the bed. "If I could, I'd howl for you."

Maybe someday he could—that is after they mated and only when he was in his wolf form. She'd heard she would be able to shift into either a wolf or a dragon, depending on her mood, and that freedom and power thrilled her—but not as much as what experiencing this amazing man would be like.

Logan crawled on the bed, his gaze never leaving her face. He stretched out on top of her and rested on his elbows. As if he was working hard not to devour her, he nipped her chin, and then kissed her nose. His groan came out deep and sexy.

"I think we're overdressed." Wendy needed to be sure he understood what she wanted.

"In due time, my impatient mate. I want to savor every second of our first time together."

Could the man be any sweeter? Okay, sweet might not be the right word, but right now, her lust was clouding her ability to string even a few coherent thoughts together.

Kiss him, already, her wolf said.

I plan to.

Wendy reached up, planted her hands on each side of his head, and drew his lips to hers. When their tongues touched, her wolf came out to play as did his dragon. Heat shot straight to her core. His exploration was slow but sure, as if he'd had a lot of experience knowing how to turn on a woman.

The more they probed and twisted, the brighter his scales flashed under his skin. She wanted to unleash that animal inside him, but only if he didn't shift. That could prove disastrous.

His breaths came out fast, and Logan broke the kiss. "I didn't think it would be this intense."

Wendy totally understood. "I had no idea either."

He rolled off to the side. "I need you naked."

"I need you naked more." Though she worried she'd just stare and drool when what she really wanted to do was touch him all over.

When he tossed off his shirt, Wendy was sure her eyes turned pure amber. Her mouth had definitely gapped open. From the way he wore his clothes, she could tell he was fit, but seeing those abs and his powerful pecs made her speechless. Whoever was responsible for pairing her with Logan deserved her undying loyalty.

"Now it's your turn," Logan said. As she was starting to take off her T-shirt, Logan stayed her hands. "I meant, it's my turn to get you naked."

"Oh."

When his knuckles brushed against her heated skin, her pulse soared. She wasn't even sure she could remain still while he lifted the material off her body, yet somehow even after her top found the floor, she hadn't moved—until now. Not waiting for an invitation, she reached out and undid the top button of his jeans.

He shook his head. "That comes later."

"That's not fair," she shot back.

"I'm happy to see someone's in a hurry."

Like he wasn't? Fine, she could control her more prurient urges, or so she hoped. What she hadn't expected during this undressing process was for Logan to slip his fingers under her bra and lift it over her breasts, keeping the back latched.

"Mmm," he murmured as he blew out a breath and then pounced.

He plucked a nipple between his teeth and tugged enough to create incredible tension without it being painful.

Wendy had to touch him. She ran her hands across his shoulders and down the upper part of his back, loving how his muscles moved every time he licked and pulled on her tiny nub.

Logan switched to the other breast. Having him pluck the first sensitive tip between his fingers while he drew the other one into his mouth made her arch her back. Climaxing within seconds of their lovemaking was not acceptable. Then again, no one before had ever had such an effect on her.

Her nails extended, and she dug them into his skin, trying not to draw blood. "Take off my pants," she pleaded.

Logan looked up. "Don't worry, I will."

"How can you be so calm?"

His jawline tensed. "You have no idea how hard I am working to take my time. I'm afraid the moment I take off your clothes, I won't be able to keep from impaling you."

That was what she wanted, but making this last a bit longer would be nice too. "Then how about I undress you?"

A smile spread across his face. He rolled over again and divested himself of his jeans and briefs. "I can do it faster."

He was naked in a flash. Whoa. Wow. No way. Before she had the chance to enjoy the view more fully, he crawled back on top of her. Instead of continuing to pay attention to her breasts, he slid lower. He unzipped her pants and tugged them off. Because they were snug, her panties were lost in the removal process. So much for him waiting, but she certainly wasn't about to complain.

He inhaled and closed his eyes. "I love your scent," he said.

Not knowing if she should say thank you, Wendy kept quiet.

While she was still reveling in his comment, he sunk a finger straight into her, causing waves of erotic lust to light her up from the inside out. If she'd been a dragon shifter, her interior scales would have been flashing so brightly they would have blinded them both.

His finger movement increased in pressure and speed, and Wendy writhed under his masterful touch. Logan then pressed on some spot that sent her soaring even higher. Her vision blurred, and her breath caught. When her wolf scratched her insides and threatened to erupt, she had to momentarily move her focus away from her near climax. Thankfully, her animal backed off.

As if Logan knew that he'd almost pushed her too far, he removed his finger and replaced it with his tongue. Joy, bliss, and total elation infused every cell of her body. How was this possible?

He's your mate, silly. It's what I've been telling you would happen.

I'm glad I held off then. I never would have written a word if I had made love with him any sooner.

The moment Logan flicked the tiny tip again, she lost all ability to keep her climax at bay. She heard her strangled cry though she didn't remember initiating it. A few seconds later, Logan lifted his head and crawled up her body.

When the waves of pleasure waned a little, she threaded her fingers through his short hair, the texture stimulating her further. "That was amazing," she said.

"I've only just begun."

He reached over to the nightstand and snatched the condom. Before she could ask to let her put it on, he'd rolled to the side, torn open the packet, and pulled it down on his cock. Considering his girth, he was probably better suited for the job.

"I wanted to return the favor," Wendy said, nodding to his sheathed dick.

"Not going to happen tonight. Tonight, is all about me giving you pleasure."

"I so appreciate that. By all means, sacrifice away."

Logan returned to his dominant position, grinned, and then devoured her lips, clearly determined to brand her as his own—and Wendy couldn't be happier.

Chapter Eighteen

H AVING WENDY IN his arms was everything Logan had imagined and more, but he wasn't sure how long he could keep it together. Her responsiveness thrilled and excited him beyond anything he'd thought possible, and his dragon had never been happier either.

"What are you waiting for?" she asked with a glint in her eye.

Sure, he'd been with aggressive women before, but Wendy brought out a deep-seeded need in him to possess her fully like no one else before. Not mating with her tonight would be one of the most difficult things he'd ever had to do.

Did he want to bite her neck and claim her as his? Hell, yeah he did, but he wouldn't, at least not before he believed she wanted to spend the rest of her life with him. For that to happen though, he needed to do whatever it took for her to fall in love with him.

His impatient imp wrapped her legs around his back. "Take me."

"You don't have to beg." He loved teasing her.

Her mouth opened in protest, and Logan took advantage of it. Not only did he kiss her, but he slid his cock right into her slick opening. The moment the tip found her back wall, something morphed inside him. It was as if his dragon was being energized by their joining. Heat seared his insides, and his scales flashed faster and brighter than ever before. Nothing had ever excited him like this.

Wendy's eyes widened, and only then did he realize he should have delved in slower. Logan eased out, and her chest deflated. He broke the kiss. "Breathe."

"I'm trying." A moment later, she nodded and then lifted her hips to virtually impale herself on his dick once more.

That one move caused his control to fly away. Logan cupped her face and kissed her again. Their tongues dueled and explored fervently as he hammered his cock into her. Her eyes watered, and her breaths came out faster. She was close. Really close.

So are we, his dragon said, clearly on the brink of losing it.

"Come for me," Logan whispered.

He lowered his lips to her neck, pretending they were about to mate. Fearing he might scare her with his sharpened teeth, he made sure not to scrape the edges against her delicate skin.

Wendy's nails turned sharper as she dug them into his back. Thankfully, his dragon healed him as fast as she destroyed the surface. She tilted back her head and clamped down hard on his cock. Just as she let out a primal scream, indicating her climax had consumed her, he came hard, with more force than ever before.

Her inner walls continued to pulse—or else that was him still pumping. When he was done, Logan lowered his face and rested his cheek on her shoulder. He wanted to hold her like this forever. And he would have too if Wendy hadn't lowered her legs and moaned.

"That was better than I could ever have imagined," she said in between breaths.

"I couldn't agree more."

After they'd both calmed a bit, he slipped out to find something to clean them up with.

Once he finished, Logan sat on the bed and wiped her damp hair from her face. "As much as I would like a repeat of that, we need to eat before the restaurants close."

"There's always the diner where we went last time. I think it's open twenty-four hours."

"I wanted to have a finer dining experience than that. Come on. Get up and get dressed." He leaned over and brushed a kiss against her lips.

She stuck her tongue out at him but then climbed out of bed. "I feel kind of different."

"That's because you've never experienced a Guardian before." Logan held his breath, hoping that little tidbit wouldn't put her off. If they were going to mate, she needed to know everything about him.

Her eyes widened. "You're a Guardian, as in that dragon clan that saves people?"

"I'm not sure I'd characterize us as a clan, but yes, we protect and help those in need." She said nothing for a minute, but her gaze that was focused on something above his head slightly unnerved him. "Are you okay with that?" She'd better be, since it wasn't something he could give up.

Wendy blinked. "Yes. Completely. I mean who doesn't want a hero for a mate?"

He chuckled. "That is a relief."

She blinked a few times. "You really are telling the truth."

"I am. Why would you doubt it?"

"I've been formulating a theory. I thought I was crazy, but it might be real."

Logan wasn't following her logic. "What theory?"

"It seems that ever since I was poisoned, when I hear a lie, I see a gray halo above that person's head. At first, I thought it might have been because we were mates, but I spotted it above a woman at the store."

He searched his memory for that magical talent. "I've never heard of anything like that before. I know my sister's mate Blake can sense a person's aura, but not whether they are telling the truth."

"I'm not positive that is what my gray halo theory means," she said. "I need to test it out some more."

"Maybe you should ask Danita. She might know."

"I plan to as soon as we return."

He recalled Wendy's look of amazement when they were sitting at the kitchen table at the safe house. "After you recovered from the poisoning, and we were in the kitchen, you detected something similar to this, right?"

"Yes."

He figured something was up when she ran a hand over the top of his head. "Was it when I said Camden was asking about you?"

"Yes." Her voice escalated.

"I wasn't really lying. I just didn't tell you the whole truth."

She nodded. "Perhaps that was why the halo faded so quickly."

Her talent could come in very handy if she could detect the truth. "How about this?" He lifted his chin. "I don't find you attractive at all." He had to work to keep from rolling his eyes.

She lifted her gaze and then squinted. "I saw a quick flash of gray. I'm guessing that the person has to believe it in order for it to stay gray."

"I'll keep that in mind, but I don't intend to ever lie to you. It was why I told you about my true identity."

Wendy said nothing for a moment. "I can't believe you're really a Guardian. Is that why you and your family helped save all those men in the mine or was it really because your copper sales were down?"

From the way her eyes were searching the room, she was putting all of the pieces together. "Both, actually. I'm kind of surprised Danita never mentioned that Griffin was one."

"She never did. He must have told her not to. And I won't say anything either."

"Thank you, though you can talk about it to Danita or Greer or anyone else in my family. I mentioned it in part because I don't want you to worry about me. I told you I was trained, and that is true. In fact, I've been developing my skills since I learned to fly. My cousin Thane makes us do mock battles all the time. Coupled with our magic, no one has taken us down—at least not yet."

Wendy blew out a breath and moved closer. She placed her hands on his chest, stood on her toes, and kissed him. "Good to know."

She spun around before he could hold her again. When she

dragged down her bra and then slipped on her panties, he dressed too.

As soon as they were ready, he double-checked that the windows were secure. It was a habit he couldn't ignore. At the front desk he spoke with the clerk. "We are here on police business. Please don't let anyone enter our room, regardless of what or who they claim to be." He flashed his badge. The desk clerk didn't need to know it was a temporary one.

To the clerk's credit, he merely nodded. Outside, Wendy looked up at him. "Are you really expecting trouble?"

"No, but I don't want to take any chances when it comes to your safety."

She smiled. "You always say the nicest things."

Score one for him.

WALKING THE STREETS of Sawmill was like being in a dream. Not only had Logan revealed an incredibly well-kept secret, he'd woken up her body in ways she never could have imagined. Parts of her were probably glowing—at least they seemed to be doing that, even if it was only on the inside.

"Did you also research which restaurant to go to?" Wendy asked. Logan almost didn't need a computer. He seemed to instinctively know things.

"Remember Stone and I came here before you arrived, and we found a really nice Hearndian food restaurant."

"Sounds great."

Even though she'd put on a light jacket to keep from getting cold, it turned out she didn't need it. Her afterglow from making love was enough to keep her warm.

"Here we are," Logan announced all too soon.

"Fancy."

"Only the best for you."

She tightened her grip on his arm. The inside of the restaurant was lit with warm yellow lights, and the cloth-covered tables were adorned with glowing candles. There were only about ten tables, most of which were empty, but that added to the romantic ambience. The soft, soothing music was the perfect touch.

They stepped up to the hostess station. She looked up from her computer and smiled. "Table for two?"

"Yes. Mind if we sit away from the window?" Logan asked.

She didn't react. "Of course."

Once seated, they both quickly looked over the menu, but Wendy's mind wasn't really on food. She would eat because she needed her strength to approach Deke tomorrow. Her plan was to go to his workplace where hopefully Becky wouldn't be present. Wendy couldn't wait to see Deke's reaction when she waltzed in with Logan, a far more handsome and viral man than her former boyfriend.

"Your mind is spinning," Logan said as he placed a napkin on his lap. "Tell me. And remember, there are no secrets between us. Secrets are the same as distancing our hearts from each other."

He was right. If the two of them were to spend the rest of their lives together, she had to be honest. "Okay, I'll tell you. I'm trying to figure out the best way to confront Deke."

"I've been wondering the same thing. Just so you know, talking to him is fine, but asking Robert Darnell if he poisoned two teenage boys as a way of enacting his revenge is definitely not."

She let out a breath. "Even I think that would be too dangerous."

His brows rose, and his lips lifted slightly. "I'm glad to know you can be reasonable."

She smiled sweetly. "I can be."

Their server stopped by, and Wendy picked one of her favorite fish dishes.

"Red or white?" Logan asked. "I'm assuming white since you are having fish."

"Regardless of the meal, I'm a red girl."

"Works for me." He rattled off a brand she'd never heard of to the waiter and then chose a meat platter for himself. "Tell me about yourself, Wendy Oprander."

She huffed out a laugh. "Don't you think it's a little late for introductions?" She was kidding, but only slightly. Danita had filled her in a bit about his family, so Logan wasn't that big of a mystery to her. He didn't know anything about how she'd grown up. When she did tell him, she worried he'd change his mind about her.

"I do love your sense of humor," Logan said. He pointed to the imaginary crown on his head. "Remember, I can't lie in any way or you'll know. I just wish I had the same ability to know when someone else isn't telling the truth."

He might once they mated. "You won't ever see a gray halo above my head either, because I'll always tell you the truth."

"Then by all means, tell me who Wendy, the journalist, really is."

She inhaled. "Unlike your family, my parents were poor, mostly because my dad had a gambling addiction. In fact, he still does. The man loves to bet. Truth be told, he's actually quite the card shark, but even the best can lose." She fiddled with her napkin. Wendy wasn't sure she'd ever laid out exactly what her life had been like to anyone before—not even to Deke. Sure, Danita knew her background, just not all of the details.

"Go on."

"Our financial ups and downs were hard on my mom in part because my dad was often on a gambling binge. She had a few jobs to help us out, but she basically had to raise me herself. That meant she had to do the shopping, the cooking, the cleaning, and take me to all of the after-school stuff that kids need, while dad gambled and drank. That made having a full-time job tough for her. Don't get me wrong. Mom would work for a while but then lose the job when she failed to show up a few times—mostly when I was sick or had to be someplace important."

"Your father didn't work?"

"It depended on the day."

"I can't imagine what that was like. My mom was always there for us kids, and my father worked hard to set up the mines."

Wendy smiled. "My mom wanted to be there for me too, but we needed money. Thankfully, she only had me, or we'd have been living on the streets."

"Ouch. You said she became ill when you were young?"

"Yes. The summer before I turned thirteen, mold got in her lungs from working at a factory, and it was something she never recovered from. She died less than a year later, though I suspect it was partly from a broken heart. The man she had loved and married failed to be there for her."

Logan reached out and grabbed her hand. "That will never happen to us. We are mates. I will never leave you."

"My parents were mates too. At least that was what my wolf father said. Mom was human. I think that's why she never talked to me much about what it was like to be a wolf shifter and have that erotic pull that grows so strong you can't resist it when you find your mate."

Logan leaned back in his seat. "I think you understand what being a mate feels like very well. In fact, I don't think I've heard anyone explain it any better."

Heat rushed up her face. "Thank you."

They talked a bit more about her life after she moved away from home. Before she'd finished telling him, their meal arrived. Wendy dug in, and the first bite made her moan. "This is incredible."

He smiled, and once more her libido sat up and took notice. "I'm glad you are enjoying it."

They had eaten most of the food and had drank half of the wine when his cell rang, but like the gentleman he was, Logan ignored it.

Wendy appreciated that he wanted them to have an uninterrupted romantic dinner, but it could be important. "Answer it already."

He chuckled. "If you wish." He pulled his cell from his pocket and frowned. "It's Anderson." He placed the phone to his ear. "Hey, what's up?"

As he listened, Logan dragged a hand over his head, his frown deepening. "Is it about Darnell?" she mouthed.

Logan nodded. "He's what? How? Okay, thanks. We'll head over to the Thedia station right now." He hung up but said nothing, clearly trying to process what he'd heard.

"Logan, what is it?"

"Robert Darnell is dead."

Chapter Nineteen

LOGAN WOULDN'T LIE to Wendy. While he debated not telling her everything, that was almost the same as lying. She needed to know the truth. Logan inhaled and leaned forward, not wanting anyone to overhear their conversation. "Darnell was murdered."

"Are you kidding me? He was a dragon shifter. How could he be dead?" Wendy huffed. "I don't see him engaging in a sky fight at his age. Was he shot in the heart ten times or did someone stab him in that soft spot you dragons have?"

Logan had told her that he, at least, was fairly indestructible. "I don't know all of the details, but Anderson said that someone ripped out Darnell's heart."

She gasped. "How horrible."

"I agree. It had to be a terrible way to die. Unfortunately, it still means a murderer is on the loose." To think he had decided that Mr. Darnell was the criminal behind everything.

"A murderer who we can't be sure had anything to do with the boys' deaths," she said as she stared at her mostly eaten plate of food.

Logan waved to their server. They hadn't finished their meal, but he doubted Wendy had any appetite left. Logan sure didn't. "Anderson asked if we'd meet him at the Thedia station."

"By all means, let's go." Wendy shoved back her chair.

"Hold on. I need to pay the bill first."

Wendy sat back down. "Sorry. I wasn't thinking straight. This is such a shock. Do the police have any idea who did this?"

"No." The waiter came over with the check, and Logan paid. After donning her jacket, they exited. "It's not far. You okay to walk?" he asked.

"I love to walk."

"Good to know. Likes red wine and loves to walk. Check."

She rolled her eyes, and her lips briefly lifted into a smile. "If I get bored, I'll write my autobiography, so you'll have all the sordid details of my life."

Thankfully, her comment held some cheer. "In all honesty, I'd rather learn everything about you bit by bit in person."

Wendy fully smiled this time, and his libido once more shot to life. Because that was totally inappropriate, he forced himself to think about Darnell's death, which helped calm him.

When they entered the Thedia police station, the noise level was rather high, and he suspected that had to do with the murder of a high-profile citizen.

At the front desk, they showed their credentials and were then shown to a conference room. Anderson was seated at the large table along with a few policemen. The shocker was the presence of Deke Darnell who looked just like all the photos he'd seen of him. Wasn't he a person of interest? After all, it was his father who'd been killed.

Anderson nodded to them. A detective asked Anderson to introduced them. His cousin explained they were Avonbelle deputies, called in to work on this case. When Logan checked to see Wendy's reaction, she was looking everywhere but at Deke, and Logan wasn't sure how to react. They took a seat across from his cousin and Wendy's former boyfriend.

Deke's eyes narrowed. "Wendy, since when did you become a deputy? This is a murder investigation, not a chance for some story," he said in a low, harsh tone.

"There are a lot of things you don't know about me, and it's Deputy Oprander to you."

Go, Wendy!

Before Deke had the chance to respond, the door opened, and another policeman escorted in a man who appeared to be in his mid-forties.

The detective on the other side of Anderson motioned he take the seat next to Wendy.

"Wendy, this is a surprise," the man mumbled as he pulled out the chair and sat down.

Before she said anything, the detective in charge continued. "Now that Mr. Landry is here, we can begin."

Landry? What was a newspaper man doing on a crime-solving panel? At least Wendy had been deputized. Nothing about this murder investigation was making any sense.

"Mr. Landry," the detective said, "will you please tell us what you found when you visited Mr. Darnell this evening."

He pulled a handkerchief from his top pocket and patted his forehead. "I had an appointment with Mr. Darnell at seven p.m., but when I arrived, I found him on the floor of his office. Dead." He shook his head. "It was horrible. His chest was clawed open and blood was everywhere." The poor man's voice trembled.

Considering the circumstances of Robert Darnell's death, a shifter was responsible, and given Landry was human, he hadn't done this. The cops asked the newspaper editor a ton of questions about whether he saw anyone when he entered the office building or if he'd heard anything after he arrived, but Landry didn't know much of anything.

All Logan could say for sure was that either Mr. Landry was an excellent actor, or he truly was distraught over the man's death.

"If I may," Logan said, needing to ask some questions. "Why were you meeting with the deceased after business hours?"

Mr. Landry sniffled. "I planned to write a story on his upcoming candidacy. He'd said nothing publicly to any paper yet, because Mr. Darnell wanted to keep it quiet for the time being."

What candidate wants to keep quiet?

The son's forehead furrowed. "Dad never mentioned he planned to run for office again."

Landry looked over at Deke and tilted his head in apparent sympathy. "He was waiting for the right time to tell you."

Wendy slipped a hand under the table and grabbed Logan's leg, sending his head in the wrong direction again. He glanced over at her, but he couldn't tell what she wanted to tell him. If only they could communicate telepathically, this would be easier.

"Mr. Darnell," the detective said to Deke. "Will you tell the group where you were tonight?"

He looked at each member of the team. "I was working on a document on my computer at home—a document that has a time stamp on it."

The detective nodded. "I asked Mr. Darnell to show me the computer. He did, and it proves he was at home."

The man could have worked on a document, rushed out and killed his father, and then returned home, but for the moment, Logan would keep quiet.

Wendy released the pressure on Logan's thigh. It was almost as if she was trying to indicate who was lying and who wasn't. He could only hope her ability to see a gray halo over the liar extended to that of her former boyfriend.

"What about Becky, your mate?" Wendy blurted.

From a few wide eyes, he suspected most of the detectives in the room were unaware of who she was. Logan didn't know why Wendy asked that question, but he had to assume she suspected something. However, he couldn't imagine what motive Deke's mate would have for harming Robert Darnell.

"I don't know," Deke said. "I needed to do some work, and she said she was on deadline too. I guarantee you Becky would never harm my dad if that's what you're thinking."

"Just curious, that's all. When you were informed of your father's death, you called her, right? Or can you telepath with her now?"

Bitterness laced her tone, implying Wendy might still have some feelings for the cad.

"We are not at that stage of our relationship, but I did call her. It went to voicemail."

That would be easy enough to check, and Deke would know that. Maybe he was telling the truth.

The detective cleared his throat. "If you please. Mr. Darnell, you said you and your mate were close. Is it usual for her to be out of contact with you?"

Deke's fingers formed a fist. "No, but I'm sure there was a good reason. She might have turned off her ringer so as not to be disturbed. She is a busy woman."

"What does Becky do for a living?" Wendy asked, clearly wanting or needing answers.

"Ms., ahh...," The detective glanced down at his tablet. "Ms. Oprander, I am extending you the courtesy of being here because Detective Caspian asked me to, but remember Mr. Darnell is not a person of interest."

She held up her hand. "I'm sorry. I'm only trying to understand all the aspects of this crime. I have one more question. If I may?"

The detective's lips pressed together. "Go on."

"What kind of shifter is she?" Wendy asked.

"A wolf. Why?"

It was possible Deke was unaware how his dad had been killed. Until they analyzed the size of the claw marks on the body and test some hair samples, it could have been almost any kind of shifter.

"Thank you."

A knock sounded on the door, and then an officer stepped inside. "Sir, may I have a word?"

The detective in charge pushed back his chair. "I'll be right back. Let's suspend with the questions until I return."

Chatter broke out in small groups, giving Logan a moment to find out what Wendy was up to. "What was all the thigh squeezing about?" he whispered.

"It means I saw a gray halo." She leaned closer. "Though Landry's was close to dark gray for much of it."

Interesting, but why would a newspaper man lie? "Keep up the good work, but I didn't understand the questions about Becky?"

"I'll tell you later," she said just as the door opened and the detective returned, his face even more dour, if that was possible.

He pulled out his chair and sat down. "Excuse the interruption, but my officer informed me that we have video footage taken around the area of the warehouse that is owned by the deceased. A suspicious looking truck leaving was detained around the time of Mr. Darnell's murder."

The room turned deathly silent. No coffee cups were being set down, no scraping of china sounded on the wooden table, no shifting in seats, and no rustling of clothes. Even with Logan's near perfect hearing, he could only detect rapid breathing.

"What did you find?" Deke asked, his voice low, filled with what sounded like fear.

"Drugs, Mr. Darnell. Crenathum to be exact."

The silence broke as Deke, for one, shoved back his chair. "My father was selling drugs?"

Logan waited for Wendy to tighten her grip on his leg again, but her fingers only twitched.

"Yes, Mr. Darnell. I take it you had no idea?"

It wasn't like Deke would admit it, or would he?

He lowered his chin, inhaled deeply and then looked up. "He promised he wasn't dealing anymore."

Anymore? That was a surprise.

"When did he deal drugs?" the detective asked.

Deke blew out a breath. "Two or three years ago. I overheard my father bitch about some banker who had refused to extend his loan payments a few years ago. My dad felt like he had no choice but to turn to some illegal activities—selling drugs to be exact—in order to get back on his feet. When I found out, I confronted him, and my dad swore he would stop."

"And you believed him?" the detective asked.

"I know he stopped. I did a lot of asking around. What I was unaware of was that he'd started up again." Deke's lips pressed together. He must be telling the truth or else Wendy would be squeezing the hell out of his thigh.

"Mr. Darnell," the detective continued. "The building where your father was murdered had security. We will need to access the footage. The killer might have been picked up on it either coming or going."

"Of course." Deke didn't hesitate.

Logan might have to reassess his opinion about this man, though there was still the issue of the two attempts on Wendy's life. Now, however, wasn't the time to bring that up. He would mention it to the detective later when they were alone. Considering all that had gone down tonight, Logan and Wendy might be staying in Sawmill a few more days than he'd intended.

The detective stood. "Anyone is welcome to join us. Over the years, I've learned the more eyes the better."

Even though he and Wendy had temporary badges, he was surprised the detective was okay with a journalist being there. Anderson must have told him what she did for a living. Perhaps he didn't care since he seemed to welcome Thedia's own Editor-in Chief of the local paper.

When Logan tapped her on the shoulder and nodded toward the exit, her eyes brightened. She acted as if he'd given her the best present ever. He figured he might as well escort her. His curious journalist would somehow find a way to look at the tapes even if he told her not to.

The office was located several miles away so walking was out of the question. When he asked for directions, Deke told Logan just to follow him since he planned to fly. While Logan didn't like having to depend on anyone, it wasn't a good time to argue. A plus would be Logan would learn what Deke's dragon looked like.

The trip to the warehouse was short, and the three of them were the first to arrive. As soon as Logan set Wendy down, both he and Deke shifted. Before he could stop his mate, she rushed up to her former lover. For the smallest of seconds, he thought she would hug her ex-boyfriend. Thankfully, he was wrong. So very wrong.

Chapter Twenty

WENDY'S MIND SCRAMBLED. While Deke appeared to be telling the truth about his lack of involvement in his dad's death, there were a lot of holes in his story, and the only way to plug them was to ask. Before Logan could stop her, she rushed up to Deke and planted her hands on her hips. "I have some questions for you."

"I imagine you do. Look, I'm sorry I never called after I left."

She waved a hand. "I don't care about that." His eyes widened. "Did you ever tutor a boy by the name of Tom Sanderson in Edendale?"

Deke sucked in a breath and glanced at the sky, probably trying to decide how much of the truth he should reveal. "I did."

She hadn't expected the confession. "Why didn't you tell me? You know I'm a big fan of volunteer work."

Logan stepped next to her, but he said nothing. He too seemed interested in what Deke had to say.

"I didn't tell you because, well, my motives weren't the best."

"What do you mean?" she asked, her heart speeding up.

"Before I moved to Edendale, I was about to knock on my dad's office door when I overheard him talking rather loudly to someone on the phone. Dad was complaining about a man by the name of Sanderson. He said this guy was some banker who had refused to extend one my father's loans. To be honest, I didn't think my dad needed loans. I mean, he always seemed flush with cash."

"I've heard he vowed revenge against this banker. Do you know anything about that?" Wendy wasn't about to say some Fairy told her, and she was thankful Deke didn't ask for her source.

"Not at that time. Dad must have sensed I was standing outside the door and abruptly hung up. He then whipped it opened and told me to come in. From the way his face was still flushed, he was angry with me for eavesdropping."

"What does all of this have to do with tutoring Tom Sanderson?"

"My dad told me about the banker's refusal to extend his loan and asked that I find Mr. Sanderson's son and offer to help him in some way."

She could put the pieces together. "I gather it wasn't to help some high school student get better grades, but rather to spy on the family?"

Deke dragged his hands down his face. "Yes."

"What was your father planning to do with the information? Find the best time to kill Tom's dad?"

Deke held up a hand. "I swear I don't know. I told him that I didn't want to be his spy, but he said he'd cut me off if I didn't. By that I mean, no money. No job. No inheritance."

"So you sacrificed a young boy's welfare for your own well-being?" What had she seen in this guy?

"I didn't know someone would kill the kid!" The strain in his voice and the lack of gray halo implied he was telling the truth.

Logan piped up. "Do you know who poisoned the teen?"

Deke shook his head. "I have no idea. I swear."

Wendy stood up taller. "Where did I fit in your plan?"

Car engines sounded. The police were arriving.

"My father asked that I keep an eye on you."

An eye on her? So she was just a job to him? Wendy wanted to shift and claw his heart out, but Logan would surely stop her if she tried. "Why? He never met me."

"He knew you were sniffing around the Ted Yancy case."

Her heart pinched, and her mind spun. "What did Ted Yancy have to do with Tom and Mike? I mean, I know he worked for your dad, but I found no evidence your father was involved in his death."

"My father said that the circumstances of his employee's death needed to be kept a secret, only he wouldn't tell me why."

Logan stepped forward. "Did your father kill Ted Yancy?"

"No. We were together for a father-son weekend during the time Ted was killed, if you can believe the irony of that." Deke shook his head. "It was the first time he'd ever asked me to go fishing with him. Hell, I don't recall him ever fishing before. It was something I liked to do."

Logan huffed. "He wanted you as his alibi."

"That's my guess too."

Wendy's sympathy swelled, but only for a short time. Deke was still scum. "All the time we were together, you were merely following your dad's orders?"

Even though Logan was standing there, Deke gently clasped her shoulders. "Wendy, I loved you. Why do you think I left in such a hurry? Dad asked me to, ah, kill you, if you learned any more about the case."

"Seriously? You knew your father was a murderer, and yet you ran back to the man? Who are you?" Her knees buckled at the outrage. It was Logan who was there to keep her upright.

Car doors slammed, and the rest of the round-table crew descended before she could question Deke further. It wasn't too hard to fill in the blanks though. Right now, if Deke's dad hadn't been dead, she'd have killed him herself.

The police detective motioned them toward the building. "Can you show us to the security room, Mr. Darnell?"

Deke glanced at her once more and then strode toward the detective. "Sure."

Logan stopped her. "We don't have to go in if you don't want to. I'm sorry about the betrayal."

"It's okay. It's because of the betrayal that I have to see this through."

"Then come on."

Logan was the best. He kept proving it time and time again. The group followed Deke inside, passing through the building's large interior and then continuing down one flight of stairs. Using a keypad to unlock the security room door, Deke opened it up. Because the space was rather small, only Deke and the detective entered.

Once they were inside, Logan moved them off to the side and wrapped an arm around Wendy's waist and leaned in close. "As much as I wish you had never met Deke, I'm sorry you did so under false pretenses."

"Thank you. While Deke's confession shocked me, I'm actually angrier at myself for thinking he cared," she said.

"He did care. You heard him. He could have killed you, but he chanced the wrath of his father by returning to Thedia."

"He should have stayed to protect me. If his father wanted me out of the way, didn't Deke think his father would just send someone else?" She cupped Logan's cheeks, pulled him a bit closer, and brushed his lips with hers. They were there for business, not sexual excitement, which was why she kept the contact brief, but she needed to drink in his goodness. She leaned back.

As much as Wendy wanted to peek in and see what they were doing, Mr. Landry and another officer had wedged themselves in the doorway, blocking most of the view.

While it was difficult to make out what Deke and the detective were saying, it was evident their voices were becoming more and more animated.

"There I am," Landry called out from the entranceway.

"Yes, you are," the detective said, his voice directed toward the exit. "The time stamp indicates it probably was after Mr. Darnell was dead."

Wendy looked up at Logan. "Someone had to have entered the building at some point. He didn't rip his heart out of his own chest."

Logan's eyes flashed. "If his face doesn't show up in the feed, it's possible the killer was in the building already. Did Deke ever say what his mate did for a living?" he whispered.

"No, just that she was very busy with work."

"Could she work here?"

Now that was an idea. "When he comes out, I'll ask him."

Someone shouted inside the room. "Who is that?" the detective asked.

Silence.

"That's Becky," Deke responded in a cold, flat tone.

"Can you zoom in any closer?" the detective seemed to be speaking to the technician in charge of the feed.

Wendy clasped Logan's arm. "We could really use Meena right now. She could transform into bits of light, fly in there, and see what is going on."

"That would be a great talent—one I wished I possessed."

Her imagination ran rampant. "Nah. You'd lose the bad boy look if you were a firefly. I'm not seeing it."

His smile was brief. Several people were talking at once, and Wendy couldn't make out most of the details. So much for wanting to have more eyes on the video. A moment later, the detective and Deke exited the room. Hopefully, they found something.

Deke grabbed the detective's arm to stop him. "I'm telling you, it can't be Becky."

"Let. Go."

Deke lowered his arm. "What are you going to do?" Deke asked the detective, his voice a bit shaky.

"Look for your girlfriend and bring her in for questioning. She is a werewolf, and your father could have been murdered by one. We'll know more after the autopsy."

"A wolf shifter could never overpower my father."

"We'll see."

They suspected Becky? She had to agree with Deke. Wendy didn't think a slip of a woman could get the drop on a strong dragon shifter. It didn't matter if his dad was in his human form at the time or not.

Once the entire party exited the building, Logan placed a hand on her shoulder. "Let's let the cops search for Becky. What do you say we head back to town to grab a drink and maybe some decadent dessert before retiring? I know I could use the relaxation. My mind is spinning with possibilities."

Wendy couldn't say no to his plea. So what if she wasn't in the mood to celebrate? She did need to unwind and talking about the case might help her sort things out. While she had wanted to ask Deke a few more questions, she suspected Logan would have been against it, and he might be right. "Sounds good."

In the now-empty parking lot, he shifted and then picked her up. A few minutes later, Logan landed in the park where he'd first taken her after the hotel fire. "Do you have a place in mind for this drink?" she asked. Logan seemed to have every aspect of his life planned out.

"No." He slipped her hand into his and guided her across the street, moving away from the burned-out hotel. Logan pointed to a well-lit restaurant/bar two blocks down the road. The lamps on either side of the door lent the place elegance. "Want to try this one? First drinks and dessert and then maybe some fun between the sheets?"

That made her laugh. "Do you always have sex on your mind?"

"Me? Never. I blame it all on my dragon. Don't tell me you have no interest." He wiggled his brows, clearly trying to bring some levity to the overwhelmingly confusing situation of tonight's events.

While possibly inappropriate considering a man had died today, Wendy enjoyed flirting with Logan, but she wasn't sure how far to push it, especially since their relationship was so new. "I might consider it if you treat me right."

Logan smiled, leaned over, and lightly kissed her on the lips. The next thing Wendy remembered was flying through the air and landing hard on the sidewalk, her head bouncing on the cement. Her forward momentum propelled her another ten feet, tearing up her palms and knees on the rough surface. When she came to a stop, her pulse had skyrocketed, and her body burned. Nothing fully registered for at least three seconds. Had someone just tried to kill her? Or had it been a chance accident?

Her thoughts jumped to Logan. Oh, no! Had he been hit too?

"Logan?" she called out, her voice a mere squeak.

When she was finally able to lift her head and look around, all she saw was Logan sprawled out on the sidewalk in a pool of blood. Her heart dropped to her stomach. Fear and injustice raced through her. Even though her body was screaming, she forced herself to sit up.

Shift so I can heal you, her wolf demanded.

I have to go to Logan first.

Wendy's bones ached, and her skin was on fire, but he needed help. Standing—or at least rising somewhat to her feet—took a lot of effort because of the sharp pains. After stumbling a few times, she made it over to him. Wendy squatted down and shook his shoulder. "Logan?"

He couldn't be dead. Nothing short of removing his heart or stabbing him in that soft spot would kill a dragon shifter or so he'd said.

He moaned, and her hopes soared. "Can you shift?" she asked, even though part of him would land in the street if he did.

Since there weren't any cars traveling in either direction at the moment, he could do it. Then he could fly somewhere to heal.

Logan started to push up using his hands but then dropped back down. "Fuck."

"Are you okay?" That was a stupid question. "Do you know what happened?"

With a lot of grunting and wincing, Logan rolled onto his back, his breaths coming out fast. "I was hit by a car. I can't believe I didn't hear it especially when the tires hit the curb."

"Damn. If it jumped the curb, this probably was no accident." No car was in sight, nor was anyone running to their rescue, which implied the hit and run had been on purpose.

"I'm glad I was able to push you out of the way," he said.

The gentle but forceful shove on her back filtered into her memory. "You saved me! Again."

Logan draped one arm across his stomach, and using what appeared to be his uninjured arm, pushed up to a sitting position. "Give me a sec. I'll shift and head on over to the park where I can heal. I'd carry you, but with only one good arm, I fear I might drop you."

"Don't worry about me. I'll meet you there." It was only a block away.

"O-kay." While Wendy's head was still pounding and blood was dripping down her cheek and legs, nothing appeared to be broken. Even though she was insanely stiff, she rose once more and stepped back.

Wendy would have offered to help him up, but Logan had too much pride to accept it. She waited until he was on his feet—make that wobbly feet—and hoped he had enough strength to shift.

To her relief, Logan went from human to dragon in a few seconds. While his flight didn't reach much more than twenty feet above the ground, it was sufficient for him to make it the park.

Noting where he'd landed, Wendy looked both ways before crossing the street. She could have shifted, but it would be less painful if she waited a few minutes.

At the park entrance, Wendy followed the path to where she believed Logan had landed. Before she could locate him though, a woman stepped into her path.

"Hello, Wendy."

Oh, shit. It was Becky.

Chapter Twenty-One

EVEN THOUGH EVERY nerve ending was firing, Wendy had learned how to control her response to unwelcomed events. "Becky, what are you doing here?" she asked with amazing calm.

"Looking for you."

Wendy's pulse soared even higher. This wasn't good. "I'm guessing Deke told you we spoke?"

There was no way he had, unless he'd secretly texted her. If Deke believed Becky had killed his dad, he would be searching for her, not aiding her escape.

"We didn't talk, but he did sneak a text to me to warn me that you were on the warpath."

On the warpath to find a killer. Wendy couldn't think of a reason why Deke would even contact Becky, but maybe it was a trap he and the detective had set—at least she hoped it was something like that.

"Listen, I'd love to hear why he claimed I'm on the warpath, but I need to go to my mate. Someone tried to run him down tonight, and he's somewhere in the park in his dragon form healing."

Wendy hoped that if Becky knew Logan was near that she wouldn't try anything.

"Trust me, I was aiming for you." Becky moved closer. Out of instinct, Wendy took a few steps back. She might have considered yelling, but no one seemed to be in the park at this late hour—at least she hadn't sensed any shifter signatures other than Logan's.

"Why would you want to kill me? I barely know you. And Deke left me, not the other way around."

Becky shook her head. "I didn't take you for someone so naïve. Of course, Deke only has eyes for me, but since you are going to die for real tonight, I might as well tell you my reasons for needing you dead."

Really? Becky thought she could just rip out her throat? Not likely. Wendy was a good fighter. She had to be, growing up with a father like hers. The issue right now was that her body had yet to heal from being knocked down. However, the longer she kept this crazed woman talking, the more chance her wolf would have to build up her strength.

"Before you start, may I ask if you were responsible for setting the hotel fire or poisoning me?"

Her brows rose in appreciation. "Close. Actually, Landry set the fire. I was with Deke at the time. I'd say ask him, but you won't live long enough for that."

Confident, wasn't she? "Landry? Why would he want to harm me? He was trying to hire me."

Becky's laugh sounded maniacal. "Landry is behind everything."

Wendy expected to see a black halo above Becky's head, but instead the only thing behind her was the light pouring down from the lamp post. "He's a human."

"Yes, a human who found out Robert Darnell's drug dealings and was extorting money from him. Landry would go to any lengths to keep that man's secret—including taking you out. Why do you think he wanted to hire you?" Becky waved a hand. "It was the old saying: keep your friends close and your enemies closer."

Wendy's already turbulent stomach churned, and bile rushed up to her mouth. She swallowed and then inhaled. "I know Landry didn't kill Robert Darnell. So who did?"

"For a journalist, you aren't very bright. I did, silly."

Truth or brag? Wendy wasn't sure she could trust the lack of a halo. "How? Darnell is a dragon shifter, and Deke said you were a wolf shifter."

Becky pulled out what looked like a small dart gun and waved it.

"With this. It contains a paralytic. The poor man was awake the whole time I removed that vital organ, but he wasn't able to move a muscle." She grinned. "It was glorious."

It was horrifying. Becky was insane. Wendy might claim to be a cool and calm person, but seeing the paralytic gun scared the shit out of her. "What about Deke? Didn't you think it would tear him apart when he learned of his father's death—especially when it occurred in such a violent way?"

She laughed. "Deke is so much better off without that controlling man. Did you know his own father threatened to cut Deke out of everything if he didn't kill that Sanderson boy so Robert could have his revenge?"

Meena's words came back to her. They made sense now in light of what Deke had said earlier. "Revenge because a banker was doing his job?"

"So you say."

"Whatever. Did it ever occur to anyone that maybe Deke's dad didn't deserve to have his loan extended?"

"Possibly, but the lack of funds caused Robert to turn to dealing drugs, something he said he didn't enjoy."

Good. "A lack of funds didn't *cause* him to do anything. He chose to deal drugs," Wendy said.

Becky lifted a shoulder. "Maybe. I didn't know him back then, but he was angry how things had turned out."

"That's no reason to kill anyone," Wendy said. "Did you say that Deke killed the Sanderson boy? And Mike Evans along with him?"

She waved the hand holding the dart. "No. His father ordered him to, but that weakling wasn't capable. That's why I had to do it."

Wendy doubted Becky would confess to protect her boyfriend. She seemed too cold-hearted. "You? I'm impressed. How did you do it?" Wendy was proud that she could keep shooting questions at the egotistical woman. Clearly, Becky loved to brag.

Good job. Keep her talking. I'm working fast to heal you, her wolf said.

"Easy. I knocked out their maid and took her place at the party as their server. When the two boys went into one of the bedrooms, I came in with the drug and told them one of their friends asked me to deliver it. When they asked what it was, I said it was something to get them high. In reality, it was a bottle of Crenathum laced with rat poisoning that Robert had given me. Once they ingested it, I left. I heard they didn't last long."

There was no regret in her voice, and Wendy became furious at the injustice. Then more pieces of the puzzle fell into place. "You put rat poisoning in my tea, didn't you?"

"I did. Apparently, I didn't put enough in your tea. Then again, I didn't want you to become suspicious. You do have a good sense of smell."

Even though Becky claimed Wendy might die tonight, her journalistic spirit was alive and strong. "What about Ted Yancy?"

Becky waved the paralytic. "The truck driver? That was Landry's doing. He would do anything to keep the money flowing, and that meant eliminating anyone who wanted to take down Robert Darnell."

This was so sick, her stomach nearly erupted once more. "If you and Deke are mates, how could you do all of this—to him?"

Once more she laughed. "We are not mates. His dad paid me to tell people that. It provided me with an excuse to keep a watch on Deke. I was hired to make sure he didn't interfere with his dad's business of selling drugs—or worse, turn him into the police."

A small part of her was relieved but only because it meant there was a bit of decency in Deke, albeit not much. "How could Deke not know you two weren't fated?"

"He knew, but he didn't care. After all, we did set the sheets on fire when we were together."

That was information she didn't need to know. Her head was still throbbing, but the cuts on her hands and knees were healing, and most of the aches had disappeared. The big question was, was she ready to fight?

Hell, yes she was—but unless Wendy could stop Becky from using what was in the vial, nothing she did would make a difference. The only way to succeed was to shift now and be the attacker, hopefully knocking the paralytic gun from Becky's fingers. Then Wendy would have a fighting chance.

Given this woman was a crazy mercenary, no telling how well trained she was. That meant Wendy's best chance of success was to find a distraction.

Wendy looked behind Becky and waved. "Oh, Logan! We're over here."

Thankfully, her adversary fell for the trick and partially turned around. It was at that moment that Wendy shifted and charged. The look of surprise on Becky's face when she realized she'd been fooled was priceless.

As if a new power emerged inside her, Wendy bared her teeth and catapulted herself into the air, aiming for Becky's arm. Too bad, Deke's fake mate still had enough time to lift her arm and take aim. Just as Wendy bit down on Becky's wrist, she pressed the plunger. The dart hit Wendy, but somehow bounced off her furry skin. Victory! Although it was a short-lived one.

Becky jerked her arm upward as gravity forced Wendy back to the ground. A moment later, Becky was in her wolf form too. One eye was circled in black, but the rest of her coat was a combination of browns and grays. For someone so pretty in her human form, Wendy expected Becky to be a more vibrantly colored wolf. Some might say her ugly interior was showing.

Focus, her wolf reminded her.

Her wolf was right. Her appearance was the least of her problems. During those few seconds when Wendy let her mind wander, Becky got the drop on her. She had leapt onto Wendy's flank and was biting down hard. She yelped but then became more determined than ever not to let this vixen get the best of her. Correction: this three-time killer—get the best of her.

How could Deke have been so blind about this murderous

woman? Or was he so driven by greed that he was willing to let his girlfriend do his dirty work for him?

Before she could tackle that issue, Wendy needed to dislodge Becky who was gnawing at Wendy's side. Spotting a lamp post a few feet in front of her, Wendy came up with a plan.

Using much of her reserve energy, she dragged the two of them down the path. When they were within inches of the post, Wendy gripped her nails against the rough pavement and charged, taking Becky with her.

As she hoped, Becky's rear slammed against the metal structure, and the subsequent thwack sound was so rewarding. Too bad, that one bite Becky had taken was wreaking havoc on Wendy's stamina. Not one to cower or run away, Wendy spun around and despite the crippling pain, went on the offensive once more. As she charged, Becky jumped up and came straight at her. As they passed each other, Wendy was able to nip at the back of Becky's neck. Too bad her adversary broke free a second later and dug her nails into Wendy's hind quarters.

Another searing ache raced through her veins, draining her of most of her remaining energy. Even though she was losing, Wendy would do whatever it took to prevent Becky from attacking her throat.

Being weakened from the loss of blood, Wendy needed a new tactic. She dropped to the ground and then onto her back, forcing Becky to let go of her strong grip. The problem was that now Wendy's throat was exposed.

Think! Wendy dropped her jaw to protect that vital area and with nails extended, lashed out with all four paws.

To Wendy's frustration, Becky seemed unaffected by the damage she was able to inflict. The crazy wolf continued to jam her nose between Wendy's chest and snout, finally giving her enough room to go in for the kill. Just as Becky opened her mouth in order to tear out Wendy's throat, she pushed on Becky's chest, shoving her off just enough to enable Wendy to roll onto her side. As her adversary stumbled backward, Wendy jumped up and pounced, latching onto Becky's throat. Yelps and screams rent the air, but she wasn't sure if they came from her or Becky.

Before Wendy could finish the kill, some great force lifted her off the killer. A giant claw then grabbed Becky and flung her aside.

Logan! In all his dragon glory.

He looked down at Wendy as if to ask if she was okay. Since they couldn't communicate telepathically yet, she howled.

Logan looked up as retreating nails scraped against the cement path. No! Becky was getting away. How was that even possible? She'd landed with such a thud. Determination swamped her. Wendy couldn't let this killer escape. Just as she was about to take off after Becky, Logan flew down the path and shot a stream of fire at the fleeing figure. The stench, howls, and slowly dying screams of the burning wolf would be something Wendy would never forget.

As much as she wanted to run over to the pyre to make sure the horrible woman was dead, Wendy's strength gave out.

When she opened her eyes, she was lying on soft grass in her wolf form, sheltered from the elements by a large dragon wing. She inwardly sighed, knowing she was safe. Wendy fell back to sleep, urging her wolf to heal her fully.

She wasn't aware how much time had passed, but when she woke up again, Logan was cradling her in his lap and stroking her head.

"Welcome back." He smiled, and all residual pain and fear disappeared.

Thrilled that they both seemed to have healed, she eased off his lap and shifted. Logan rose and hugged her. "Thank you," she said.

He leaned back and grinned. "Aw, it was nothing. You had it in the bag. I just didn't want you to have the guilt over killing someone, though I would like to know who I incinerated."

She loved this man. "That was Becky. And boy do I have a tale to tell."

Chapter Twenty-Two

L OGAN WANTED TO take Wendy back to the hotel and check out her injuries, but considering how long she'd been in her wolf form, he had to agree with her assessment that she'd healed just fine. After having fought a hard battle, she told him all she wanted to do was shower.

"Before we head back to the hotel, can you call your cousin though?" she asked. "I need to tell him what Becky revealed to me."

"Don't tell me she confessed?"

"You have no idea what the chatterbox said. I'm not sure why she told me, but I had the feeling she was taking pleasure in showing me that she had won the grand prize—Deke—while I would die a painful death. It's possible she even wanted me to marvel at her ingenuity. All I know is that she was positive I wouldn't be the one walking away from the fight."

"I'm so glad you did. It's rare for someone just to blurt out their crimes like that."

"I got lucky, I guess. While you are reaching Anderson, I need to find that dart containing a paralytic that she shot. It will prove that she killed Darnell and tried to kill me. I don't want there to be any doubt that my attack on her was motivated by anything other than self-preservation."

"I can help you look and talk at the same time."

"I'd appreciate that."

He called his cousin, and Anderson answered on the first ring. "It's late," his cousin said as a way of a greeting, his voice thick as if the call had woken him up. Logan was sure it wasn't the first time his sleep had been disturbed by a call.

"I know. I'm sorry, but I have good news for you."

"What is it?" This time his voice wasn't as gruff.

"We found Becky." Silence. "You there?" Logan asked.

"Yes, where is she?"

"At the moment, she is a pile of smoldering ashes in some park near the burned-out hotel. She and Wendy got in a tussle and I—or rather my dragon—went crazy and stepped in. Can you meet us back at the Thedia police station? Wendy can fill us in with all of the details. Once we get there, I can show you on a map where to find our killer, or rather find what's left of her." Wendy bent down, and using the hem of her shirt, picked up the dart. She looked up at him and grinned. He gave her a thumbs up. "And we'll bring proof that Becky killed Robert Darnell."

Anderson whistled. "Well, I'll be damned. I knew I was right in deputizing you and your mate."

Logan laughed. "Actually, Wendy did all the work." She looked up and smiled. "See you at the station." Logan disconnected and faced her. He told her that Anderson would meet them. "Even though the station isn't far, flying will be faster."

"I trust your arm is good enough to carry me?"

He'd had more time to heal than she had. "I'm in perfect working order. Guardians have special magic healing abilities."

She pressed her lips together in apparent appreciation. "I'm glad."

Logan shifted and flew them the mile to the station. Normally, he wouldn't think of landing in the middle of a street, but this late at night, there were enough breaks in the traffic that he was willing to chance it. As soon as his claws touched the pavement, he set her down and then shifted.

Wendy jogged to the sidewalk, and he was pleased to see the ease with which she moved. He joined her and rejoiced that almost all of his leg pain was gone. Once inside the station, he asked to speak with the lead detective on the case since Anderson wouldn't have had time to arrive yet.

"What is this about?" the desk officer asked.

Logan explained that a murderer had been caught, and that during her escape, he had to use fire to stop her. "I'm afraid the fugitive is dead."

The officer's eyes widened. "I'll give the detective a call." He motioned another officer to escort them to a conference room.

Once in the room, Wendy located a coffee stand where she extracted a napkin from the holder and used it to transfer the dart she was holding with the end of her shirt to the table.

"Now we wait," she said as she pulled out a chair and dropped down, looking rather fatigued.

"How about I pour us some coffee? I know I could use some."

She looked back over at the coffee station. "Only if the pot is hot. I'm not a lukewarm coffee drinker person."

He flashed her a smile. "Got it."

Thankfully, the brew looked relatively fresh. He poured two cups, carried them over to the table, and sat down next to her. "Want to tell me what happened?"

She lifted her cup and took a sip. From the way she closed her eyes for a second and sighed, the brew hit the spot. "After you shifted and headed to the park, I hobbled across the street to find you."

"Why didn't you shift?" he asked.

"It would have been less painful if I waited. I planned to shift as soon as I found you, but when I was partway down the path, Becky showed up. To say the least, I was surprised."

"I can only imagine. Did you think you were in danger at that moment?"

"From the look in her eyes, absolutely. Don't forget, the video showed her leaving the building. Not proof she killed Darnell, but it meant it was a strong possibility. I had to stall her until my wolf had a chance to heal me a bit more. I also wanted to satisfy my curiosity as to whether Becky was responsible for anything that had happened. I never expected her to tell me she'd killed Robert Darnell. She also said that she'd tried to run us down, though she meant to harm only me."

He whistled. "I was so focused on you that I wasn't paying attention to any approaching cars. If I hadn't leaned over to kiss you, I might not have seen her out of the corner of my eye. I'm just happy that we weren't injured more seriously."

Wendy reached out and squeezed his leg. That one touch elicited a series of lustful pleasures. "Thank you for saving me. Again."

The door opened and Anderson rushed in. "Are you two okay?"

He appreciated his cousin's concern. "We're fine. We've had enough time for our animals to do their magic."

"Good." Anderson took advantage of the coffee and then sat across from them. "Tell me everything."

Wendy was halfway through her reveal when the detective in charge barged in. His hair was mussed, and he needed a shave. Apparently, Logan's request had resulted in him being roused out of bed too.

"Sorry." He nodded to each of them. "What did I miss?"

Wendy was a trouper and started from the beginning. When she was done, she finished off her cup of coffee. From the way her shoulders were sagging though, telling the tale a few times exhausted her.

"And this?" the detective asked nodding to the dart.

"That was what Becky had in her hand. She said it contained the same paralytic that she used on Robert Darnell. She planned to use it on me, but I got the jump on her first and caused her to miss."

The detective whistled. "I have to say, Ms. Oprander, I am impressed. How you managed to survive was admirable."

"Thank you. I'm just glad this is over."

"Where were you, Mr. Caspian, during this altercation?" the detective asked.

"In the park in my shifted form." He explained he was healing from when Becky tried to run them over. "Had I not seen her coming at the last second, we might not have healed so fast."

"Good thing for fast shifter reflexes."

"Totally."

Anderson looked over at the detective. "If what Becky said was true, and Landry killed Ted Yancy, we should be able to check his whereabouts by either using cameras or possibly tracing his credit card charges. I doubt he drove from Thedia to Avonbelle to kill the driver."

"We'll do whatever it takes to find the truth," the detective in charge said. "If Landry is guilty, he won't get away with it." The detective nodded and then turned to Wendy. "You said that Becky told you Darnell paid her to kill Tom Sanderson?"

"Yes."

"What else did she say about her arrangement with Darnell?"

Wendy inhaled. "I'm having a hard time remembering everything. It's not every day you believe your life is about to come to an end, but she did tell me how the boys died." Wendy explained that Becky had made sure their normal maid called in sick, and she took her place during the party. "Apparently, Darnell supplied the poisonous drug in liquid form that the boys willingly ingested."

"Does that mean Mike Evans was collateral damage?" the detective asked.

"She didn't explicitly say, but that would be my guess."

The detective glanced over at Logan's cousin. "I think my department can take it from here, Detective Anderson. We'll do a check on both of their bank records to see if there was any transfer of funds."

"If you want to bring down Landry," Wendy said, "I would check his payments to Becky. I got the sense that Landry asked her to take me out of the picture by poisoning me."

Logan clasped Wendy's hand to give her some support.

Anderson whistled. "That was one cold-hearted bitch."

That was an understatement. Logan would never understand what Wendy had ever seen in Deke Darnell in the first place, especially if he claimed to have Becky as his mate. Personally, the guy seemed like a pansy, but that relationship was in the past. Wendy was now his. And most likely, Deke's involvement in all of this mess would be questioned again. Only time would tell if the cops could prove anything against him.

Logan pushed back his chair. "If you don't mind, we've both had a long day and an even longer night."

"Of course," the detective said. "The Thedia Province Police thanks you for all of your help. Will you be around for another day perhaps? We might have some more questions."

Logan looked over at Wendy. While he could guess that she'd want to go home, having a relaxing day in Thedia might be good for both of them. "Wendy?" he asked.

"Sure." She half chuckled. "At least I won't have to make that phone call to Mr. Landry and turn down the newspaper job."

Everyone smiled.

It was time to put Wendy to bed. As much as Logan wanted to make love with her for hours, he had to let her body and mind heal.

WHEN WENDY OPENED her eyes, sunlight was streaming in the window, and the rich smell of coffee was wafting in the room. She pushed up on her elbows to find Logan standing next to her with a tray in hand. Wow. "What is this? Breakfast in bed?"

"Only the best for my mate." Logan set the folding tray over her legs and then gently sat down next to her. "How are you feeling?"

She narrowed her eyes and grabbed his hand. "I know you mean well, but we need to clear up something. You have to stop asking me how I'm feeling."

He tossed her an exaggerated pout. "I worry about you."

She rubbed his arm. "And I worry about you, but by asking me every few minutes how I'm doing, I get the feeling you think of me as some weak person. And I'm not."

Logan held up a palm. "You're right. I wasn't thinking. I won't ask again unless you are practically dead."

That made her laugh. "Deal."

The right half of his sexy lips lifted in a half smile. "You know, when we mate, I won't have to ask. I'll be able to feel if something is wrong."

She had heard that. "That will be a bonus, but for me, the best part of mating will be the ability to communicate telepathically. Trust me, I wished we'd been able to do that so many times of late— like when Landry was lying, and I wanted you to know."

"I figured it out with all of the leg squeezing, but I hope the best part of mating won't just be the ability to communicate telepathically or sense what the other is feeling."

"There is the shifting part," she said, enjoying where this conversation was headed.

"And?" He cocked a brow.

"Having mad passionate sex with you all of the time, of course." Wendy almost giggled.

Logan grinned. "That's my girl. Are you ready to be fully mated to me?"

"Hmm." Wendy didn't need even a second to think about it, but she wanted to draw out the tension. She sipped her coffee and moaned. "I trust that our relationship is more than just lustful animal attraction?"

Okay, that was a shameless act of looking for a compliment, but right now she needed it.

"A lot more," he said with disbelief in his voice. "You have to know that I love you, Wendy Oprander. You are everything to me. I haven't been able to have a decent nights' sleep from the first time I found you at the mine."

Her eyes widened. "Why didn't you say something?" He dipped his chin. "Never mind. You wanted to, but I was too stubborn to even go out with you."

"Precisely."

"How about I have a few bites of this breakfast and then do

something to make it up to you?"

"That is music to my ears," he said with a smile in his eyes.

"I am sorry I made you wait. I think being captured by Malpan took a bigger toll on me than I realized."

He rubbed her arm. "Having someone try to harm you no less than four times in two months couldn't have been easy."

Four times? Oh, yeah. Malpan was one, and then Becky and Landry made up the other three times. "No, but that is in the past, and I for one would like to concentrate on the present."

"I like the present much better too."

In between bites, she remembered something and snapped her fingers. "Did I mention that Landry had proof that Darnell was dealing drugs and transporting them across province lines? Not that it matters much now that he's dead."

"If you told me, I've forgotten. Knowing you were in peril for so long kind of short-circuited my brain."

"I should let the detective know. It will be more proof that Landry was blackmailing Darnell." She held up a finger. "But first, let me see if I can help you find your mental sharpness again."

As quickly as she could, she scarfed down her breakfast, not caring that the sheet fell and exposed her naked breasts. Even though she'd been dead tired last night, both of them had showered when they arrived back at the hotel, and that helped refresh her a bit. As much as she had wanted Logan to join her in the shower, being naked inches from him would have resulted in more hot sex. While she had yearned for that, her wolf had demanded she heal first. And now she had.

As she was finishing the last bite of toast, Logan stripped and then lifted the tray off of her lap. After he placed it on the desk, he crawled into bed and cupped her breast. "I hope you can believe me now when I say we belong together forever."

Those were the sweetest words to her ears. "Yes, so what exactly happens next?" No one had ever mentioned any kind of ceremony, just some hot loving followed by them biting each other. She hoped she didn't mess up that part.

"We let our animals guide us and form that final bond."

She couldn't believe today would be the day she would become Logan Caspian's mate.

Chapter Twenty-Three

L OGAN'S EYES GLAZED over as they morphed from hazel to teal, lust and love blending in the perfect combination. It didn't matter that they'd made love before, this would be the ultimate joining, the one that would bond them for life. Given the rush of hormones running through her body, Wendy wasn't sure she could keep from biting him in the next thirty seconds. She was that excited to have this union complete. Logan Caspian was everything she wanted in a man: Protective, understanding, loyal…and did she mention hot?

"Where did you go?" Logan asked, as he dragged a finger across her forehead, pushing aside an errant strand of hair.

"Just thinking how lucky I am to have met you."

One eyebrow rose. "Is that so? How about less talk and more show then?"

"You read my mind."

Wendy rolled onto her side and pressed her body against his. Oh my. The arm that was pinned under her body just happened to be in a position to cup his balls—which of course she did. With her free hand, she stroked his cheek, enjoying the light show of teals, blues, and oranges swirling in his eyes.

Logan moaned and then leaned closer. He kissed her softly at first and then with more passion. He draped his arm across her hip and drew her nearer so that nothing could come between them. The added pressure of body meeting body surely made her eyes turn amber. While Logan's interior scales were flashing that pretty blue, her nails were growing by the second.

Logan ran his tongue across her lips, and Wendy opened up, giving him full access. As she plunged her tongue into his mouth, he immediately met her thrust for thrust. Needing more contact, she dragged her hand down his shoulder, loving how his muscles bunched and flexed every time he moved.

Not breaking the kiss, Wendy pressed on his shoulder to roll him on his back before crawling on top of him. Logan moaned once more and then closed his eyes briefly. She broke the kiss and slid downward.

"You're playing with fire," he said, his eyes flashing.

"Give me a sec, and you'll see that I'm not playing. I plan to engage in some very serious business."

He grabbed a lock of her hair and tugged, ratcheting her desire close to her limit, but Wendy was determined to hold out until the big bite.

"Don't take too long. I want you, or rather I need you," Logan said, his eyes now hooded.

She smiled. "I'll settle for both wanting and needing."

"You've got it, wolf lady."

Dragging her sharpened nails down his chest, she slid lower until her lips were hovering over his engorged cock. She then licked her lips in anticipation while inhaling his lemony scent.

Perhaps in need of something to hold on to when she went down on him, Logan clasped her shoulders. With a delicate touch, she dragged her tongue from his balls to the tip. His grip tightened as his blue scales went off in intermittent patterns, lighting the way. Even if it had been nighttime, she'd have been able to see because of the way he was flashing. Wanting to torture him a bit, she dragged a finger up and down his dick, and then rimmed the tip with her nail.

Logan sucked in a big breath. "Remember, turnabout is fair play."

While she loved being the focus of his tongue, even Wendy had to admit she wouldn't last long if he returned the favor. Deciding not to prolong this, she grabbed the base of his hard shaft and drew him deep into her mouth.

He let go of her shoulders and clasped the sheets. "Wendy, please."

Logan Caspian begging was the last thing she expected, but it only proved that he loved what she was doing. Being a mischievous person, Wendy pumped her fist several times as she swirled her tongue around his girth.

A second later, Logan flipped her onto her back and loomed over her. "Like I said, if you play with fire, you could get burned."

Wendy grinned. "It's all good."

"I'll show you good."

When Logan went down on her, it was as if the sun had suddenly come out after days of rain. Every fiber of her being vibrated the moment he flicked her sensitive clit. Oh, how she loved that every one of his touches was a loving one.

As Logan continued to tease her tiny nub, he reached up and nabbed her nipple with his right hand, and the combination of the two sent her closer to her climax. Now it was her turn to beg.

"Logan, please."

It was as if he never heard her, because he lowered his right hand and slid two fingers into her opening, sending spikes of ecstasy through her so hard that she lost control. An overpowering orgasm claimed her and stole her breath away.

With her back arched, Logan slowly let up on the pressure and then crawled halfway up her body. Wendy thought he would slide right into her, but instead he nabbed a taut nipple between his teeth, sending more sparks of desire cascading over her skin, and the onslaught of lust nearly toppled her once more.

To keep from coming again, she clamped down on his head with one hand and his shoulder with the other. With each nip and lick, Wendy soared higher, angry with herself for not taking advantage of this amazing man sooner. She must have been blind not to have recognized what an incredible person Logan was.

He continued to drive her crazy with his gentle—and sometimes not so gentle—tugs as well as the occasional lick. She ran her hand over his head, stimulated by the short bristles on the sides, and thrilled that this loving man could take her to such heights.

Logan switched his attention to her other breast and cupped the one he'd been teasing. The added sensation pushed her even higher.

"I'm ready," she pleaded.

"Uh-huh."

Surely, he wanted this too. Needing to take things to the next level, she wrapped her legs around his back and lifted her hips. If that wasn't a hint, she didn't know what would be. The hand massaging her breast slid upward until he cupped her cheek. A second later, he elbowed his way upward.

Glory be. This was it. As if his dick had built-in radar, he slid into her and stretched her wide. The slight pain added to the delicious intensity. Wendy tightened her leg hold, only now her heels were resting on his hard rear instead of his back. When Logan drove into her several times in a row, she lowered her feet to the bed and lifted to meet each of his thrusts.

His lips collided with hers, and the kiss that followed melted her insides. Logan Caspian was everything she could ever want in a mate and more. Instead of trying to compete for dominance, their tongues did a delicate dance, heightening her emotional commitment to him. When Logan broke the contact and slid his lips to that sensitive spot between her shoulder blade and neck, she stiffened.

"Shh. It's okay," he soothed. "Seal our mating with a kiss of your own."

Kiss? Surely, he meant a bite. Wendy had never been comfortable with the idea of driving her teeth into someone's flesh, but she'd heard that the mating bite was different somehow. The hormones in her body would ease the way, and she hoped it was the same for Logan.

His hands slid down to her hips, and he held her still as he eased out of her almost completely. The sensation was so stimulating that she barely felt the scraping of his teeth along her skin, even though goose bumps formed. Every conceivable emotion from love to a bit of fear to an intense desire to be with him forever consumed her. As if her animal had taken over, her mouth found the perfect spot on his neck.

She didn't remember him signaling her in any way, but they both seemed to know that now was the right time. Wanting all of him, she pressed down with her heels and lifted her hips. Their sharpened fangs plunged at the exact same time and was quickly followed by the frenzy of his cock hammering into her. Endorphins shot through her system, disabling her ability to control anything. Her climax came so hard and fast that Wendy's breath shot out. Logan closed his eyes and opened his mouth, but no sound escaped. Her vision blurred and heat infused every cell in her body. It was almost as if they were transferring their shifter magic into each other.

Wendy remembered nothing after that until the bed dipped and Logan returned to clean her up. He gently licked at the mating bite on her neck before passing the cloth between her legs.

"How are you feeling?" he telepathed. Or at least she thought she'd heard his words in her head.

"Did you ask me a question, or am I going crazy?" Wendy wasn't sure how to communicate using telepathy, but she figured all she had to do was think the thought and mentally direct it at her mate.

Logan crawled next to her. "You are not going crazy, and I know how you feel, because I feel the same way."

"Oh, yeah? And how is that?"

"Wonderful, amazing, full of love. All I know is that I'm a lucky bastard."

She laughed. "Yes, I feel the same way."

Logan leaned in and pulled her closer, their lips inches from each other. "I wish I could fully express how much I love you."

She smiled. "I think you just showed me—and very well at that." With his luscious face so near though, Wendy had to kiss him again.

He groaned. "Be careful. Now that we are mated, my animal seems to have woken up from a long sleep. I want you again."

"I want that too, but...my body needs a break. Give me a minute?"

He smiled. "Take as long as you need."

She didn't believe him. "How about a week?"

His brows pinched. "I was thinking more like ten minutes."

Wendy could tell their life was going to be consumed by work and sex, and that wasn't a bad way to live.

AFTER THEIR MARATHON love making last night, Logan wanted to do something special with Wendy today. She asked that they stop at the station to tell the detective a few things she'd remembered.

"We can do that. Afterward though, I thought we'd take a little trip," he said.

"Ooh. Sounds fun. Where to?"

"Have you ever seen snow?" he asked as he watched her thread her legs into her panties, getting ready to start the day.

"Snow? Not in person."

"Would you like to take a first-hand look? The mountains around here are amazing."

She stepped into her jeans and then pulled on her bra. "I don't think my jacket will keep me warm enough."

"Not a problem. You've never been a dragon before, because understandably we haven't left the hotel room—but your body should have a built-in heater now. Besides, I'll be carrying you. If you get chilled just tell me, and I'll hold you closer to my heart."

She smiled. "I like that idea. Maybe afterward, you can teach me to fly like a dragon."

"I can try, but you already know how to shift. My cousin Declan mated with a wolf shifter. At first, all he had to do was picture the animal he wanted to turn into. Now, it's like his animal automatically does it depending on what he needs to do."

"Cool, though I'd still like some help."

Logan embraced her. "We'll do it any way you like. I have to practice being in my wolf form too."

"I like that idea."

Logan kissed the top of her head, not trusting himself to do anything more. "We'll grab some breakfast downstairs, fill the detective in about Landry having proof that Darnell was a drug dealer, and then take a trip to the mountains. We don't even have to touch down. Those shoes will get too wet in the snow if we do."

"True, unless we shift into our wolf forms and run up and down the mountains."

"I love that idea. I've never had that luxury before." Logan was excited to try this new form.

Wendy quickly finished dressing, acting as if she was really excited about testing out her new powers. As soon as she tied her shoes, she stepped closer to him, and then dragged a hand down his chest. His dragon roared.

Kiss her, his animal demanded.

If I start, I can't stop.

So?

She needs to rest.

His dragon harrumphed.

Only when Wendy's fingers threatened to latch onto his cock did he stop her. "Behave. I don't want to make you sore."

"Spoilsport," she telepathed.

He laughed. "You should be thanking me."

Logan escorted her downstairs. It seemed as if today the lobby was brighter and people were happier. He suspected mating with Wendy had a lot to do with his newfound joy.

THE VIEW OF the mountains in the distance took Wendy's breath away. She'd never seen anything so tall or so majestic. *"It's incredible!"* she telepathed.

Logan dipped his head and took them lower. *"I haven't been here in a long time, but I have to say, I want to run around in the snow."*

"We should do that, but you'll need to find a spot that isn't too

steep."

"Let me know when you see the perfect place," Logan telepathed.

She was checking out the rugged terrain when a loud screech rent the air.

"Logan, what the hell was that?"

Before he could answer, something large collided with Logan from above. He didn't have to say anything, because a strong wave of anger swept through her as if she were upset—which she was only because Logan was trying to get out of this other dragon's way.

"Hold on," he telepathed.

Oh, shit. There was no way he could do battle with her in his grasp. From what Deke had told her a dragon's claws were its best weapon. When the attacker swung around in front, she froze. *"It's Deke."*

"Why am I not surprised?"

Wendy wanted to yell at Deke and ask him what in the realm he was doing, but considering how fast he was approaching, this was his plan all along. No doubt he'd learned that she—along with Logan—had killed his girlfriend. Either Deke was in cahoots with her, or he was one dumb, horny dragon who fell for the likes of Becky.

Logan dove at the last second, narrowly avoiding a collision, and the sudden drop made the bottom fall out of her stomach. Shit. He should let her go and hope she could shift and fly. It would be the only way to defeat Deke. But what if it took more than the mere image of being a dragon to make the shift work? She looked down. They were hundreds of feet in the air.

"I'm going to set you down," he telepathed. *"Then I want you to shift and hide."*

"Okay."

Relieved there was a solution, Wendy slightly relaxed—that was until Deke attacked from behind. She wasn't quite sure what came first: the screech or the opening of Logan's claws.

All she knew was that she was falling.

Chapter Twenty-Four

A SWOOSH OF air blew upward beneath her, most likely from some air current coming off the mountains. The extra bit of wind helped keep her afloat for a few more seconds, but it was inevitable that she would crash.

Wendy wanted to look upward to check that Logan was okay, but at the same time, she had to look down to see how much time she had before she slammed into the ground.

"Shift into a dragon," came an interior voice that didn't sound like Logan at all.

The advice was sound nonetheless. It was do or die time. She closed her eyes and pictured Logan's magnificent dragon form.

"Shift," she screamed, though Wendy wasn't sure who she was talking to—her wolf or the dragon she'd never met. All she could hope was that her new animal realized the danger she was in and showed herself.

"Open your wings," said a new voice—it was Logan!

Not sure exactly what to do, she opened her arms, and when she looked, they weren't arms or paws at all, but wings. Holy crap. She slowed down a little, but the ground was still fast approaching. Duh. She needed to flap her wings. With much effort, she lifted her giant wings and then drew them downward.

The ground stopped approaching. Holy goddess. She was flying!!! Actually flying.

Because Wendy had no experience, she didn't want to attempt any daring maneuvers like flipping over so she could see where Logan was.

A sudden and sharp pain sliced across her wing, but when she looked around, no one was even near her.

"Wendy, you have to land and shift into your wolf."

As much as she wanted to help Logan fight off Deke, she remembered Logan saying no one in his family had died in battle. Deke had never bragged about being an accomplished fighter, so she had to trust Logan could handle him.

After a quick survey of the ground, she found a flat spot, dipped her head, and aimed for it. To say her landing was unorthodox was an understatement—as in she ended up doing a face plant in the snow—but at least she was down and appeared to be unharmed.

More screeches sounded above her, but when she glanced upward, all she saw was a dragon with orange tipped wings. *"Where are you, Logan?"*

"I'm a bit…ah…busy right now. Hide!"

She wasn't going to figure anything out by gawking. Wendy needed to shift into her wolf form. If she could transform into a dragon by picturing one, she should be able to become a wolf without having to transform into a human in the process. She planted the image of her animal in her mind. A second later, she sunk deep into the snow, her snout buried deep in the cold flakes. She'd take the win. Now to hide.

There were some trees in the distance but reaching them would take some doing. Logan had said to hide, and that was what she would do. If Deke decided to come after her—which she suspected was his original plan—she'd be an easy target for a dragon, especially with her dark coloring against the pristine white snow.

Focusing on the nearest copse of trees, she took off, working hard to not look up as she plowed through the deep snow. Wendy was halfway to her destination when a humongous body fell ten feet in front of her. She froze. All she could see was a black head, a large humped back, and half a wing sticking out of a snowbank—a wing with an orange tip.

A soft whoosh landed behind her, and Wendy spun around.

When she saw it was Logan, and that he looked okay, joy filled her. She loped up to him. Because she was still in her wolf form, Wendy only came up to his legs.

"Give me some space to shift," he telepathed.

Wendy moved to the side, careful to avoid Deke. Whether he was dead or not, she didn't know, but she wanted to be careful. Logan shifted and opened his arms.

Wanting to feel every inch of his body against hers, she shifted into her human form and ran toward him. Even the icy snow burrowing into her jeans and wedging its way down her shoes couldn't dampen her excitement at seeing him. She wrapped her arms around his neck and kissed him. For the first time, Logan didn't even ask if she was okay. He must have sensed her joy that they'd survived.

Logan broke the kiss and nodded behind her. She turned around just as the dragon lifted itself out of the snow.

"Stand behind me until we see what this knucklehead plans to do."

"Not a problem."

She hadn't gone more than a few feet when Deke changed into his human form. His arm was hanging by his side and blood caked his cheek. For one second—and only one second—she wanted to ask if he was okay. Then she remembered that he was the one who'd attacked them.

Wendy didn't wait for Logan to address Deke. She had to know why he came after her. "What is wrong with you?" she nearly shouted as she stepped from behind Logan.

"What's wrong with me? You killed Becky."

She figured that would be his issue. "After she threatened to kill me by using a paralytic—like she did on your dad. She planned to render me unable to move before she tore out my throat. Of course, I killed her."

Logan piped up. "Actually, I killed your girlfriend—or rather your paid-for girlfriend."

There was a sincere look of disbelief on Deke's face. "What are you talking about?"

"Talk to the detective. He has all of the information about how your dad paid Becky to make sure you didn't turn him in for selling drugs. I'm sure the police will want to interrogate you about some things you were involved in too."

"Like what? I've done nothing wrong."

Denial was ugly in any form. Wendy almost debated turning around and suggesting they leave. Sure, the unanswered questions would drive Deke crazy, but that wasn't the type of person she was. "Nothing wrong? Tell that to the parents of the boy you tutored. Both he and his friend are dead!"

His mouth dropped open. "I told you. I had no choice."

"Sure you did. You could have done the right thing and said no to your dad. You're smart. You could have found another job."

"You don't understand."

Wendy turned around and faced her mate. "Can we go home?"

He glanced between Deke and her. "Don't you want me to kill him?"

Logan would never kill someone who wasn't actively attacking him. Her mate was just being nice. With Deke's bad arm and other injuries, he didn't stand a chance. "He's not worth the effort."

"How true. Want to fly or be carried?"

"It's not all that far, but my ability to land really sucks. I don't want to wipe out a playground in my attempt to reach the ground." She turned back to Deke. "You might as well turn yourself in now because we are going to tell them how you attacked us."

Deke said nothing, but his glare told it all.

Logan bowed slightly. "Your chariot awaits you."

Chariot? The only ones she knew about were in books from Earth that she'd read as a child. Wendy stood back while Logan shifted. She refused to even look at Deke. That chapter in her book was so closed.

THE NEXT TWO days were whirlwinds of activity. The trip back to Sawmill was thankfully uneventful. Before they headed to the hotel though, they took a quick detour to the police station to let the detective in charge know they had spoken with Deke—or rather fought with him. Even though her former boyfriend truly believed he'd done nothing wrong, she was pretty sure the judicial system in Sawmill would think otherwise.

Because the case involving the two teens was solved, Logan suggested they head home, and Wendy couldn't be happier.

"The trip is a fairly long one. I suggest you take advantage of my personal transportation service once more—at least until you learn how to maneuver and land," Logan said.

"I would love that."

After they checked out of the hotel, he escorted her to the park that now kind of gave her the creeps. He shifted, picked her up, and took off. Being pressed against his body was wonderful, but her inner wolf—or maybe it was her inner dragon—kept suggesting she ask that they stop somewhere before Edendale so they could satisfy their needs. It was difficult to feel his heat and not want to indulge in his hotness, but there would be plenty of time for that later.

When they arrived home, Logan took her back to his place. This time, she didn't even question it, because it was where Wendy belonged. She never wanted to spend a night apart from him again.

THE NEXT EVENING, Logan stepped out of the bedroom wearing tight black jeans and a white button-down shirt. "Aren't you going to change?" he asked.

"In a minute. I need to finish this paragraph." Wendy had her computer out on the dining room table, working on her new big story—one she hoped would garner her a full-time writing gig.

Logan stepped behind her, and when he placed his hands on her shoulders, his scent messed with her train of thought and forced her to stop typing. "How is it going?" he asked.

Wendy saved her document and looked over her shoulder. "I'm not done with my story of murder and corruption, but I'm pleased with my progress."

"I'm glad the words are flowing. Did both of the boys' parents give you permission to use their names?"

She looked up and smiled at him. "They did. I have to say, it makes for a more emotional story."

"I'm thrilled, but enough writing for now. You need to get ready. My parents are big into promptness."

The dinner party. Yikes. Wendy was nervous. She'd be meeting his folks tonight, as well as the rest of the family, for some kind of big dinner. "Want to help me pick out something to wear?" she asked as she slipped off the chair, stood, and faced him.

Logan dipped his chin. "We don't have time."

"What do you mean?"

As if he lost total control over his body, his eyes flashed teal. "In order for you to put on something for dinner, you'll have to take off the clothes you are wearing."

Wendy laughed. "And we don't have time to enjoy some wanton behavior. I get it."

"Just to be clear, it wouldn't be as much wanton as loving. But you're right. We don't have time. But afterward, I have something in mind." Logan winked.

"I like the way you think."

Not wanting to tempt fate, she rushed into the bedroom. Logan was dressed in a casual but classy way. Not wanting to match his outfit though, she put on a form-fitting black dress. The right jewelry and makeup would make it fancy, but she opted for a simple emerald pendant. It had been her mother's, and the only thing Wendy had left to remind her of her mom. Her dad had hocked everything else of value.

Refusing to dwell on the past, she went into the bathroom and freshened up her lipstick and blush. For shoes, she wanted to be tall—or rather taller—since his siblings had height in spades. Just as she finished dressing, her cell rang. Sheesh. Danita had already called to say she'd done some research on the gray halo effect. Apparently, no one had ever heard of it. As for Logan, he hadn't inherited the talent of being able to detect if someone was lying, but it was still early.

She didn't want to be late to dinner, but when she saw it was her hopefully future boss at the paper, she had to take it. "Mr. Everhart."

"Wendy. I hear congratulations are in order. Helping to find who murdered those boys is amazing. Nice job."

Her pulse soared. "Thank you, but trust me, I had a lot of help."

"When will the article be finished?"

He must have assumed she'd be writing it. "In two days."

"Fantastic. I hope you are ready to start working for us full-time then."

Her knees almost buckled. "Oh, my goodness. Yes. Of course. Thank you, but don't you want to read it first?"

"I'm sure it will be spectacular." Some noise sounded in the background. "Stop by when you are done."

"I will, and thank you."

When she hung up, a bit of shock raced through her. Oh my goddess. She was now a bona fide journalist. Wendy rushed to the living room to tell Logan.

He was standing at the bay window, looking out with his phone in his hand. He spun around and whistled. "How am I supposed to keep my hands off of you during dinner?"

He was only kidding, or so she hoped. "I would think being at your parents' house would be enough to dampen your lust."

"I doubt it."

"Guess what?"

"What?" he asked as he moved closer.

"I am now a full-time employee of the Edendale Herald."

"For real?" She nodded. Logan picked her up and spun her around. "I am so proud of you. When do you start?" he asked as he set her down.

"As soon as I turn in the article." She nodded to the phone in his hand. "Did someone call?" She thought she heard him talking.

"Anderson. I'll fill you on the way."

His folks lived a little bit outside of town, and for some reason, he wanted to drive there. Not wanting to have her hair mussed by the wind, she agreed.

"Tell me about what your cousin said."

"Mr. Darnell's computer was a treasure trove of information. Apparently, Deke's father wanted to make sure he could keep a leash on his son at all times, so he kept very careful notes of the times Deke helped him traffic drugs, noting dates and everything."

She whistled, happy he wasn't going to go unpunished. "What happens to Deke now?"

"He's been arrested and will stand trial. If he helps the Thedia police with other criminals, he might get a reduced sentence."

"He had the chance to get out from under his father's grasp but didn't. He was too greedy," she said.

"I agree. With that bit of business out of the way, I wanted to ask if you had any objections to me announcing that we are not only bonded mates, but that we are living together."

"Not at all. You already told Greer, Stone, Camden, and probably the rest of your siblings. I can't imagine your folks don't know."

He pulled onto the road and then glanced over at her. "You're probably right, but Mom will want to hear the announcement nonetheless."

"Will they make a fuss?" She'd grown up without much parental affection, so she wasn't sure if she would feel suffocated by his folks or not.

"It's the Caspian way, but don't worry, you'll live. If Mom corners you, I'll try to save you."

"Thank you."

It didn't take long before he turned off the main highway that cut through town into a community consisting of very large homes. Some she'd even label as castles. "You actually grew up here?"

"Yes. Remember, we live hundreds of years, and my father has had a long time to build his business. Just so you know, both of my parents made sure we children worked just as hard. Everyone has a tough job to do in the family business. Not only do we have to keep the mines going, but we have to protect the realm."

"Wow. I hadn't realized how much being a Guardian is part of who you are."

"It's a very large part."

The whole fight scene wouldn't stop playing in her mind. "Can I ask you something?"

"Anything."

"I was probably in shock after being knocked out of your grasp when you were battling Deke, but after I landed and looked up, I didn't see you anywhere."

"That's because I have the ability to become invisible when I'm in my dragon form."

She had heard rumors about dragons having that talent, but she didn't know Logan could do that. "When Deke first attacked, why didn't you shield yourself?"

"To be honest, I've never used the shield while carrying anyone before. Once I realized you were safe though, I went into stealth mode."

"Deke couldn't do that."

"No, it's one of the things that makes the Guardians special."

He pulled down a long driveway. Trees bordered either side that led to a large stone home two stories tall. In the middle of the large circular drive was a fountain spewing water. Wendy sat there in awe of the grandeur.

As soon as Logan pulled in front of the mansion, the double front doors opened, and a man in uniform exited. He pulled open her door and held out his gloved hand. "Ma'am."

Wendy wasn't sure what to say since she never expected this kind of reception. After letting the butler, if that was what he was called, help her out, Logan offered her his arm and escorted her inside, making her feel like a queen.

Okay, here goes!

Chapter Twenty-Five

A S SOON AS Logan stepped inside his parents' home, a wave of comfort swamped him. He had been so preoccupied of late that he had put his family on the back burner, and he immediately promised himself he wouldn't do that again.

Griffin and Danita rushed up to them, and the two women hugged. While they chatted excitedly, Griffin asked how the investigation went.

"Better than expected. We learned why the two boys were killed and even managed to bring the killers to justice."

"That's fantastic!" his brother said.

"I'm very pleased too." He gave his brother the shortened version of the series of events. "Yesterday, I received a call from the Thedia police detective who said they had not only found the evidence Landry had on Darnell, but the receipts from Darnell for every month he sent money to the blackmailer. He also had check receipts to Becky Edmonton for services rendered. Landry will spend the rest of his life in jail."

Griffin patted him on the back and then nodded to Wendy. "How's that going?" he asked in a hushed voice.

A broad smile claimed his face. Griffin and Nessa were the only siblings he hadn't directly told that he and Wendy were mates, though he suspected they knew. "Amazing."

His mom came barreling toward them with open arms. She hugged him first. "So glad you could make it. Your mate is adorable."

"Mate?" Griffin asked and then waved a hand. "Yeah, I knew."

Logan figured he did. He then twisted around and placed a hand on Wendy's back. "Hon, I'd like to introduce you to my mother, Iona. The tall man speaking with Greer is my dad, Laird."

For the next few minutes, his mom took over the conversation. "Wendy, do you want to help me in the kitchen while I put the finishing touches on dinner?"

Wendy looked over at him. It wasn't as if he could tell her to say no. *"She just wants to get to know you."*

To his delight, the smile on Wendy's face was as bright as he'd ever seen it. Maybe because she'd lived so long without her mom that she was happy to get a second chance.

It didn't take long before the meal was on the table. Once everyone was seated, he and Wendy spent most of the time detailing their adventure in Sawmill. "The big plus is that Wendy and I have officially mated," Logan said.

No one seemed surprised, though everyone appeared thrilled.

A cell phone rang, and everyone stilled, because phones were not allowed at the table. His mother held up a finger and picked it up. To say he was shocked was an understatement until he remembered that Declan's mate was due to deliver the first of the next generation of Guardians any day now.

His mom listened carefully and then grinned. "I am so happy. Chelsea and Celia are doing okay then?" Another smile. "Give her my love, Kaleena."

His mom hung up. "I'm sure you can all guess what that was about. Chelsea had a baby girl and named her after her mom."

Every female in the group sighed, including his mate, which meant there was something else he needed to discuss with her—children. To be honest, he wanted to spend some alone time with his mate before starting a family.

"And Kaleena?" Greer asked. "How is she doing?"

"Fine. She has another month or two before we add another girl to our family tree."

No doubt his cousin Thane's mate, Angelique, was at the delivery since she had been sent to Tarradon in the first place to make sure all of the Guardian children thrived.

His mom pushed back her chair. "Dessert anyone?"

"I can't eat another bite," Wendy telepathed. *"I stuffed myself."*

"Can we have a raincheck, Mom? It's been a rough week for us."

His mother waved a hand. "Of course. You both need to rest. Getting run over and then doing battle, not to mention any other extracurricular activities you both engaged in, must have taken a toll on your stamina."

Stamina indeed, however Logan was smart enough not to engage in a battle of wits with his mother. "Thank you for understanding."

Logan pushed back his chair, walked around the table, and kissed his mom on the cheek. "Don't get up, please. I'll see most of you at work tomorrow."

The chatter picked up again, and he escorted his mate outside.

Wendy looked up at him and smiled. "That wasn't nearly as bad as I thought it would be. In fact, I enjoyed myself."

"I'm glad. When all of the Caspians get together, it can be a bit overwhelming. The Sinclairs are a tad more reserved." He faced her. "If you aren't too tired, I have a surprise for you."

"A surprise?"

"I want some alone time with you. Are you up for that?"

"Even if I'm falling asleep, I'd be up for it."

Logan laughed, loving life at the moment. He wasn't surprised that his new mate would be willing to go on an adventure. The reason he wanted to drive to his parents' house was because landing near the base of a craggy mountain at night could be tricky, and Wendy deserved to be given a few lessons before he'd feel totally comfortable letting her loose in the air.

After she finished writing her great exposé on the drug dealer, Robert Darnell, Logan planned to teach Wendy some fighting skills. After the way she handled Becky though, he'd say his mate had a lot of promise.

"Where are we going?" Wendy asked after he passed the road to his condo.

"Someplace special."

"Ooh, I can't wait. I hope it's private."

He reached over and slid some hair behind her ear. "Very private." Because it was dark in the car, her dragon scales flashed a yellowish-amber, like the color of warm honey. "Did you see that?" he asked.

"See what?"

"The color of your inner scales."

Wendy looked down. "Oh, my goddess. I love it."

He did too. "You'll almost match your eye color when you're excited—unless your eyes glow purple like other female dragon shifters."

She smiled. "Maybe I'll have both colors."

"I can't wait to find out."

He turned down a dirt road that ended at the base of a mountain and then parked.

Logan pushed open his car door, walked around to Wendy's side, and helped her out. "What is your pleasure? Do you want to try flying or would you like me to carry you?"

"It depends. Where are we going?"

"It's about a half mile up that dirt path."

"What about shifting into our wolf form so we can run up the path? Unless of course, you don't think you can do it."

He did love his mate. She was a woman who would always challenge him. "Wolf it is."

"You can lead since you know where we're going," she said.

Logan figured if Wendy could shift into a dragon with such ease, he could shift into a wolf just as easily. She spun in front of him and was instantly in her animal form.

I trust there's a wolf inside me somewhere, he said to his inner wolf, hoping the two of them could communicate.

I got this, came a voice he'd never heard before. How cool was that to have two beasts? Or maybe not. He suspected his dragon would be challenging the wolf at every turn.

Well, I don't like it, his dragon shot back.

See? Did he know his dragon or what? Logan laughed. *Deal with it. We're all about to get some action, assuming you can contain your jealousy.*

When you put it that way, his dragon responded, *go ahead and do your thing.*

And Logan did just that. One minute he was human and the next he became this short animal. While he wasn't used to being this close to the ground, he would adjust. He had to admit he could see the advantage to being in both forms, especially if a battle was ensuing. Kaleena and her mate certainly seemed enthralled with that ability as did Chelsea and Declan.

"What are you waiting for?" Wendy telepathed.

"Just enjoying the view."

Being this low to the ground gave Logan the chance to really run. He had to admit this new ability thrilled him. Logan was constantly aware of whether Wendy was close behind, and to her credit, she had no trouble keeping up.

When he came to the cave entrance, he turned and darted inside. Wendy followed. Earlier this morning while Wendy was still asleep, he'd brought up blankets, two pillows, some candles, a bottle of wine, and a special surprise. Wanting to make this as romantic as possible, Logan shifted back into his human form, and Wendy quickly followed.

"Why are we here?" she asked.

"You'll see. Wait here. I need a second to do something."

Logan headed farther into the cave and took the second branch off to the left. While it smelled a little musty, he had taken the time to rid the area of rocks and anything else that might get in their way. All he had to do was put the flowers in a vase, light the candles, strip, and drop down onto the makeshift bed.

"Come find me," he telepathed as soon as he was ready. *"Just follow the light."*

Thirty seconds later, Wendy appeared, her eyes going wide. "You're naked. On a blanket. With candles." She glanced over at the vase. "You bought me flowers?"

"This is our first date—sort of." He discounted all the meals they had in Thedia. That was business.

"Aww. You said you only buy flowers for someone special."

"That would be you." Logan unfolded his arms from behind his head and sat up. "Join me. I'll pour the wine."

"This is incredible."

"Not as incredible as you."

Wendy giggled. While he uncorked and then poured the wine, she stripped. As much as he wanted to do the honors, he was so horny, he couldn't wait.

WENDY NEVER PICTURED Logan being this spontaneous—even though he clearly had thought this through. "After the week we've had, this is my idea of winding down," she said.

Logan poured two glasses and handed her one. "Have a drink and then let me warm you up."

She dropped to her haunches, took the glass, and drank half of it in two large gulps. Nothing tasted better—well, Logan would, but the drink did hit the spot.

He smiled, tossed back his drink, and then set it down. Logan slipped the glass from her fingers and placed it next to his. What this man did to her. She quickly took off her clothes. Now naked herself, she straddled him and guided him onto his back. When his big cock pressed against her opening, the need to kiss him overwhelmed her.

Wendy leaned over, planted her hands on either side of his head, and did just that. As he plunged his tongue into her mouth, his hands found her waist. He then held her still while he lifted his hips slightly, putting more pressure on both her private parts. Joy, contentment, and lust took over her body. Wanting his mouth on more than just her lips, she broke the kiss and offered him her breasts.

Logan's eyes glowed, and his scales flashed. She swore between the two of them, they'd created their own private light show. He cupped one breast while he suckled on the other. The act of having mated intensified every touch. Maybe it was the enclosed area that exaggerated everything, but his scent seemed different too. It smelled more like frenlen needles and fresh loam than lemons.

Wendy ran her fingers through his hair, trying not to dig her nails into his scalp. When his teeth tugged hard on one nipple, the spikes of need soared through her so hard that she nearly came.

"Your turn," she panted. Not waiting for him to tell her he'd explode too soon if she licked him, she slid down, and then bent over. She didn't have time to tease and tempt him. Instead, she drew him deep down her throat, grabbed his hard shaft, and pumped fast. With each stroke, his moans increased. When a burst of cum released, Logan grunted. Just as she was pulling away, he flipped them over with one quick move.

"I can't wait any longer," he announced. He turned her around once more, lifted her to her elbows and knees, and then pressed his cock against her needy entrance.

Waves of anticipation slickened the way. Unable to wait any longer either, she shoved her hips back just as Logan drove in. The combined movement shot her lust to levels higher than a dragon could fly, and when a cool rush of air swept into the cave, she shivered. Logan seemed to understand what had happened, because he pressed his chest against her back and cupped her breasts, his fingers twirling her distended nipples.

The frenzy that followed defied description. Their animals seemed to take over as he thrust into her over and over again, building her need to epic proportions. Wendy clutched the blanket and balled it up. When she lowered her head and flung her hair to the side to expose her neck, Logan leaned over and dragged his teeth against her skin. Never in her wildest dreams did she think she'd want a man to bite her, but the intensity it brought to their lovemaking was monumental.

As he ran his rough palms over her sensitive nipples, she moaned louder and louder. The bite to her neck that followed took her to a new plane of existence. Then on his next thrust, Logan's cock expanded. The moment he lifted his mouth, her own climax shot forth. Sparks of color burst behind her lids and waves of love and completeness filled her.

Making love in a cave had never been on any kind of wish list, but after this romantic gesture, she just might suggest it more often.

Exhausted, she collapsed onto the blanket. Logan rolled off of her and pulled her back against his warm chest.

"I could stay like this forever," he whispered.

While a highly impractical comment, she loved the sentiment. "Me too."

Birds squawked outside and some kind of animals rustled in the leaves at the entrance. "We should probably dress and clean up," Logan said, a short while later.

"I like it here." She rolled over so that their lips were close. "This was the perfect way to clear my head. Thank you."

"My pleasure. We can only hope the world will give us some peace and quiet for a few weeks at least."

"From your mouth to the universe's ears." She tapped his nose. "Did I ever mention that I love you?" she said.

"No. Never. Do you?"

"I think we have time for me to prove it to you once more, but only if I get to ride you like the dragon I am."

Logan cracked up, and Wendy fell even more in love with him.

I hope you enjoyed reading Wendy and Logan's story as much as I enjoyed writing it.

Don't forget to sign up for my newsletter *to receive three free books, as well as up-to-date information on my stories. If you prefer to only receive notices regarding my releases, follow me on BookBub.*

http://smarturl.it/VellaDayNL

bookbub.com/authors/vella-day

What would you do if you found out the man who is hotter than sin has been lying to you? Find out in Fueled By Flames, Kenton and Tory's story.

Here is a preview of chapter one. Enjoy.

"I CAN'T DO this anymore." Kenton Forrester's anxiety was already at an all-time high, and something had to give. Considering Feys were supposed to be calm under all circumstances, this abstinence wasn't helping his mental state.

After his brother placed the last dish in their cupboard, he spun around. "Can't do what?" Bevon asked, acting all innocent.

His brother knew. Kenton had been going on and on about Tory Sinclair for weeks now. "You know what. Stay away from Tory."

The left side of his brother's lips quirked upward. "I still don't know why you're avoiding her? She's your mate. I say go for it, big brother."

"And how do you propose I do that? Teleport to the middle of her jewelry store showroom and say: Excuse me, miss. You don't know me, but I was the one who saved your life over a month ago and then erased your memory after whisking you off to an unknown realm."

Bevon grinned. "That could work."

"Somehow, I don't think that will endear her to me." Kenton pointed a finger at his brother. "Then I'll add: And did I mention I made your whole family promise to never tell you what really happened after you were infected by that dark Fey?"

Bevon just shook his head. "Self-pity is an ugly trait as is sarcasm. Get over yourself. Do what everyone else does. Bump into her at a bar or on the street and introduce yourself. Oh wait. I forgot. You don't go out."

"Shut up." It didn't matter that his brother made a valid point.

Bevon moved closer. "I get it will be hard for you, but you can do this. Use your charm to get her to go out with you. And by charm, I don't mean your magic."

"Easier said than done." Kenton had no idea why this was stressing him out. He was hundreds of years old and had dated many women in his realm. On Feyrion, everyone knew he was next in line to be the king, so finding a woman to fawn over him was easy. But here? On foreign soil? Not so much.

"Just talk to her. I'm not suggesting you lie to her about her past. Far from it. I'm merely saying not to put all of your cards on the table on the first date. Bit by bit, let her know the danger she was in after her attack. You can then tell her the lengths you had to go to save her."

For once, his brother made sense. "That's actually a good idea."

Bevon hopped up on the kitchen counter, clearly enjoying being able to give advice for a change. "I know it is. On Feyrion, Tory seemed like a sweet girl, one who was the forgiving type."

"You barely saw her."

He shrugged. "I dropped by the Royal Castle a few times when she was healing from her deathly experience."

"Tory was mostly out of it."

"Not the last day. She was up and about. We spoke a bit. I got a good feeling about her. From what I could tell, Tory has a mind of her own, but she was kind too."

He'd thought the same thing. Kenton studied his brother—as in the one who had little to no restraint when it came to woman or anything else in his life. "Let me ask you this: Have you ever asked out a woman from Tarradon—one who had no idea you're nobility?"

"No, why would I when there are plenty of Feys and Fairies in Feyrion who want me?"

"That's what I thought." His brother was a hopeless playboy and not someone Kenton should be taking any dating advice from. He pulled open the refrigerator to look for something to eat. Not that he couldn't swipe a hand and create some gourmet masterpiece, but he was trying to learn to live in this realm, as backward as it was. "The problem is that Tory is my mate, so it's not like I can replace her with someone from Feyrion. I didn't plan for this to happen, you know. It just did."

His brother sobered. "All the more reason why you need to meet her like any other Tarradonian male would."

Only he wasn't an ordinary male. He was Fey—one with extraordinary powers. Kenton closed the refrigerator door. He'd lost his appetite. "You're right. I'll teleport to Edendale, cloak myself, and keep a watch out for her. When the timing is right, I'll run into her."

"I didn't mean literally."

That made Kenton smile. "I didn't mean literally either."

Bevon nodded to Kenton's clothes. "You do know she'll be able to see through those white harem pants you wear. The women here will find that offensive."

"I always wear this on Feyrion, and trust me no Fey or Fairy has ever been offended. Come to think of it, I've attracted many a shifter woman wearing it too." It was Bevon who never liked the traditional royal garb. In fact, Bevon hadn't been on Tarradon a month before he'd purchased several pairs of jeans from a store in Edendale, along with a couple of short-sleeved and long-sleeved T-shirts. Kenton thought his brother looked ridiculous, but he did blend in better than Kenton did.

He looked down at what he was wearing. "I see nothing wrong with my attire, but if you think it will make Tory uncomfortable, I'll change." With a swipe of his hand, his clothes turned from white to dark blue. He checked again to see that nothing showed. Damn. While his pants were now opaque, the protrusion made it obvious that he was thinking about her. He owned underwear but rarely wore it. He didn't like the restriction.

"You can wear a pair of my jeans," Bevon said with too much cheer in his voice.

Kenton knew when he was defeated. "Fine. And thank you, I think."

"You know where they are."

If Kenton hadn't wanted to impress Tory, he wouldn't have bothered changing. Once in Bevon's room, Kenton located a pair of jeans and dragged them on. They were heavy and uncomfortable, but he'd deal. His peasant style shirt looked perfectly fine though. Only the rebel, Bevon, opted to dress like these natives.

Not particularly pleased with having to adapt, Kenton strode back into the cabin's main area.

His brother looked up and smiled. "You look great, though I suggest you put on shoes."

"I can't please you, can I? Why don't you just tell me to teleport back to Feyrion and forget about Tory?" Not that he ever would.

"You know why. She's your mate."

Kenton blew out a breath. "I'm glad you realize that." He swiped a hand once more and was immediately dressed like everyone else in this realm. "Better?"

He didn't need his brother's permission or acceptance, but it was polite to ask. If Kenton didn't need to see Tory right now, he'd have asked one of his sisters for her opinion on how to dress more mainstream.

Bevon laughed and gave him a thumbs up—a symbol Kenton thought was as dumb as it was odd.

"Perfect. Just don't mess this up, brother. If you do, you'll be impossible to live with, and I'll be forced to move into Fay's place." Bevon wagged a finger. "On second thought, I'd ask Meena to take me in. She's the sweetest of the three."

"Even Meena won't take you. You are too insufferable. Besides, they all live together, you goof."

He grinned. "There is that."

"I HAVE BAD news." Tory's cousin, Detective Anderson Caspian, was addressing the Guardians in their conference room on the fourth floor of the SinCas office building.

Just as Tory Caspian covered her mouth to stifle a yawn, Anderson's announcement had her heart dropping to the pit of her stomach. It wasn't that the Guardians weren't used to gathering at eight in the morning to learn about some current crime spree, but the way Anderson Caspian said it had her body reacting in a not-so-good way.

"What happened?" Tory's Uncle Laird asked, his tone deep with concern.

Most of her family was seated around the twenty-person table— all except the usual suspects, like her brother Ramsey, who never was willing to leave his lab, and her cousin Camden who was just as bad. Naturally, her sister wasn't there since Kaleena and her mate, Finn, were busy having a baby. Tory didn't see her dad and that worried her. Of late, he'd participated less and less in the Guardian meetings.

"We've had four suicides in the last two weeks—all by slitting their own throats." Anderson held up a hand. "I know that's not something we usually deal with, but these deaths are different."

"How so?" Her brother Thane was possibly the most intense

member of the group, and the one who was always ready to do battle.

"My men have investigated all four cases. As you know, suicide usually occurs in those who are depressed or who have experienced some recent traumatic event. In each of these four cases, the people were successful and happy, at least according to their loved ones. One had just received a scholarship to college, another had been given a big promotion at work, the third had completed his residency at Edendale Medical, and the fourth had retired after a long and successful career in business."

That made no sense. While some rogue shifters had gone on killing sprees over the years, none had been able to make it look like suicide.

"What are you saying?" her uncle asked. "That these weren't suicides but rather murders?"

"I'm here to ask for your help in figuring out exactly what happened. When we autopsied the bodies, they all had the same unknown chemical inside their bloodstream. That hints at a connection between the deceased, even though none of the family members believe they knew each other."

"What type of drug was it?" Thane asked.

"Unfortunately, we can't identify it, which means we don't know where it came from. Even if we did find its origin, we would have to prove someone was responsible for drugging these people right before their deaths. I'm thinking this chemical caused some kind of psychotic break that made them take their life."

Laird whistled. "What can we do?"

Anderson inhaled. "I need your ears to the ground. Talk to anyone who might know if there is a chemical that would trigger suicide."

"Was it a kind of paralytic or a different scheduled drug?" her brother Declan asked.

"The composition isn't consistent with a paralytic or anything else, which is the scary part."

"I'm wondering if someone slit their throats after they were incapacitated."

"From the angle of the cut and the direction of the blood spatter on the victim's hand and arm, the victim did the deed himself. Plus, they all were standing at the time of their death. Before you ask, we don't believe anyone was holding their arm either." He turned to Thane. "I'm thinking Angelique might be able to help."

"Angelique? How?"

"Your mate is from a different realm and has dealt with dark entities. Maybe this unknown substance comes from there."

Greer grabbed Tory's wrist and squeezed hard. Her cousin's mate had been possessed by a dark entity for a short while, and the thought of another one like him roaming around Edendale had Tory's pulse soaring.

"Angelique's realm isn't like ours. It's not like they even have buildings where they can manufacture anything. Remember, these entities don't have bodies until they are released," Thane said.

More talking and buzzing erupted, but this time her family settled down quickly. Greer piped up. "Dark entities have escaped before. Could an escapee be inhabiting that person's body for a while and then cut his own throat before exiting?"

Anderson planted his hands on the table and leaned forward. "I actually had considered that, but none of the bodies had any burn marks on them, like they had when you were involved with such a malevolent creature—or rather when your mate was taken over by one."

Tory had arrived dead tired this morning, but the horror of it all had her on full alert now. "Do you have any clues or ideas where we should look?" she asked her cousin.

"None, other than my money is on the perpetrator being from a different realm. As I said, ask around."

Either Anderson was right and the killer was from another realm or else this person was some expert chemist who had injected the person with some homemade concoction. Though that would be the best-case scenario. The worst would be if it were indeed an entity from another realm. The Guardians were the ultimate fighters, in part because they trained constantly and could cloak themselves when needed. Their particular kind of magic made it difficult for another dragon to attack what they couldn't see. But other world creatures were a whole different story. Tory and her family had learned the hard way how difficult it was to battle even one dark entity. If it hadn't been for Angelique who was a light entity, Greer would not have a mate.

Her uncle looked around. "You are positive suicide wasn't the cause of death?"

"Pretty much, but if we can't find the source of this drug, we might have to tell the family we can't be sure how they died, and that won't bring any closure to them."

"I take it there were no needle marks on the body?" Tory asked.

"None that the coroner found, but I'll ask him to do another sweep." Anderson pushed back his chair and stood. "Thank you for your help."

Camden might be able to figure something out. Her cousin was a genius when it came to analyzing poisons and unique chemicals. Even though he was a dragon shifter, he preferred to do research rather than go into battle. The sad part, at least to her, was that Camden might be one of the most talented fighters in the group. Her cousin possessed a sixth sense about what his opposition was about to do before he did it.

"What a minute," Tory called, remembering what had almost killed her a month ago. Anderson and the rest stopped.

"What is it?" her cousin asked as he turned around.

"What about a dark Fey? Malpan was able to do mind control. He even convinced about twenty men to work in his mine for free. He was powerful enough to take me out for a while."

Griffin shook his head. "Good thought, but it can't be Malpan, because Kenton Forrester sent him back to his realm where his darkness was removed."

"I know that, but I was thinking there could be other dark Feys here. Didn't your mate mention a man by the name of Balkin who worked for Malpan? He could have been one."

Her brother's brows pinched as he studied her. "She did, but even if this Balkin guy is one, why would he compel strangers to kill themselves? What would be his end game?"

Tory looked around, waiting for someone to come up with an answer, but no one did. "I don't know."

"For the sake of argument," Anderson said, "let's say your theory is correct, and the victims were being told what to do. How would you explain the identical chemical in all of their bodies? Is that something a dark Fey would do?"

Why would he think she'd know? "I have no clue, but we could ask one of the Forresters. Since a few of them are Feys, they should be able to tell us."

Anderson's shoulders seemed to relax. "That's a great idea, Tory. Ask them."

Not her. She'd speak with Griffin about being the one to contact the family. After all, he dealt with them most recently. "I will."

As soon as Anderson left, Greer pushed back her chair, stood, and then clasped Tory's arm before she had a chance to go after Griffin. "Do you really think it's a dark Fey? I have to admit it makes a lot of sense."

"It could be. What bugs me is that these deaths seem so purposeless. I understood why Malpan would want to control his workers, but these victims died. They can't help anyone." Tory brushed some wisps away from her face. "Ugh. This whole thing is sad and creepy at the same time."

"No kidding."

Tory snapped her fingers. "I should have asked Anderson for the chemical composition of this drug."

"What good will that do?"

"Since locating the Forresters is no easy chore, I want to see if Camden can do a deep dive on the structure of the chemical. He might be able to figure out what it's made from and where it was made."

"That's smart, but let's hope it's not made from the killer's own body."

"That is a really scary thought," Tory said.

"No kidding." Greer checked her watch. "Hey, I have to open the store. Do you plan to investigate this mess today?"

"Probably not. I'm too exhausted to be of much good to anyone. I haven't slept in a couple of days worrying about Kaleena. Before Anderson called this gathering, I had planned to visit her in the hospital to make sure she's okay and then take a nap. After that? We'll see how I feel."

"I take it your sister hadn't gone into labor yet?"

"No. There have been two false alarms. Finn and Angelique are with her now. Kaleena's only in the hospital, because the doctor is worried about her high blood pressure." To Tory's knowledge, no dragon shifter had ever had that issue. She just hoped Kaleena's dragon was up to the task of delivering this baby.

"She'll be fine." Greer squeezed Tory's hand. "If you need to take tomorrow off so you can be with her, I'll be happy to cover for you."

Greer truly understood what a special twin bond Tory and Kaleena shared. "You are the best. Thank you. I'm hoping she delivers today. I'm so ready to be an aunt."

"You're already an aunt."

Tory's mind was fuzzed from lack of sleep. Chelsea, Declan's mate, had delivered a month ago. "I meant I want to be an aunt again."

Greer placed a hand over hers. "Then go, and make sure you are."

After a quick hug, Tory rushed out. Greer stayed behind. She always was the one to volunteer to help clean up the conference room since the Guardians were a rather messy lot when it came to leaving empty coffee cups on the table.

Tory had planned to speak with Griffin, but she wanted to see Kaleena first. She had walked at most a block when a sharp cramp in her stomach nearly made her knees buckle. It must have come from their twin link. Tory would be feeling what Kaleena felt—only on a smaller scale. *Hold on, Kaleena. I'm coming.*

Normally, Tory couldn't communicate telepathically with anyone, but when she wore their special necklace, they could. For privacy purposes, she didn't wear it often.

The intensity of that jolt had been more than either of the two before it, implying her twin might even be in labor—for real this time. Because of the quick onslaught of pain, Tory had to stop to catch her breath. While she took several deep breaths, she studied the traffic. Thankfully, it was a Saturday, and the streets weren't very crowded. The hospital was only about a mile away, and Tory believed she could drive there safely. Walking was a possibility, but that would take too long. Her last option was to fly. The problem was that other than landing on the helicopter pad on top of the hospital, there was little space around the hospital to safely set down. So drive it was. Tory just hoped the cramps didn't incapacitate her. She retrieved her keys from her purse so she could rest once she reached her car.

As she neared, a man with light brown hair pulled back in a ponytail, wearing jeans and a white peasant shirt seemed to have appeared out of thin air right in front of her. Had his body not blocked the sunlight, she might have run into him.

"I'm sorry," Tory said, as she tried to walk around him.

"Are you alright?" he asked, his voice full of sympathy.

Tory stopped. "Yes. I should have watched where I was going. Excuse me, I'm on my way to the hospital to check on my sister." When she tried to stand up straighter, her breath caught again, and her palm automatically went to her stomach.

"Let me help you."

Tory was born and bred to be independent. "I can manage myself, thank you."

Just then another stabbing pain doubled her over. Without asking permission, the man wrapped his arm around her shoulder. "Where is your car?"

Normally, she would have shrugged out of his grasp, but the waves of warmth that seemed to come from his embrace erased all of her discomfort, allowing her to actually stand upright. That was strange. Or had Kaleena had a short contraction, and it had ended as suddenly as it came?

Tory pretended to look around for her vehicle, while trying to decide her next move.

"Miss?"

What the heck. He wasn't a shifter, so how much harm could he cause? "It's the blue car at the end of the block."

"Good. Come on."

Tory could only hope she wasn't making a mistake.

HIDDEN REALMS OF SILVER LAKE (Paranormal)

Awakened By Flames (book 1)

Seduced By Flames (book 2)

Kissed By Flames (book 3)

Destiny In Flames (book 4)

Box Set (books 1-4)

Passionate Flames (book 5)

Ignited By Flames (book 6)

Touched By Flames (book 7)

Box Set (books 5-7)

Bound By Flames (book 8)

Fueled By Flames (book 9)

FOUR SISTERS OF FATE: HIDDEN REALMS OF SILVER LAKE (Paranormal)

Poppy (book 1)

Primrose (book 2)

Acacia (book 3)

Magnolia (book 4)

Box Set (books 1-4)

Jace (book 5)

Tanner (book 6)

WERES AND WITCHES OF SILVER LAKE (Paranormal)

A Magical Shift (book 1)

Catching Her Bear (book 2)

Surge of Magic (book 3)

The Bear's Forbidden Wolf (book 4)

Her Reluctant Bear (book 5)

Freeing His Tiger (book 6)

Protecting His Wolf (book 7)

Waking His Bear (book 8)
Melting Her Wolf's Heart (book 9)
Her Wolf's Guarded Heart (book 10)
His Rogue Bear (book 11)
Box Set (books 1-4)
Box Set (books 5-8)
Awakening Their Bears (book 12)
Her Wolf's Warlock(book 13)

PACK WARS (Paranormal)
Training Their Mate (book 1)
Claiming Their Mate (book 2)
Rescuing Their Virgin Mate (book 3)
Box Set (books 1-3)
Loving Their Vixen Mate (book 4)
Fighting For Their Mate (book 5)
Enticing Their Mate (book 6)
Box Set (books 1-4)
Complete Box Set (books 1-6)

HIDDEN HILLS SHIFTERS (Paranormal)
An Unexpected Diversion (book 1)
Bare Instincts (book 2)
Shifting Destinies (book 3)
Embracing Fate (book 4)
Promises Unbroken (book 5)
Bare 'N Dirty (book 6)
Hidden Hills Shifters Complete Box Set (books 1-6)

MONTANA PROMISES (Full length contemporary)
Promises of Mercy (book 1)
Foundations For Three (book 2)

Montana Fire (book 3)

Montana Promises Box Set (books 1-3)

Hart To Hart (Book 4)

Burning Seduction (Book 5)

Montana Promises Complete Box Set (books 1-5)

ROCK HARD, MONTANA (contemporary novellas)

Montana Desire (book 1)

Awakening Passions (book 2)

PLEDGED TO PROTECT (contemporary romantic suspense)

From Panic To Passion (book 1)

From Danger To Desire (book 2)

From Terror To Temptation (book 3)

Pledged To Protect Box Set (books 1-3)

BURIED SERIES (contemporary romantic suspense)

Buried Alive (book 1)

Buried Secrets (book 2)

Buried Deep (book 3)

The Buried Series Complete Box Set (books 1-3)

A NASH MYSTERY (Contemporary)

Sidearms and Silk(book 1)

Black Ops and Lingerie(book 2)

A Nash Mystery Box Set (books 1-2)

STARTER SETS

Contemporary

Paranormal

Author Bio

Want three FREE books? Sign up for my newsletter and receive MONTANA DESIRE, AN UNEXPECTED DIVERSION, and BARE INSTINCTS.
COPY AND PASTE INTO YOUR BROWSER:
http://smarturl.it/o4cz93?IQid=MLite

Not only do I love to read, write, and dream, I'm an extrovert. I enjoy being around people and am always trying to understand what makes them tick. Not only must my books have a happily ever after, I need characters I can relate to. My men are wonderful, dynamic, smart, strong, and the best lovers in the world (of course).

I believe I am the luckiest woman. I do what I love and I have a wonderful, supportive husband, who happens to be hot!

Fun facts about me

(1) I'm a math nerd who loves spreadsheets. Give me numbers and I'll find a pattern.

(2) I live on a Costa Rica beach!

(3) I also like to exercise. Yes, I know I'm odd.

I love hearing from readers either on FB or via email (hint, hint).

Social Media Sites

Website:
www.velladay.com

FB:
facebook.com/vella.day.90

Twitter:
@velladay4

Gmail:
velladayauthor@gmail.com

Instagram:
@dayvella